The ALPINE
BETRAYAL

*Also by Mary Daheim
in Thorndike Large Print* ®

The Alpine Advocate

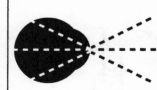

This Large Print Book carries the
Seal of Approval of N.A.V.H.

The ALPINE BETRAYAL

Mary Daheim

Thorndike Press • Thorndike, Maine

Thorndike Large Print ® Popular Series edition published in 1993 by arrangement with Ballantine Books, a division of Random House Inc.

The tree indicium is a trademark of Thorndike Press.

This book is printed on acid-free, high opacity paper. ∞

Set in 16 pt. News Plantin by Minnie B. Raven.

Library of Congress Cataloging in Publication Data

Daheim, Mary.
    The alpine betrayal / Mary Daheim.
      p. cm.
    ISBN 1-56054-874-6 (alk. paper : lg. print)
    1. Large type books. I. Title.
    [PS3554.A264A8 1993]
    813'.54—dc20
                                                    93-22678
                                                         CIP

The ALPINE
BETRAYAL

Chapter One

I wouldn't set foot in Mugs Ahoy unless it was a matter of life and death. But finding my so-called advertising manager, Ed Bronsky, came close.

Ed is not given to hanging out in bars. Strong drink has a way of cheering him up — and Ed prefers walking on the gloomy side of life. But I knew he had to clear an ad for Mugs Ahoy's promotional tie-in with Alpine's Loggerama Days. Deadline was upon us, and so were the media representatives from the new Safeway that was opening west of the shopping mall. Ed had stood up the reps, and as editor and publisher of *The Alpine Advocate*, I had a right to be annoyed. I left the Safeway people in the capable hands of our office manager, Ginny Burmeister, while I ran the full block up to Pine Street to haul Ed back to the newspaper.

If they ever sweep the floor at Mugs Ahoy, they'll probably find a couple of patrons who have been lying there since the first Loggerama in 1946. The tavern is littered with bottle caps, peanut shells, cigarette butts, and crumpled napkins. At high noon on a summer day, the place is mercifully dark. No wonder the dart board with the curling edges looks otherwise unused; between the murky light and the bleary eyes, I doubt that most patrons can find it.

Ed was at the bar, drinking coffee and exchanging glum comments with the owner, Abe Loomis. A half-dozen other customers were hoisting glasses of beer and watching a soap opera. Their faces looked jaundiced; the air smelled stale. I began to feel as depressed as Ed.

Across the bar, Abe Loomis nudged Ed and nodded at me. "Mrs. Lord. The boss." He mouthed the words, and looked as if he were announcing somebody's imminent death.

Ed swiveled his bulk slowly on the stool and peered at me through the gloom. "Hi, Emma. Can I buy you a cup of coffee?"

Ed's about as wide as he is square, but even sitting down he's taller than I am, and he weighs twice as much. As ever, when I upbraid my lugubrious ad manager, I feel like a gnat attacking a hippopotamus. This time around, I also felt a little foolish, since everyone in the tavern had turned curious, if befuddled, eyes away from the TV and onto me. After two years of small-town life, I'm getting used to being observed at close quarters.

"Ed," I began, trying to keep the exasperation out of my voice, "the Safeway reps are —"

Ed didn't exactly spring from the bar stool, but he landed with a thud that made the ancient floorboards creak. "Damn," he breathed, brushing crumbs off his plaid sport jacket, "I forgot! Sorry, Emma. I'll be right over there." He started to lumber toward the door, but stopped midway and turned back. "You don't suppose they want *color*, do you?" He asked the question as if it were immoral. Before I could answer, he waved a pudgy hand at Abe Loomis. "Oh, go ahead and check out that ad for Abe, will you? I didn't quite get around to it." Ed Bronsky creaked and squeaked his way out of Mugs Ahoy.

Gingerly, I sat down on the bar stool next to the one Ed had vacated. "Okay, Abe," I sighed, "let me have a look." Ed wasn't merely lazy, he seemed to have an aversion to selling advertising. If he hadn't been employed long before my tenure as owner of *The Advocate*, I would have gotten rid of him — or so I often told myself. The truth was I didn't have the heart to fire him.

Abe Loomis, a skinny man with deep-set eyes of no particular color, reached under the bar and produced a mock-up, two columns by six inches deep, featuring a busty blonde from Ed's clip art files. I winced at the illustration, then tried to concentrate on the copy.

I'm all for equal rights, though I consider myself more of a humanist than a feminist. However, I am definitely a supporter of good taste. Even though Alpine may not be Seattle, and the First Amendment gives Abe the right to say what he wishes, I had to balk.

"Uh, Abe . . ." I pointed to the ad, careful not to let it get doused with coffee, beer, or God only knew what other liquid that might be stagnating on the bar at Mugs Ahoy. "I think this needs a little work."

Abe's eyes seemed to sink even deeper into his skull. "Like what?" he asked in a surprised voice.

"Like shorter," I suggested. "Or maybe

more informative. Here, let's take out a couple of lines and put in something about the contest itself." I gave Abe what I hoped was an engaging smile. "Eligibility, for instance."

"You mean measurements?" inquired Abe, emptying Ed's coffee mug onto what appeared to be the floor.

I tried to avoid gnashing my teeth. "I was thinking more of age, maybe geography. You know, if they have to live within the city limits."

Abe furrowed his long forehead at the mock-up. For the next ten minutes, we rewrote the ad. He surrendered the two most offensive lines, while I let the artwork pass. As long as there were wet T-shirts and women willing to fill them, there really wasn't any other way to picture the contest.

"It should be a big year for Alpine," he said when we'd finally come to an agreement. "Especially with Dani Marsh coming back to be Loggerama queen and ride the donkey engine in the parade down Front Street."

"Right," I said, tucking the ad under my arm and slipping off the stool. "It was lucky for Alpine that her new movie is being shot on location at Mount Baldy."

"Lucky, my butt!" The hoarse female voice shot out of a darkened corner near the ancient jukebox. I turned, trying to recognize the figure sitting at the small round table. Although Alpine is made up of only four thousand persons and my job brings me into contact with the public, I still don't know half the population on sight. Abe, however, has owned Mugs Ahoy for over twenty years. He gazed at the woman with the indulgent expression typical of his trade.

"Aw, Patti, don't be so hard on the kid. She's made a name for herself, put Alpine on the map in Hollywood. You know darned well you'll be glad to see your daughter when she gets here."

"You're full of it, Abe," retorted Patti, shaking off the restraining effort of her companion, a lean, sinewy man in a red plaid flannel shirt. "I never want to see the little tramp again." She stubbed out her cigarette and got to her feet. "Come on, Jack, let's get out of here."

Patti and a man I recognized as owning a logging company, but whose full name eluded me, stalked out of the tavern. The remaining customers watched with interest while Abe made a pass at the bar with a dishrag.

I took a couple of steps back toward Abe. "That's Dani's mother?"

Abe looked up, grimacing. "Patti and Dani never got along. Patti thought Dani was a wild one." He rubbed his long jaw. "Case of heredity, if you ask me."

My cotton blouse was beginning to stick to my skin; it hadn't rained in over a month. Even the beer out of the tap looked warm. I needed to get outside. "Thanks, Abe," I said, waving the mock-up of his ad.

"Sure." He nodded absently, then lifted his head. "Say — who's your entry?"

I stopped on the threshold. "For what?"

He pointed to the banner that drooped over the bar. "The wet T-shirt contest. Most of the merchants are finding somebody to wear a shirt with their business' name on it. Then the girls can ride in the parade. Who you got from the paper?"

I made a real effort not to burst out laughing. The contest was serious business to Abe Loomis. My regular staff consisted of Ed Bronsky; Ginny Burmeister; Vida Runkel, the House and Home editor; and Carla Steinmetz, my solitary reporter. The idea of any of *The Advocate*'s female staff taking part in a wet T-shirt contest was laughable. Except maybe for Carla. It was hard to tell what Carla would do, except that she'd probably get it wrong the first time.

"I'll see," I said, trying to keep a straight face. "Maybe I'll ask Vida."

I'd expected Abe to guffaw at the image of my strapping sixtyish House and Home ed-

13

itor posing in a wet T-shirt, but Abe merely inclined his head. "She's a buxom one, all right."

"Right," I said, suddenly a little breathless, and scooted out the door.

"You *what?*" screeched Vida, rocketing back in her chair and snapping off her tortoiseshell glasses. Her summer straw hat flew off, landing in the wastebasket.

"I didn't really," I protested. "I was joking. But I thought I'd better tell you because I'm not sure how much of a sense of humor Abe Loomis has."

"Abe!" Vida rubbed frantically at her eyes, a gesture that always indicated she was annoyed or upset. "That man's dumb as a bag of dirt. If half this town weren't fueled by beer, he'd have been out of business a long time ago." She stopped trying to gouge out her eyeballs and glanced down at a half-dozen sheets of paper on her desk. "The whole thing is so silly. Vulgar, too. Here," she said, pushing the papers at me, "this is the background piece I just finished on Her Majesty, Queen Dani. Somebody called while you were out and said she and her entourage would be in around noon tomorrow. Do you want me or Carla to take pictures?"

I flipped through the story, noting the results of Vida's usual two-fingered, rapid-fire method of typing. Maybe it was time again to try to talk her into a word processor. I looked at the battered upright on the little table next to her desk and decided the right moment was probably a long way off, unless I smashed the typewriter with a sledgehammer. "If Dani and company don't get here until tomorrow noon, we won't have enough time to get a picture in Wednesday's edition. Let's just go with the studio head shot and run some new photos next week."

Having retrieved her hat and put her glasses back on her nose, Vida regarded me over the rims. "If everybody buys as much space as they promised, we may have room for a photo essay on Dani. You know — Dani arriving in Alpine, Dani on location, Dani at her old home, Dani getting ready for the parade. People love that sort of thing." Vida pulled a face and jammed her straw hat back on her head. Obviously, she didn't number herself among those people.

I considered her suggestion. Unless Ed somehow single-handedly managed to discourage Alpine's merchants from participating in the special Loggerama edition, we should be able to go at least forty-eight pages. Maybe even sixty. The sound of money jingled in my head. It was not a noise I'd heard much since buying *The Advocate*, but I liked it.

"Where *is* Ed?" Not in the newsroom; not in my editorial quarters. Nor had I seen him as I came through the front office.

Vida was putting a fresh piece of paper in the battered typewriter. "He and Ginny took the Safeway people to the Venison Inn for coffee. If you ask me, you ought to let Ginny handle this alone. Ed still thinks Safeway made a terrible mistake coming into Alpine and competing with the Grocery Basket."

I flipped through Vida's article on Dani Marsh. "That's only because he can't go on talking the Grocery Basket out of running big ads. Do you remember last Easter when he tried to convince Jake that he didn't need to advertise his hams because nobody else in town had any?"

"Oooooh!" Vida gave a tremendous shudder. "The man's impossible! Just this morning I overheard him telling Itsa Bitsa Pizza they shouldn't advertise their new special because that wife of his, who's built like a bathtub, is on a diet!"

I groaned, though it didn't do any good. All the badgering and coaxing in the world couldn't change Ed's attitude. But *The Advocate*'s balance sheets looked a little brighter now than when I'd taken over. The previous owner, Marius Vandeventer had made a good living in the halcyon days of low paper costs and hot type job printing. But new technology had moved the printing business — including that of *The Advocate* itself — down the highway to Monroe. Even more ironically, in a town that once had been dependent on logging and mill operations, the price of trees had sent newsprint costs skyrocketing. But with the help of an old friend, I'd managed to pare down other expenses and somehow goad Ed into soliciting more advertising, however reluctantly. Circulation was up, too, a source of personal pride. I expected the Loggerama edition to be our biggest moneymaker of the year. Certainly the presence of a bona fide movie star would help.

"Vida," I said, now sitting at Carla's empty desk, "where did you get this stuff about Dani Marsh?"

She turned halfway in her chair. "What? Oh, the Hollywood bilge is from some press release. The early background is off the top of my head."

Most Alpine background comes from Vida's head. She is a walking encyclopedia of local lore. Vida knows so much about the town and its residents that usually the most interesting stories aren't fit to print. The piece on Dani Marsh, however was bland in the extreme. "She was born, grew up, graduated from high school, got married, divorced, and moved to L.A." I tapped page one of the article with a fingernail. "Then you've got six hundred words of press kit. Couldn't we do more with the local angle? What about her mother?"

Vida gave another shudder, setting the paisley print of her summer dress aquiver. Fleetingly, I pictured her in a wet T-shirt. It was an awesome sight.

"Patti Marsh! Now there's a piece of work!" Vida yanked off her glasses again. "Do you know her?"

"I ran into her just now at Mugs Ahoy. She didn't seem real thrilled about her daughter's triumphal return."

Vida put out her hand. "Give me that story." I complied, and Vida put her glasses back on to scan it. "Dani was born — so far, so good. Ray Marsh allegedly knocked up Patti Erskine when they were in high school. They had to get married — or else. Ray walked out when Dani was a baby. Patti got divorced, went after Ray for child support, couldn't collect, took a job as a waitress in the old Loggers' Café, which is where the computer store is now. Patti had a string of men, but never married again. After the café closed, she went to work for Blackwell Timber. She's been seeing Jack Blackwell — or been seen with him — ever since his wife left him a couple of years ago."

I realized that it was Jack Blackwell I'd seen with Patti at Mugs Ahoy. "And?"

"And . . ." Vida ran a finger down the page. "Not a very stable upbringing, but I can't say that, can I?" She shuffled paper. "High school — let me think, Dani got suspended at least twice, for drinking and being naked during study hall. Not inside the school, I mean, but in somebody's pickup across the street. Still," she added grudgingly, "the girl graduated. Then she married Cody Graff."

That name rang a bell. Somehow, I connected him with Vida or one of her numerous kinfolk. Half of Alpine was related to the Runkels, her late husband's family, or her own branch of Blatts. I must have been looking curious, because Vida nodded. "That's right, Cody is engaged to my niece, Marje Blatt, the one who works for Doc Dewey. By coincidence, Cody is also employed by Blackwell Timber."

It was a coincidence, but not an amazing one. Although the original mill closed in 1929, logging had continued as a major enterprise, right up until the recent — and most serious — controversy over the spotted owl. The two smaller mills, located at opposite ends of the town and supplied by gyppo loggers, were outstripped by Blackwell's operation between

19

Railroad Avenue and the Skykomish River. Jack Blackwell also owned some big parcels of land — on Mount Baldy, Beckler Peak, and along the east fork of the Foss River. It struck me as odd that I hadn't met Blackwell until today.

"Does Blackwell live here?" I asked.

"Part of the time. He's got operations in Oregon and Idaho. Timbuktu, for all I know." Vida spoke impatiently, going through the rest of her story. Jack Blackwell was obviously a side issue. "So Dani and Cody got married when they didn't have enough sense to skin a cat, and they had a baby — a full nine-month one, I might note — but the poor little thing died at about six weeks. Crib death, very sad. Then about two months later, the marriage blew up and Dani flew south. Five years later, with some big-shot director's backing, she's a star." Vida gave an eloquent shrug. "How much of that do you want me to put in?"

I accepted defeat gracefully. "I was hoping she'd starred in the senior play or something. How did the press kit cover her background?"

Vida waved a hand. "Oh, some tripe about how she came from a quaint Pacific Northwest logging town up in the mountains with snow on the ground half the year and deer sleeping at the foot of her trundle bed. You know — the sort of nonsense that makes us look like we've got moss growing around our ears and we're still wearing loincloths."

I inclined my head. Having spent all of my life in Seattle, Portland, and Alpine, I was accustomed to the attitudes of outsiders. Let them think we ate raw fish for dinner and held a potlatch instead of hosting cocktail parties. Maybe it would keep them away. I allowed Vida to put her story in the copy editing basket.

"What's the name of this picture Dani's doing?" I asked, feeling a bit passé. The life of a single mother running her own business didn't leave me with a lot of leisure time for moviegoing.

Vida, another single working mother, albeit with children out of the nest, had to look down at the press release on her desk. "Let me see . . . here it is. 'A film by Reid Hampton, starring Dani Marsh and Matt Tabor. *Blood Along the River*' Ugh, what a stupid title."

I had to agree. Maybe they'd change it. It never occurred to me that it might be not only stupid, but prophetic.

Chapter Two

Durwood Parker was under arrest. Again. Durwood, who had once been Alpine's pharmacist, was probably the worst driver I'd ever had the opportunity to avoid. Drunk or sober, Durwood could nail any mailbox, hit any phone pole, or careen down the sidewalk of any street in town. Since not all the streets in Alpine have sidewalks, Durwood often tore up flower beds instead. His latest act of motoring menace had been the demolition of Francine Wells' display window at Francine's Fine Apparel on Front Street. Francine was in a red-hot rage, but Durwood was stone-cold sober. For his own protection, Sheriff Milo Dodge had locked Durwood up overnight.

"We have to run it," Carla Steinmetz announced the following morning as she went over the blessedly short list of criminal activity for the past twenty-four hours. "It's a rule, isn't it? Any name on the blotter is a matter of public record, right?"

I sighed. "I'm afraid so. Poor Durwood. Poor Dot. His wife must be a saint."

"She's got her own car," put in Vida. "She'd be crazy to go anywhere with Durwood. Did you know he drove an ambulance in World War II?"

"Who for?" I asked. "The Nazis?"

Vida's response was stifled by Kip MacDuff, our part-time handyman and full-time driver. Kip was about twenty, with carrot red hair and cheerful blue eyes. He was, he asserted, working his way through college. Since I had never known him to leave the city limits of Alpine, I assumed he was enrolled in a correspondence school.

"Hey, get this!" Kip exclaimed. "Dani's coming in by helicopter! She's going to land on top of the mall! The high school band is coming out to meet her!"

I gazed at Vida. "I guess you'd better get a picture."

But Carla was on her feet, jumping up and down. "Let me! This is incredibly cool! When I was going to journalism school at the University of Washington, I never thought I'd get to meet a movie star in Alpine!"

And, I thought cruelly, her professors probably never thought she'd get a job in newspapers. But here was Carla, now in her second year as a reporter on *The Advocate*. Why, I asked myself for the fiftieth time, did all the good ones go into the electronic media? Or were there any good ones these days? Was I getting old and crotchety at forty-plus?

Vida was only too glad to let Carla take the assignment. "I've been looking at Dani Marsh since she was waddling around in diapers and plastic pants. Just make sure you load the camera this time, Carla. You remember what happened two weeks ago at Cass Pidduck's hundredth birthday party."

Carla, who usually bounces her way through life, looked crestfallen. "I left the film in the car."

Vida nodded. "At least you had it with you."

Carla's long dark hair swung in dismay. "So I went out to get it, but when I came back, Mr. Pidduck had died."

"Yes, I know," said Vida, "but his children liked that shot of him slumped forward in his birthday cake. They said it was just like old Grumps. Or whatever they called him," Vida added a bit testily. "Frankly, the Pidducks never did have much sense. Cass may have been long in the tooth, but he was short in the upper story."

Accustomed to Vida's less than charitable but often more than accurate appraisals of Alpine residents, I withdrew to my inner office. The usual phone messages had accumulated, including one from my son, Adam, in Ketchikan. After two years and no foreseeable major at the University of Hawaii, my only

24

child had decided to go north to Alaska. He was spending the summer working in a fish packing plant, and had a vague notion about enrolling for fall quarter at the state university in Fairbanks. I looked at Ginny Burmeister's phone memo with my customary sense of dread whenever my son called in prime time.

He was staying in a dormitory owned by the fish co-op, which meant that I was put on hold for a long time while somebody tried to determine if he was on or off the premises. For ten minutes, I counted the cost and perused the mail. Adam should be at work in the middle of the day. Maybe he'd had an accident. Or had gotten sick. I lost interest in the numerous bills, press releases, irate letters to the editor, advertising circulars, and exchange papers that jammed my in-basket — especially on Mondays. At last Adam's clear young voice reached my ear:

"Hey, Mom," he began, "guess what? Fairbanks is seven hundred miles away! I thought I could take the bus to campus."

Adam's sense of geography, or lack thereof, was astounding. Indeed, I had tried to explain the vastness of Alaska to him before he flew out of Sea-Tac Airport. I might as well have saved my breath.

"Is that why you're calling at two o'clock on a Monday afternoon when you ought to be at work?" I demanded. "Bear in mind, Fairbanks is so far away it's in another time zone, twice removed."

"I worked Sunday," Adam said, sounding defensive. "Didn't I tell you I'm on a different shift this month?"

He hadn't. Adam was well over six feet tall, weighed about a hundred and seventy pounds, was approaching his twenty-first birthday — and still qualified as my addled baby. One of these days, I'd turn around and find him gainfully employed, happily married, and the father of a couple of kids. And maybe one of these days I'd fly to Mars on a plastic raft.

"So you just discovered you couldn't commute to Fairbanks?" I said, wondering whether to be amused or dismayed. At least he'd never suggested taking a degree in transportation.

"Well, yeah, but that's okay. I'll just move there next month. I can take a plane." His voice dropped a notch. "If you can advance me the price of a ticket."

"So why are you working? I thought you made big bucks in Alaska."

"I got tuition, room and board, you know — I didn't count on having to pay for an airline ticket." He sounded faintly indignant, as if it were my fault that Alaska was so spread out.

"I'll see what I can do." I didn't have the remotest notion how much it cost to fly from Ketchikan to Fairbanks. It appeared I'd have to dip into savings. At least I still had some, thanks to a fluke of an inheritance that had allowed me to buy both *The Advocate* and my green Jaguar. Still, it crossed my mind that this was one of those times when it would have been nice to have Adam's father around, instead of off raising his own kids and taking care of his nutty wife.

"Thanks, Mom." My son spoke as if the ticket purchase was a *fait accompli*. "Hey, I just talked to some guy who's leaving for Seattle this afternoon and then going on to Alpine. Curtis Graff. You know him? He works here in the cannery as a foreman."

The name rang a bell, but it was off-key. "Cody Graff I know. At least I know who he is. His name just came up a few minutes ago." There was no point in boring Adam with details. "How old is Curtis?"

"Oh — thirty, maybe. He went to Alpine High, worked in the woods, was a volunteer fireman, and went out with the daughter of the guy who owns the Texaco station."

Adam's thorough account amazed me. Usually, I was lucky to get the last name of his acquaintances. But I still couldn't place Curtis Graff, unless he was Cody's brother. Vida would know. "What's he bringing down?" I inquired. Surely Adam couldn't pass up the chance to have somebody hand-carry videos that were six weeks overdue, a broken CD player, or a torn jacket that only Mother could mend.

"Nothing," my son replied, sounding affronted. "I just thought it was kind of strange that there was somebody else up here from Alpine. It's not exactly the big city."

"True," I agreed, thinking wistfully of the metropolitan vitality I still missed since moving to Alpine. But my years on *The Oregonian* in Portland and my upbringing in Seattle seemed far away. I had committed my bank account to *The Advocate* and my soul to Alpine. My heart was another matter.

We chatted briefly of mundane concerns before Adam announced he had to race off and help somebody fix an outboard motor. I turned my attention back to the other phone messages, the mail, and the print order for the weekly press run in Monroe. It was after one o'clock when I realized I'd skipped lunch. I said as much to Vida, who had already consumed her diet special of cottage cheese, carrot and celery sticks, and a hard-boiled egg.

"You eat alone too much," she announced, depositing two wedding stories with accompanying pictures on my desk. "I'll come with you. I could use a cup of hot tea."

"Good." I started to sign the print order just as Carla returned, bubbling like a brook.

"Dani Marsh isn't much taller than I am," Carla declared, dancing into my office. "She's in terrific shape though, works out for two hours a day, and drinks nothing but cabbage extract. Her skin is *amazing!* But you ought to see Matt Tabor! What a hunk! He's six-two, with the greenest eyes ever, and muscles that ripple and bulge and —"

Happily, the phone rang, cutting short Carla's bicep recital. The mayor, Fuzzy Baugh, was on the line, his native New Orleans drawl characteristically unctuous. He wanted to make sure we included an article about the celebrity bartenders who were going to be on duty at the Icicle Creek Tavern during Loggerama. He and Doc Dewey Senior; Dr. Starr, the dentist; and Sheriff Milo Dodge would make up the star-studded cast of mixologists, unless they got lucky and enticed somebody from the movie crew to take part. That struck me as dubious, since the Icicle Creek Tavern makes Mugs Ahoy look like the Polo lounge. Located at the edge of town, the rival watering hole is famous for its Saturday night brawls which usually involve raucous loggers hurling each other through the windows. I frankly couldn't imagine Fuzzy or any of our other more dignified citizens having a beer at the place, let alone serving the rough-and-tumble clientele. But this was Loggerama, and apparently a truce was in effect.

I was still listening to the mayor's long-winded description of how he planned to give civic-minded names to his libations (*citizen schooner, mayor's mug, political pitcher* — I didn't take notes) when Ed Bronsky staggered in, looking as if he'd been attacked by wild beasts.

"Inserts!" he wailed, clutching at the doorjamb. "In color! Every week! It's worse than I expected!"

Inwardly, I was elated. Enough color inserts might pay for Adam's ticket from Ketchikan to Fairbanks. But between Fuzzy yammering about his Beer à la Baugh, the star-struck Carla still twittering to Vida, and Ed now threatening to have an aneurism over Safeway's advertising temerity, I was anxious to escape. Hastily, I shoved the print order at Vida to sign for me while relented and took down the dates and times that the various so-called celebrities would be at the Icicle Creek Tavern. At last I was able to hang up, console Ed, listen to Carla, and get out the door before some other obstacle rolled my way.

"Burger Barn," I said, feeling the full impact of the sun overhead. *The Advocate* wasn't air-conditioned, but its proximity to the Skykomish River gave an illusion of cold water and fresh air. Outside, I could see the dry foothills of the Cascade Mountains. Even the evergreens seemed to droop. To the north, Mount Baldy was bare of snow, with wild heather blazing under the blank blue sky. The forest fire danger was extreme, and all logging operations had been curtailed. After over a month without rain, we natives were beginning to feel as if our own roots were drying up and withering our souls.

The Burger Barn is both restaurant and drive-in, located two blocks west on Front Street, across from Parker's Pharmacy, once owned by the wayward Durwood. Fleetingly, I wondered how he was managing in jail. In Alpine, the county prison consists of six cells in the building that houses the sheriff's office. Usually, the only inhabitants are drunk drivers, transients, and the occasional spouse batterer. Durwood probably had the place to himself. I mentioned the fact to Vida, who snorted loudly.

"He'll probably ask to stay an extra day. Dot Parker talks like a cement mixer. Nonstop, just grinding her jaws away." She took a stutter step, then waved, a windmill gesture that might have stopped traffic had there been

31

more than three cars on Front Street. "Marje! Yoo-hoo!"

At the entrance to the Burger Barn, Vida's niece, Marje Blatt, returned the wave. She was accompanied by a lanky young man wearing cutoffs and a tank top. As coincidence would have it, he was Marje's fiancé, Cody Graff. Introductions were made, but before I could inquire about Curtis Graff, Vida whisked us inside the Burger Barn.

"We might as well sit together," said Vida, heading for an empty booth that looked out toward the bank across the street. "I'm just having tea."

Marje and Cody looked a little reluctant, but docilely sat down. "I'm on my lunch hour," said Marje. She was in her mid-twenties, with short auburn hair, bright blue eyes, and a piquant face. Unlike her more casual counterparts in many big city medical offices, Marje wore a crisp white uniform. She scanned the menu as if it were an X-ray. "Why am I looking at this?" she asked, pitching the single plastic-encased sheet behind the napkin holder. "I'm having the Cobb salad."

The waitress, a pudgy middle-aged woman named Jessie Lott, stood with order pad in hand, blowing wisps of hair off her damp forehead. Cody asked for the double cheeseburger, fries, and coffee. I opted for a hamburger dip au jus, a small salad, and a Pepsi. Vida requested her tea. The waitress started to wheel away, but Vida called her back:

"There's a minimum per table setting, right?"

Jessie Lott shrugged. "Really, that's just when nobody else orders more than —"

"In that case," Vida interrupted, "I'll have the chicken basket with fries, sauce on the side, and a small green salad with Roquefort." She threw Jessie a challenging look and deep-sixed the menu. "Well," Vida said, eyeing her niece and Cody, "when's the wedding? I heard you ordered the invitations last week."

"October nineteenth," replied Marje in her brisk voice. She didn't look at all like her aunt, but some of their mannerisms were similar. Both were no-nonsense women, devoid of sentiment, but not without compassion. "We're going to Acapulco for our honeymoon." She turned her bright blue eyes on Cody, as if daring him to differ. "We'll love it."

Cody, who had been toying with the salt and pepper shakers, gazed ironically at his beloved. "Yeah, sure we will, Marje. Especially the part where we both get the Aztec two-step."

"Don't believe everything you hear," Marje retorted. "You just don't drink water

33

out of the tap, that's all. Or eat in strange places. Good Lord, Cody, don't be such a wimp!"

Cody drew back in the booth. He was sharp-featured, with straw-colored hair, restless gray eyes, and a sulky cast to his long mouth. Though he was narrow of shoulder, his bare upper arms were muscular, and I supposed that younger women would find him attractive, especially with that petulant air. He struck me as spoiled, but I hoped — for Marje's sake — that I was wrong. Certainly she seemed to be getting her way about the honeymoon.

"You just wanted to go fishing in Montana or Wyoming or some godforsaken place," Marje was saying. "As if you don't hotfoot it out to the river every chance you get around here."

"Fishing stinks in this state," declared Cody. "There isn't a river in Washington that isn't fished out. I haven't caught a trout bigger than eight inches since I was sixteen. And steelheading is a joke. You're lucky if you get one of those babies every season."

Cody wasn't exaggerating, but I kept quiet, not wanting to take sides. But Cody wasn't finished with his griping: "Everything stinks around here these days," he proclaimed, flexing his biceps for emphasis. "Take all these wimpy environmentalists trying to wipe out the logging business. How does a guy like me live in this state? I don't know how to do anything but work in the woods. Do they want me sitting on a street corner with a tin cup and a sign that says WILL WORK FOR FOOD? Work at *what?* It pisses me off."

It was pissing off an increasing number of people in the forest products industry, though I noticed that Cody seemed to take the environmentalists' concerns very personally. I supposed I couldn't blame him, but I had an urge to point out that there were two sides to the story, and that while I sympathized with him, he was not alone in his outrage. Vida, however, intervened.

"Just be glad you can afford a honeymoon at all," she admonished them. "And the time. How long will you be gone?"

"A week," replied Marje. "That's all I can take off at once from Doc Dewey's office. It's too hard to get anybody to fill in for me in this town. In fact, he'd rather I went next week because he's going to be gone." She pulled a face at her aunt. "Frankly, I don't think he wants me to go at all. Doc's been real cranky lately."

"We ought to elope," said Cody, his ruffled feathers apparently smoothed. "With the logging operation shut down and that bunch of dorks making a movie up there on Baldy, this would be a good time for me to take off." He jostled Marje's arm. "What do you say, honey, want to slip off to a J.P. and forget about all those flowers and champagne glasses and ten pounds of gooey cake?"

"I sure don't," Marje countered crossly. "Between Doc's constant advice and your weak dose of enthusiasm, I wonder why we're getting married in the first place. It may be old stuff to you, but I've never had a wedding before. Besides, I don't know how long Doc's going to be away this time."

Vida leaned across the table, scenting gossip. "Where's he going?"

Marje lifted her slim shoulders. "Seattle, I think. Frankly, he's been sort of vague. Mrs. Dewey's going with him, though. Maybe it's just a getaway. He could use it — that's probably why he's such a crab. Doc doesn't take much time off for a guy his age, especially when he's got his son to rely on to back him up."

Vida sniffed. "His son has too many peculiar ideas, if you ask me." She paused as Jessie showed up with our order. "Last Friday, Amy took Roger in to see young Doc Dewey," she went on, referring to her daughter and grandson. "Amy and Ted think Roger is hyper." Vida rolled her eyes and pounced on her chicken. "Hyper what, I asked? He's just a typical spirited nine year old. But young Doc Dewey is putting him on some kind of medication. Doesn't that beat all?" She bit into her chicken with a vengeance.

Marje looked as if she were trying to keep from smiling. "Well, Roger *is* pretty lively. Amy told me how he tried to microwave Mrs. Grundle's cat. And put a garter snake in the bank's night depository."

"Kid stuff," asserted Vida. "Roger has an active imagination, that's all."

The truth was that Roger was a terror, but Vida doted on him all the same. Although her three daughters had provided her with a running total of five grandchildren, only Roger lived in Alpine. Familiarity did not breed contempt, as well it might, given Roger's proclivity for mischief.

"Somebody," said Cody, who had seemed temporarily lost in his world of double cheese and fries, "ought to smack that kid. At the family Fourth of July picnic, I caught him putting cherry bombs in the barbecue pit. Remember those big explosions?"

Marje nodded, but Vida gave Cody her most severe expression. Before she could defend the errant Roger, however, the sound of honking horns blasted our ears. We all craned our necks to look out toward Front Street.

"What is it?" asked Marje, whose vision was blocked.

Cody had gotten to his feet, dropping a couple of french fries in the process. "Jeez." He turned pale under his summer tan as the honking grew louder, competing with the whistle of the Burlington Northern, heading east. "It's that ballbuster Dani."

I was sticking to my clothes and my clothes were sticking to the booth. I leaned out as far as possible, but could see only the rear end of a big white car, no doubt a demo on loan from the local General Motors dealership. "They got in about noon," I said in what I hoped was a neutral voice.

Cody sat down, looking more sulky than ever. He picked up his napkin, crumpled it into a ball, and threw it in the direction of the empty booth opposite us. "That bitch is going to be here for two weeks!" He gave a violent shake of his head, straw-colored hair quivering. "Why couldn't she go away and stay away? What's the point of coming back just to get everybody riled up?"

Marje gave Cody a cool look. "As far as I can tell, you're the only one who's riled up. Ignore her, Cody. All that was five years ago." She pushed at his plate. "Eat up, I've got to get back to the office."

But Cody wasn't so easily mollified. With

one furious gesture, he swept the plate off the table, sending it crashing to the floor. I jumped and Vida tensed. Marje opened her mouth to protest, but Cody was on his feet, yelling at her:

"You don't know squat about that slut! She's not fit to set foot in this town! Wait and see. She'll be lucky to get out alive!" He started to heel around, slipped in a puddle of catsup, and caught himself on the edge of the table. The gray eyes glittered like cold steel. "If ever a woman deserved to get herself wasted, it's Dani Marsh! Don't be surprised if I kill her with my bare hands!" Having steadied himself, Cody Graff stood up straight and looked down at his clutching fingers.

They looked as if they'd fit neally around Dani Marsh's throat.

Chapter Three

Carla insisted that I go with her to Mount Baldy and check out the movie company. Despite some confusion about the print order, the press run was underway in Monroe. Ordinarily, I should have had my weekly bit of slack time on a Wednesday, but the extra work caused by Loggerama was interfering with our routine. I demurred, but Carla was adamant.

"Come on, Emma, you got your sixty pages," Carla argued. "Ed came through for once. Celebrate. How often do you get to see real movie stars?"

How often do I want to? was the retort that almost crossed my lips. But Carla was so enthusiastic that I finally gave in. It wasn't that I didn't admire actors — I am actually a devoted film buff — but the idea of seeing them in the flesh has never thrilled me. Maybe I don't want my illusions spoiled. Maybe I want to keep the on-screen magic untarnished. Or maybe I figure those celluloid gods and goddesses will turn out to be every bit as human as the tabloids insist they are. Why make a pilgrimage to meet somebody who is just as flawed as I am?

But I went, piloting my precious green Jaguar across the Skykomish River and down to the highway and veering off onto a switchback logging road leading up the side of Mount Baldy. I noticed that what was known as Forest Service Road 6610 had been recently resurfaced, perhaps even widened. When we stopped at about the three thousand-foot level, I saw why: four enormous truck-trailers rested at the edge of a meadow miraculously covered with snow. Even under the afternoon sun, I marveled at how much cooler I felt. Phony or not, the delusion seemed to lower the actual temperature by at least ten degrees.

Carla was hopping about, looking for someone she recognized. Although there must have been thirty people milling around, I saw no sign of either Dani Marsh or Matt Tabor. But Carla had zeroed in on a lion-maned man wearing a straw hat, cowboy boots, and faded blue jeans.

"Mr. Hampton!" she called. "It's me, the press!"

Mr. Hampton's teeth sparkled in his tawny beard. "Carla, my favorite media personality! Are you here to do a behind-the-scenes feature? Maybe you'll get it picked up by the wire service."

Carla's petite body jiggled with pleasure. Proudly, she introduced me to Reid Hampton, a director whose work I've sometimes admired but rarely enjoyed. Hampton's pictures tend to be gloomy, not so much film noir as Kafkaesque. Come to think of it, Ed Bronsky would love them — if he ever stopped watching *Mister Ed* reruns long enough to see a movie.

"*Road Weary* was very provocative," I said, knowing it was his most recent directorial effort. In truth I had seen only the trailer. Two hours of watching three derelicts beat each other over the head with tokay bottles had not impressed me as entertainment. But Reid Hampton was still holding my hand and beaming that dazzling smile.

"It was a statement," he said in as modest a tone as his deep, rumbling voice would permit. "I hope George Bush saw it."

Personally, I hoped the president had better things to do, but I, too, kept smiling. "Is this picture a statement?" I inquired, feeling my fingers shrivel.

He finally let go and made a sweeping gesture. "*All* my pictures are statements. Poverty, politics, sex, violence — the whole human condition. The camera not only conveys truth; it demands a response from the audience. What did you think of Little Louie?"

"Ah . . ." Little Louie, Big Louie, even

Medium Louie were all outside my frame of reference. Whoever Louie was, he probably had been one of the three grubs in *Road Weary*. "Vulnerable," I said, taking a guess. "Strong, though, in many ways. Under the surface," I added hastily.

Still grinning, Reid Hampton slapped his hands together. "Exactly! It isn't every cocker spaniel you can get to put those emotions across. Cockers in particular aren't too bright. I should have used a collie, but then everybody thinks *Lassie* and all that sentimental crap. On screen, animals always have a —" He stopped and looked over my head. I turned to see Carla outside one of the big trailers talking to a slim blonde who had to be Dani Marsh. Hampton took my arm. "Come on, you must meet our star, your own hometown heroine. Dani's great, a real talent, absolutely catches fire in front of the camera. And Matt Tabor — together they'll scorch the screen. I've been trying to put this package together for over two years."

Dani Marsh was one of the most beautiful women I've ever seen. She had honey blonde hair, limpid brown eyes, and not-quite-perfect features with a mouth too wide and brows too thick, but the overall effect was stunning. I realized I had never seen her in a movie, but according to Vida's reworking of the studio press release, Dani had zoomed to the top of the heap with only three major roles, two of them in pictures directed by Reid Hampton.

Dani was almost as expansive as her director. She shot out a hand and gave me a dazzling smile. "Ms. Lord! Carla has told me all about you! I think it's wonderful that a woman has taken over from that old curmudgeon, Marius Whatsisname. Is he dead?"

"No," I answered, finding her forthright manner irresistible. "Just retired and moved away. Marius Vandeventer is indestructible."

Dani laughed, a lovely, tinkling sound that made Carla's frequent bouts of giggling sound like a car crash. "I've so much catching up to do in Alpine. Five years! And it *has* changed. I'm so glad I talked Reid into doing some location shooting up here." She threw back her head and looked up toward the twin, flat crests of Mount Baldy. "I used to go berry-picking up there. My mother and I would make pies and jam."

From what I'd seen of Patti Marsh, making book would have been more like it. Fleetingly, I wondered if Dani had attempted a reunion with her mother yet. I tried to see any resemblance between Dani and Patti, but my recollection of the senior Marsh was fogged by the dark smoky interior of Mugs Ahoy.

At the edge of the meadow, activity was suddenly underway. Cameras were being moved into position, equipment was being set up, a background — which looked to me like a replica of the view I was looking at — had even been dropped in the middle of the fake snow.

"Excuse me," said Dani, "I have to get into my costume." At the moment, she was wearing a dark green leotard that displayed finely toned and roundly contoured body parts. I had an insane — and fleeting — urge to exercise. "Believe it or not," she laughed, "I have to put on a parka and ski pants. I may melt before this picture is wrapped!" With a graceful little wave, she climbed the four portable stairs that led to the trailer that housed her dressing room.

Reid Hampton was off consulting with his assistant director; Carla was hobnobbing with a bald man behind the camera; and descending from the cab of the trailer was Matt Tabor, carrying a can of diet soda. I allowed myself to stare. I have seen Matt Tabor in at least four films, and although his acting range may be limited, his sexual attraction is not. Matt had been cast in the heroic mold, with chiseled features, wavy black hair, a terrific torso, and those seductive green eyes that had earned rave reviews from Carla and fifty million other females. Indeed, Matt Tabor was so incredibly good-looking that I not only stared, but laughed out loud.

He shot me a curious glance, and I actually flushed. I felt fourteen instead of forty-two. As he strolled in my direction, I seriously considered bolting. Then I remembered how unimpressed I was by movie stars and that I was a newspaper publisher and that I had once met Gerald Ford. Somehow, the comparison was inadequate, especially since Ford had seemed far more at a loss for words than I had been.

"Are you from the logging company?" Matt Tabor's famous baritone echoed off the evergreens.

It was the last question I expected. "What?" I sobered quickly. "No, I own the local newspaper. Do you mean Blackwell Timber?"

"Right." He was wearing some sort of black vest over his bare chest and had on a pair of very tight black pants. I tried not to notice. "Those jackasses can't make up their minds," Matt remarked, not necessarily to me. He was wearing his brooding look, which had served him so well in *Beau Savage*.

"Oh?" I pretended we were having a conversation. "You mean Jack Blackwell and his crew?"

He nodded, the black forelock somehow

staying in place. "I guess that's his name. He tells us we can use this place for the location shoot, extorts twenty grand for the privilege, then pitches a fit because we cut down eight lousy trees." Matt Tabor sneered. I remembered the expression from *No Mercy at Midnight*. "What the hell, he can't log anyway because his workers get too hot. Or something like that." He gave a contemptuous shrug of his broad shoulders, just the way he did when he walked out on the heroine at the end of *Jericho in Jersey*.

"It's because it's too dry," I said, trying to keep my eyes on Reid Hampton and a tall redhead with what looked like a script in her manicured hands. "There's a danger of forest fire."

"Hell." Matt Tabor reached inside his vest and pulled out a pack of cigarettes. "Where's Smokey the Bear when we really need him, huh?" For the first time, he looked directly at me as if I were really there. I looked at his cigarettes. Even after three years of not smoking, I hadn't lost my craving. But maybe it was safer to lust after Matt Tabor's tobacco than the rest of him. "Who are you?" he asked, in a tone that implied I might not know.

"Emma Lord. I own *The Alpine Advocate*." Matt was puffing away, and I resolutely returned my gaze to the preparations in the meadow. I decided I must be seeing double. Two people who looked exactly like Matt and Dani Marsh were standing knee-deep in snow while several others peered, prodded, and conferred. It dawned on me that the man and woman were the actors' stand-ins, helping the crew get ready for the actual shooting.

Reid Hampton was coming toward us, a copy of the script under his arm. "Bundle up, Matt. We're almost ready."

"Hell." Matt Tabor dropped his half-smoked cigarette but didn't bother to stomp it out. I watched it nervously and as soon as he turned away, I pounced.

"Is it true," I asked, hoping Hampton would find my safety zeal contagious rather than laughable, "that Matt Tabor and Dani Marsh plan to marry?"

Hampton's smile seemed to stick, rather than merely stay in place. "So I hear. We'll see if they survive the picture." He tipped his cowboy hat, then moved off to speak with his cinematographer. Carla had settled into a folding chair, obviously keen on watching the filming. I strolled around the meadow's edge, looking for wildflowers.

The mating of Dani Marsh and Matt Tabor struck a discordant note. Visually, they were a perfect pair: beautiful blond Venus; dark and handsome Adonis. But Matt Tabor seemed like a first-run version of Cody Graff. Surely five years and dazzling success in Hollywood should have changed Dani's taste in men.

Standing next to an old-growth Douglas fir and hearing the cedar waxwings chatter among its branches, I could believe they were talking about me. Who was I to criticize Dani Marsh's love life? In over twenty years, I not only didn't have a new man in my life, but I'd never gotten over the one who got away.

Out in the snow, under the bright, hot sun, the two people who so resembled Matt and Dani were embracing. In their heavy parkas and ski pants, they didn't look like they were having much fun. All the same, the idea of embracing appealed to me. A lot. Maybe it was time to call the sheriff.

Milo Dodge was too busy with Loggerama to have dinner with me. Or so he began, speaking in his laconic voice from the sheriff's office just before five o'clock. Carla had endured a bee sting and I had fought off boredom to see less than thirty seconds of film finally ready to go into the can. It had taken almost three hours, with Reid Hampton no longer so genial, Matt Tabor cursing a blue streak, and even Dani Marsh beginning to show signs of impatience under her fur-lined hood.

"If we went about eight o'clock, I could do it," Milo finally allowed. "I've got to check on Durwood on the way home. I let him out this morning if he promised not to drive for a month."

Whatever spark of passion I'd felt igniting in the meadow had been doused by Milo's lack of enthusiasm for my company. To be fair, Milo and I weren't exactly an item. We were friends, comfortable together, mature adults who didn't feel the need to leap into the sack to keep close. At least that was the theory.

"I could fix dinner here," I offered. Occasionally, within the past year, Milo and I had traded home-cooked meals. He was good with the basics, but God forbid he should have higher aspirations. After five months, his beef tournedos were still a bad memory.

"What?" asked Milo.

"Whatever. I can stop at the Grocery Basket on the way home." It occurred to me that after this weekend's grand opening, I could stop at Safeway. Maybe they wouldn't have gray meat.

"I feel like chops," said Milo.

"Pork or lamb?"

"Lamb. Wait — which one is the real little kind?"

"Lamb." I winced. According to the Grocery Basket's ad, which even now lay before me in the new edition of *The Advocate*, pork chops were on special. Lamb would cost me about three times as much. "Say, Milo — who is Curtis Graff? I meant to ask Vida, but I forgot."

"Curtis? He's the older Graff kid. You know, Cody's brother. I think he went to Alaska." In the background, voices erupted. Milo apparently had visitors. "I've got to go, Emma. Mrs. Whipp just broke her Mixmaster over Mr. Whipp's head up at the retirement home. See you around eight."

The Whipps had recently celebrated their sixtieth wedding anniversary at the VFW Hall. Vida's account had omitted the part about Mr. Whipp trying to drown Mrs. Whipp in the punch bowl.

Maybe it was just as well that Milo and I weren't madly in love.

Ten minutes later, I was about to head for the Grocery Basket when Carla and Ginny Burmeister flew into my office. To my amazement, Carla's eyes were red-rimmed and Ginny was showing signs of deep distress.

"Carla's poisoned," Ginny declared, her usual composure in disarray. A tall, thin girl whose thick auburn hair was her best feature, Ginny was an ardent adherent of order and

51

routine. Carla was adroit at ruining both. "Look!" Ginny grabbed Carla's left arm and thrust it at me as if it were a haunch of meat. Irreverently, I wondered how much it would cost a pound at the Grocery Basket.

"It's that bee," gasped Carla. "I must be allergic."

Sure enough, Carla's forearm was flaming red and swollen twice its normal size. Lightly, I touched the bright flesh. "It's hot, all right. Have you ever been stung before?"

"Sure," gulped Carla. "Lots. At least when I was little."

"Maybe it wasn't a bee," I said, flipping through my Rolodex for Doc Dewey's number. "It may have been a wasp or a yellowjacket, especially at that elevation."

To my relief, Marje Blatt answered. Obviously, at least one of the Deweys was still around. Young Doc was at the hospital, waiting for Mr. Whipp and his concussion, but Doc Senior was just getting ready to go home. Could we come right away?

We could and did, all three of us jamming into the Jaguar. Carla moaned a lot as we drove the four blocks from the newspaper to the medical-dental clinic. Since Alpine is built on a sidehill, most of the streets going away from the downtown area are fairly steep. I geared down as I approached the intersection at Third and Cedar; a logging truck, minus its rig, had the right of way and was going much too fast for town driving. BLACKWELL TIMBER was painted in bold black letters on the cab's door. I recognized Jack Blackwell in the driver's seat, with Patti Marsh at his side. From this angle, Patti didn't look much like her famous daughter. One of these days maybe I'd get a close-up in good light.

I hadn't seen Doc Dewey Senior since the high school commencement exercises in June. He had always been a small but robust man of about seventy, with a brusque bedside manner masking a gentle soul. Yet as I watched him tend to Carla, he looked as if he had shrunk. His white hair seemed more sparse and the sparkle had gone out of his blue eyes. Doc's expertise was intact, however, as he administered a shot of adrenaline to Carla.

"Yellowjacket, that's my guess," Doc Dewey announced while Carla flinched and moaned some more. "I'll write you a prescription for an antihistamine. Don't cheat on it, girlie."

Doc, whose first name was Cecil, always referred to female patients, regardless of age, as *girlie*. Males were addressed as *young man*. I wasn't sure if there was sexism involved, since his overriding attitude was that all his patients were idiots, regardless of gender.

Doc was at his desk, scribbling away. "Where'd you get that, girlie?" he asked, looking back at Carla over his glasses.

Breathlessly, Carla explained. "I didn't notice much at the time," she concluded. "I was so caught up in the cinematic experience."

"The what?" Doc had gotten to his feet and was looking at Carla as if she were delirious. "You mean those Hollywood people?" He all but spat. "Stupid, just stupid! Dani ought to know better than to come back to Alpine. What's that poor girlie thinking of?"

Ginny, who had been holding Carla's hand, eyed Doc curiously. "What do you mean, Doc? Carla says she's very sweet."

Doc made a whistling sound through the excellent dentures constructed for him by his fellow tenant, Dr. Starr. "Never mind. Let's just say some things are better left alone. It would take God Almighty himself to sort out that mess, though it makes a body feel guilty not to lend a hand. Here, take this over to Parker's Pharmacy. They don't close until nine." He thrust the prescription not at Carla, but at Ginny. I guessed that Doc knew instinctively which of them was more reliable.

At the moment, I wished I knew what Doc was talking about. It seemed to me that Carla was right — Dani Marsh was a very genuine, pleasant person. But a lot of Alpiners didn't seem to agree. Maybe Dani was acting. It was, after all, her profession. In the two weeks that she would be in Alpine, I might be able to find out what the real Dani Marsh was like.

It didn't occur to me then that there might be reasons why I wouldn't want to know.

Chapter Four

Except for an occasional Clint Eastwood video, I don't think Milo Dodge has seen a movie since his wife left him for another man. The location shooting up at Baldy held no fascination for the sheriff of Skykomish County. Milo loved his lamb chops, but he wasn't much interested in the return of Dani Marsh.

"She was in school with one of my kids. I think," he added a bit doubtfully.

If Milo was right, Dani had probably been a classmate of his oldest daughter Tanya. I'd met only one of his three children — Brandon, who had spent most of July with Milo before going to Bellevue to stay with his mother and her second husband. Tanya lived in Seattle with an aspiring sculptor Milo referred to as Flake Nuts. The youngest of the Dodge offspring was still in high school. Milo usually went to Bellevue once a month to see her and to avoid Old Mulehide, the mother of his brood.

"Dani's twenty-four, according to her press release." I noted, shoveling out more green beans for Milo. "Tanya's the same age, right?"

"I guess so," Milo replied vaguely. Birthdays were more of a mystery to the sheriff than was the criminal mind. He was polishing off his third lamb chop and eyeing the empty platter wistfully. A big, shambling man with sandy hair and hazel eyes, Milo Dodge did a pretty good imitation of a bottomless pit.

Since dessert didn't exist, I offered him more bread. Obviously, I wasn't going to get anywhere interrogating him about Dani Marsh. Vida, as usual, would have to be my primary source. I changed the subject to Loggerama and saw Milo's long face grow longer.

"Let's just hope we don't get a bunch of tourists overrunning the town," he said, slapping much butter and a lot of jelly onto his bread. "The ski lodge is already full, what with the movie people staying there, and both motels have been booked for a month. I wish they'd hurry the hotel renovation along. We could use some extra space in the summers."

Milo referred to the restoration of the old Alpine Hotel, which until this past winter had housed a few elderly tenants and an occasional transient who could afford the twenty dollar minimum. A California consortium had bought the property, however, with intentions of restoring it to its former Edwardian glory. They were taking their time about it, perhaps somewhat daunted by the discovery that the hotel's glory days were a figment of some glib realtor's imagination. The Alpine Hotel had never been anything more than a boarding house with a lobby.

"I'd like to have a lot more than five deputies," Milo grumbled. "I'm thinking of scouting around for some volunteers."

"What are you expecting? A riot at the base of the Carl Clemans statue?" My tone was dour: old Carl was not likely to incite pandemonium. As the town's founder and owner of the original mill, he was always described as a benevolent, if shrewd, human being. "This will be my third Loggerama. I don't recall any big problems the last two years."

Milo's plate was now bare, except for three bones. I halfway expected he'd grind them up with his teeth. Pushing away from the table, he stretched out his long legs. "Maybe I'm just nervous because I've got an election coming up this fall. I hear that Averill Fairbanks is thinking of running against me."

I got up to fetch the coffeepot. "Averill is gaga. He reports a UFO sighting about once a month. Nobody would take him seriously."

"That's not necessarily so. Crazy Eights Neffel runs for the legislature every two years, and even though he's certifiable, he's never gotten less than ten percent of the vote in this district. Back in '64, Dolph Swecker ran his goat for city council and beat A. J. Iverson by thirty votes."

I glanced back into the little dining room to see if Milo was joking. He didn't look like it. Small towns are strange places, hell-bent on preserving their individuality. It wouldn't have surprised me to find that the goat had been impeached for embezzling. It wouldn't be any stranger than the man up on Burl Creek Road who had gone through a wedding ceremony last May with a deer named Cora.

"I wouldn't worry about Averill," I said, pouring us both more coffee. It was beginning to cool off inside the house. I had both doors open and several of the windows, too. My two-bedroom home is built of logs at the edge of the forest. Tonight, no breeze stirred the tall evergreens, but their sheltering branches helped protect me from the sun. Feeling guilty over the lack of dessert, I suggested a brandy with coffee. Milo looked at his watch.

"Better not, Emma," he said. "It's after nine. I've got to be up at the crack of dawn to help with the parade route."

"What do you mean, parade route? They start at one end of Front Street and stop at the other. This isn't Macy's Thanksgiving extravaganza, you know."

Milo took three quick gulps of coffee and stood up. "All the same, I'd better run." He avoided my gaze. "Did I have a jacket?"

"In eighty-five degree weather?" I was following him into the living room. "Gosh, Milo, you're jumpy tonight. You shouldn't let Loggerama get to you. It's supposed to be fun." Casually, I placed a hand on his arm. Maybe it really was the upcoming election that was bothering him. But Milo was already finishing his second term. I hadn't been in Alpine when he'd run for office before, but I knew he'd won handily. "Who is it?" I asked, looking up at him. Surely there had to be another, more credible candidate in the offing than Averill Fairbanks and his UFOs.

Milo's reply rocked me: "Honoria Whitman. She's a potteress in Startup." Milo was looking miserable as he put a big hand over mine. "I meant to tell you about her, Emma, but I didn't have the nerve."

I was gaping at him. "A *potteress?* You mean you're seeing someone?" My voice sounded shrill. I pulled my hand away and stepped back.

Milo swallowed hard. "I met her last June when I was fishing down on the Skykomish River. She owns a place just off the back road that hooks up into the Sultan Basin. I guess she's been there about a year, up from California."

"California!" It figured. Even though I

60

knew all Californians didn't have horns and forked tails, I wasn't reassured. The Pacific Northwest had been invaded by Californians for the last two decades, jamming our cities, crowding our highways, polluting our air, and even daring to introduce a work ethic. Honoria Whitman, with her crude clay pots and organic compost heap, was no doubt lounging around in Startup wearing flowing ethnic garments and hoping to improve the lot of the pitiful natives.

"Your private life is your own business," I told Milo frostily. My brown eyes shot daggers. "Are you bringing Honoria to Loggerama, or would she find it too vulgar?"

"I told you: I'm working the whole damned time," Milo replied, his annoyance as plain as my own. "In fact, this might be the only night I'll be able to see her until Loggerama is over."

"Then," I demanded, as he edged toward the door and I stalked him with arms folded across my breast, "why the hell didn't you have her feed you? Or don't you like Tofu Helper?"

Milo gazed at the beamed ceiling. "Wednesday nights Honoria teaches a class in pottery at Everett Junior College. She doesn't get home until almost ten." He seemed to be talking through gritted teeth.

My rational self told me to calm down. There was no reason for me to be angry with Milo. His private life was indeed his own. We had never exchanged so much as a kiss. Why then did I feel betrayed? Was it only my ego and not my heart which was wounded?

I threw up my hands. "It must be the lamb chops," I confessed sheepishly. "They set me back fourteen bucks. If you'd asked for hot dogs, I'd have told you to bring Honoria along."

Milo appeared partially convinced. Or else he was just anxious to make his peace and be gone. "You'd like her, Emma. She's very soothing company."

On drugs was the evil thought that flickered through my mind. But I tried to smile. "Go on, have a good time. I'll see you at the Loggerama kickoff banquet tomorrow night."

If Milo hadn't already been wearing his cotton sports shirt open at the neck, I swear he would have run his finger inside his collar. Instead, he gave me a lopsided grin and an awkward wave, then loped out the front door. With a sigh, I went out on the porch, conscious as ever of the fresh scent of pine on the clear mountain air. Milo was climbing into his Cherokee Chief. He was a nice man, and I ought to wish him well. Certainly he wasn't the sort I'd want to spend the rest of my life with. He was too rough around the edges, too small-town in his outlook, too anti-intellectual and too unsophisticated.

But even more than what he was, there was what he wasn't: Milo Dodge wasn't Tom Cavanaugh, and that was that.

Front Street was lined with bunting and banners, looking more festive than the Fourth of July, more colorful than Christmas. Just as Milo had feared, tourists were beginning to arrive in Alpine. Traffic on Front Street was unusually heavy, which meant there were cars in both lanes. I made a mental note to have Carla do a story on the visitors, with perhaps two or three interviews included.

Having walked to work, as I often did in the summer, I greeted Ginny Burmeister, who informed me that Carla wasn't coming in. The yellowjacket sting was less swollen, but the reaction had upset her stomach. She hoped to be back to work tomorrow.

Vida hadn't yet arrived, and Ed was at a Kiwanis breakfast meeting. I went into my editorial office and made a haphazard attempt to clear my desk. Among the leftovers from this week's edition were several glossy photos of the movie crew — Dani Marsh, Matt Tabor, even Reid Hampton. I started to pitch them into the wastebasket, but it occurred to me that there might be some fans around town who'd appreciate having the pictures as souvenirs. I left them to one side, then sorted through the notes Ginny had left on my desk. As always on a Thursday, there were repercussions from the previous day's paper. Several people had responded — unfavorably — to my article on the danger of flooding caused by clear-cutting timber. Never mind that I'd tried to balance the piece. In a town that leaned on lumber for much of its economic stability, it was hard to present any other point of view.

Most of the criticism, however, had to do with the historical pieces we had run in the special Loggerama section. The turn-of-the-century silver mines had been worked by Chinese, not Japanese. The Japanese and possibly some Koreans had worked on the Great Northern Railroad because the Chinese had been excluded by a federal act in 1882. That, asserted Grace Grundle, was why Alpine had originally been named Nippon. The largest steelhead ever caught in the Skykomish River was thirty-two pounds, three ounces, not thirty-three pounds, two ounces. And the year was 1925, not 1924, insisted Vida's eldest brother, Ralph Blatt. The correct spelling of the name of the Norwegian emigrant who had helped Rufus Runkel found the ski lodge was

Olav Linritsen, with just one *n*, not two, said Henry Bardeen, the current resort manager.

No matter how certain a reader may be, it doesn't pay to accept criticism on faith alone. I would check and recheck each correction. I never ran a retraction, never suppressed a story, never allowed anyone to censor the news — but I always owned up to mistakes.

I was verifying the spelling of Olav the Obese's surname when I heard the newsroom door open. Vida, I thought, without looking up. But it was Patti Marsh, tramping purposefully toward my inner sanctum.

"You bitch!" she flared, leaning on my desk and showing her teeth like a she-wolf. "You defamed me! I'll sue your butt off!"

Being threatened by furious readers wasn't a novelty to me. Usually, however, they resorted to the telephone, being timid about facing me in person. But Patti Marsh was bold as brass tacks, glaring at me from about three feet away.

"What's the problem?" I asked, turning slightly in my swivel chair and staring right back.

She jabbed at a copy of *The Advocate* that lay on my desk. "That's the problem, right there on page four! You said my husband left me! That's a lie, I threw the bastard out! Nobody leaves Patti Erskine Marsh!"

Calmly, I pulled the paper out from under her hand and opened it to the offending page. I read Vida's copy aloud:

"When Dani was less than a year old, her father left Alpine. Patti Marsh raised her only daughter alone, working at the Loggers' Café. After Dani's graduation from Alpine High School in 1985, she married . . .' " I stopped and shrugged. "Excuse me, Ms. Marsh, it doesn't say he left *you;* it says he left *Alpine.* That's not exactly the same."

"The hell it isn't!" Patti Marsh waved a sunburned arm in repudiation. Up close, in the daylight, I could see a faint resemblance to Dani. The brown eyes were similar; so was the aquiline nose. But the bad perm and the tinted blond hair didn't do much to enhance her features. I judged her to be about my age, but there was a lot more mileage in her face than mine. She was short, like her daughter, but carried an extra twenty pounds. The polka dot halter top and the skintight white pants showed that most of the added weight was well-distributed. It was too bad that her head seemed to be empty.

"Look," I said, standing up but staying behind the desk which I always thought of as the moat that kept my public at bay, "you're trying to interpret the sentence. Why? It just says that Dani's father left town. Some other reader might figure that you chased him off with a two-by-four. Did you?"

Patti was still wild-eyed, but she was beginning to lose steam. I gauged that she was the sort of person who can bulldoze her way through life as long as there's nothing very substantial in her path. In my guise as editor and publisher of *The Advocate*, I always felt fairly substantial. It was in my other roles that I sometimes felt like a will-o'-the-wisp.

"This town's full of gossipy old bitches — the men, too." Her brown eyes raked over my small cluttered office. Patti Marsh had a skittish, nervous gaze, as if her emotions were in charge of her vision. "How many calls have you had?"

My own stare turned blank. "About what?"

She pointed again at the paper. "About me. And . . . Dani." It seemed she could hardly get her daughter's name out.

"None. It's a pretty tame story, Ms. Marsh."

The expression of scorn she bestowed on me might have withered a person who wasn't used to letters that started "Dear Knucklehead." Or worse. "Hey, kiddo, you don't know the half of it," asserted Patti, with a toss of her bleached hair. "This whole ball of wax is anything but tame." She started to heel around on her black thongs, then her mouth twisted into a nasty little smile. "If you ask me, we'll all be lucky if somebody doesn't end up killed." Her eyes dropped to the stack of glossy photos at the side of my desk, "Who's that?" she demanded, looking startled.

I glanced down. Reid Hampton's picture was on top of the pile. "The director. Why?"

Patti Marsh gave herself a vigorous shake. "Hunh. So he's the one who's been pushing Dani. I wonder why." There was a sneer in her voice, then she strutted out of the office, almost colliding with Vida, who was just coming in. I didn't hear the exchange between them; I was too busy trying to figure out what on earth Patti Marsh was talking about. Whatever it was, I assumed it had nothing to do with Loggerama.

Vida surged through the newsroom, heading straight for my office. Her sailor hat was tipped over one ear. At least she didn't have it on backward, as often happen with Vida's headgear. Behind the tortoiseshell glasses, her eyes were afire. "If I didn't think all you Catholics were a bunch of smug hidebound hypocrites, I'd convert so I could be eligible for sainthood. Any normal person would have put Patti Marsh's nose in her navel."

Accustomed to Vida's fulminations against

any religion but her own Presbyterian sect, I merely grinned. "Got you riled, huh? What's really eating that woman?"

"Woman!" sniffed Vida, plopping down into one of the two chairs on the other side of my desk. "Patti doesn't qualify. Real women aren't so hare-brained." She stopped fuming, then cocked her head to one side. "You're right, Emma. What *is* wrong with Patti? Oh, she and Dani were always at sixes and sevens, but that doesn't make for such bitterness. Patti's the type who'd hitch her wagon to a star, especially if the star's her daughter. Five years have gone by, and it sounds as if Dani has grown up considerably. I can't help but think they ought to have worked through their differences by now."

Not knowing either mother or daughter, I was in no position to speculate. Admitting as much, I let Vida continue her mulling out in the newsroom while I answered another rash of post-publication calls. By ten o'clock, I was mired in conversation with Alpine's oldest rational citizen, Elmer Kemp, 101 years old, who had come to town as a teenager to work in the sawmill. Elmer had a laundry list of omissions from the historical coverage, and paid no heed to my attempts to remind him that we were limited in terms of space. He didn't much like the implication that clear-cutting was bad; he objected to a reference to the Lumber Trust of the post-World War I era, claiming there never was such a thing; he asserted that the big price hike back in 1919 was due solely to an unprecedented demand for lumber in the mysterious East — i.e., New York, Boston, and Philadelphia.

I was taking desultory notes for a possible feature when Ginny Burmeister signaled from the outer office, mouthing something I couldn't understand. At last, she whipped out a piece of paper and scrawled her message in red pen:

"Reid Hampton on line two."

Getting rid of Elmer was no mean feat, and I was finally forced to resort to the promise of an interview, perhaps in early September. "I should live so long," huffed Elmer. He finally hung up, giving me no opportunity to point out that having already reached 101, his chances of being around in another month might be better than mine.

The telephone only served to amplify Reid Hampton's booming voice. "You're a busy woman," he remarked in what I took to be a chiding tone. It was likely that Reid Hampton was rarely put on hold.

"The paper came out yesterday," I explained, holding the phone a half-inch from my ear. "We always get a lot of feedback.

Like a movie premiere."

His hearty laugh rumbled along the line. "But unlike the picture business, it's too late for you to make any changes."

"Yes. Journalism is real life." I felt my voice tense.

"And movies are *reel* life," Reid Hampton noted with a deep chuckle.

At least he hadn't condescended to spell *reel*. We were making small talk, and I couldn't see the point.

Reid Hampton went straight to it: "Are you free for dinner tonight?" The question was posed on a softer note.

"Why — yes." Taken by surprise, I blurted out the truth.

"Where can we get a decent meal within a fifty-mile radius?" He sounded pleased with himself.

I was nervously shuffling papers on my desk. I didn't particularly want to have dinner with Reid Hampton. But how often would Emma Lord, small-town newspaper publisher, have a chance to go out with a famous Hollywood director? How often would old Emma have a chance to go out at all? Alpine wasn't exactly a hotbed of eligible middle-aged men who were sufficiently sophisticated to know they were supposed to sniff, not chew, the wine cork.

"There's a good French restaurant just a few miles down the highway," I said, gathering courage. "It's run by a Californian and a Provençois," I added, hoping to give the place credibility.

"French food via Rodeo Drive? That sounds fine to me."

We settled on seven o'clock and I gave him directions to my home. Then Reid Hampton was off, presumably to tell Dani Marsh how to shiver in eighty-six-degree weather. I had regained my poise and was smiling, a bit wryly. Take that, Milo Dodge, I said to myself. I, too, can strike California gold.

It was busier than usual Thursday, with all the Loggerama doings. I filled in for Carla at the Miss Alpine pageant rehearsal in the high school gym, stopped by the football field to catch the trials for the timber sports competition, and checked out the parade floats being assembled in an empty warehouse by the river.

Since I was afoot, I was hot and tired by the time I dropped off four rolls of film at Bayard's Picture-Perfect Photo Studio, where we do most of our developing work. Buddy Bayard is efficient, competent, and contrary. He will argue any issue, any time, choosing any side you're not on. I cut my stay at his studio short and dragged myself the last two blocks along Front Street to the *Advocate* office.

Vida was already gone, leaving a note atop a pile of copy. Ed was going over an ad with Francine Wells for Francine's Fine Apparel. Francine was set on buying half a page to show the first of her new fall line; Ed was determined to cut the ad by half.

I stopped at his desk, greeted Francine, and admired the sketches she'd brought along. "Terrific separates," I gushed, wondering how anyone could contemplate woolens in July. "What are the colors this season?"

Francine brightened; Ed blanched. No doubt he had visions of Francine wanting a special four-color insert. But before Francine could respond, a tall, lean young man with sun-streaked blond hair came through the door, carrying a bouquet of tiger lilies, gladioli, and asparagus fern. He looked vaguely familiar, but I couldn't immediately place him.

"Excuse me," he said in a soft, diffident voice. "Could someone tell me where I could find the movie people?"

My first reaction was that the film crew probably preferred not to be found. But perhaps this self-effacing young man had a reason for going to the location shoot, such as delivering his flowers. "Do you have some connection with the company?" I asked, making an effort to sound friendly.

"Hey," said Ed, looking up from Francine's ad dummy, "aren't you Curtis Graff?" He rose awkwardly from his chair, lumbering across the room to shake the new comer's hand. "I remember you from the fire department. You rescued a couple of kids from a burning house out on Burl Creek Road."

Curtis Graff smiled in a modest manner. "I had help." His smile grew wider. "I don't think those kids wanted to come out, though. They'd been playing with matches and were more afraid of their parents than the fire."

I backed off, allowing Curtis and Ed to get reacquainted. Francine sidled up to me, her carefully styled hair and her white sleeveless dress somehow keeping unruffled in the heat of the day. "He's better-looking than Cody," she whispered. "Maybe Dani should have married him instead."

Francine was right. The weaknesses in Cody Graff's features weren't evident in those of his older brother. Perhaps it was a matter of character. Curtis Graff struck me as more serious, with a touch of melancholy. At any rate, he didn't look as if he were prone to pouting.

"I just got in from Alaska," Curtis was saying. "I'm staying with some friends." He turned to me and his dark blond eyebrows lifted. "Say — are you Adam Lord's mother? He asked me to have you send him a few things when I go back up north."

"Surprise, surprise," I murmured. "Just let me know what and when. Are you looking for anyone in particular with the movie or did you just want to watch the filming?"

Curtis, who was wearing knee-length shorts and a T-shirt, shifted from one foot to the other. "I know someone who's making the movie. I just didn't know how to get hold of anybody. Do they stay around here at night?"

"They're all up at the ski lodge," I said without further hesitation. The movie company's lodgings were no secret. Indeed, a lot of locals — and maybe a few tourists, too — had probably made their way by now to the location site.

"Great," said Curtis Graff. He offered us his diffident smile. "Thanks. I'll get back to you in a couple of days, Mrs. Lord. Adam gave me a list, but he said he might call you about some other stuff he forgot."

I inclined my head. Curtis Graff moved quickly out of the office, giving the impression that he was making an escape. "That's odd," I remarked, more to myself than to Ed and Francine. "I wonder why he isn't staying with Cody." My ad manager didn't pay any attention, but Francine's bright blue eyes fastened on me.

"If my memory hasn't failed," said Francine, "there's no love lost between the brothers. Their parents retired to the San Juan Islands about the same time Curtis went up to Alaska. I never knew the boys very well, but Hetty Graff was always hanging around the sale rack. She never bought anything unless it was at least forty percent off."

Ed's head shot up. "Forty percent off? Gosh, Francine, don't tell me you're having a clearance sale!"

Francine's carefully plucked eyebrows lifted slightly. "Not yet, Ed." She gave him her sweetest smile. "I thought about having a renovation sale after Durwood wiped out my front window, but I'll wait until September. Do you think I should take out a *full page* ad?"

Ed reeled against the desk. Trying not to laugh aloud, I crept into my office.

My walk home was uphill. I arrived at my cozy log house in a weary, wilted state, hoping that the shelter of the evergreen trees had kept the interior cool. Clutching the mail I had retrived from my box by the road, I went inside and discovered that though there was no breeze, the temperature in the living room seemed at least ten degrees below the heat outdoors.

I got a Pepsi out of the refrigerator and poured it over a tall glass of ice. Collapsing on the sofa, I scanned the mail. The usual bills, ads, catalogues — and a single letter. The return address put my heart in my mouth: a well-heeled residential street in San Francisco. Hurriedly, I ripped open the plain beige envelope.

This was the third letter I had received from Tom Cavanaugh since he had visited Alpine the previous autumn. He had come to town to give me advice on running the newspaper. He had also expressed an interest in investing in *The Advocate*, since buying into newspapers was one of the ways he had built up the considerable fortune his wife had inherited. I had not been keen on a partnership, no matter how silent, and Tom had respected my wishes. But he and I were already partners in another far different enterprise: Tom was Adam's father, and in this letter, he was insisting on playing a bigger role in our son's life.

"With my other children virtually raised and on their own, I feel honor-bound to help you with Adam," Tom wrote on his word processor. "I haven't pressed you about this because I know how hell-bent you are on being independent. If you don't want to tell Adam about me, you don't have to, but in good conscience, I can't go on ignoring my responsibilities. It's not fair to Adam, and it's not fair to me."

Bull, I thought to myself angrily. None of it was ever fair to anybody. It wasn't fair that Tom had married a wealthy heiress before I met him. It wasn't fair that we had fallen in love and that his wife and I had gotten pregnant about the same time. And it certainly wasn't fair that Sandra Cavanaugh had turned out to be a raving loony.

"I can see you wadding this letter up and throwing it across the room while you swear like a sailor," Tom went on in his usual wry — and perceptive — manner. "But I'd like you to at least think about this. I may be coming up your way in the early fall again, so maybe we can have dinner. Meanwhile, there are a couple of recent developments that came out of a publishers' meeting last month in Tampa . . ."

He went on to enlighten me about a new way of billing advertisers and how small newspapers could become the middlemen in job printing. I didn't pay much attention. All I noticed was that he signed the letter, "Love, Tom."

And I still did.

Perhaps I'd give his proposal some thought.

After Loggerama. I might even consider his suggestions about the paper. Certainly I would think about having dinner with him if he came up from the Bay Area in the fall.

One thing I would not do: I wouldn't crumple up the letter and throw it across the room. But I did swear like a sailor.

Chapter Five

My dinner with Reid Hampton was a dud. The food at the Café de Flore was excellent as always, the wine list was extensive and impressive, and the service was superb. But the company was definitely second-rate.

To be fair, I suppose a lot of women would find Reid Hampton fascinating. Certainly he had traveled a lot, read widely if not deeply, and knew everyone who had graced the covers of *People* magazine in the past year. But by the time the main course arrived, I was already full — at least of Reid Hampton, who was so full of himself. It's an occupational hazard of journalism that much of one's career is spent listening to other people tell you the stories of their lives. So maybe just once, I was hoping that in my off-hours, I'd find someone who might want to hear mine. As it turned out, Reid Hampton didn't. He didn't even ask any questions about Alpine, which struck me as strange — certainly a director who was setting a film in a small town should want to know what life was really like. But I gathered that Reid Hampton preferred to make up his own version.

It was no wonder that he didn't ask to come in when he brought me home or that he made no romantic advances. I suspected that he was as glad to park me on my doorstep as I was to see him drive away. Most of the time he had talked about himself, his films, his ambitions, his philosophy. My efforts at steering him away from his ego and onto his coworkers came to naught. He remarked that the camera loved Dani Marsh, and that she was like an empty bottle, just waiting for him to fill her up with emotions. He appeared to know next to nothing about her background, except that she came from Alpine. "Cute little town," he had commented. "We'll do a couple of street scenes after all this Loggerama crap is out of the way. I should have some of those buildings repainted along the main drag. They're not right for this picture. I need more blue, some green, maybe even a splash of red. Say, Emma, how would you like to have your newspaper office take on a coat of canary yellow?"

The Advocate badly needed a make-over, but *yellow* coupled with *journalism* did not strike me as a suitable visual message. Somehow, I'd avoided a direct answer. Reid had waxed a bit more eloquently on the subject of Matt Tabor, praising the actor's "brooding presence" and "unquenchable masculinity." Matt was from Kansas and had started out as a dancer. I had refrained from asking if he'd worn ruby slippers or had owned a dog named Toto. My only revenge had been dessert, a marvelous confection of meringue and apricots and whipped cream topped with crystalized sugar.

If I had not turned Reid Hampton into a slathering beast, he had not stirred me to pulse-throbbing excitement either. It was strange, perhaps, since he was good-looking in his lion-maned, broad-shouldered way, and certainly had the trappings of power and success to provide the necessary aphrodisiac. As I slipped out of my plain black linen sheath, it occurred to me that the evening might have gone better if I hadn't received the letter from Tom Cavanaugh just over an hour before Reid had picked me up. To my addled heart, Tom would have made Erich von Stroheim seem bland.

It was not yet ten. I put on my summer-weight cotton bathrobe and went back to the living room to check my messages. Carla had called to say she'd definitely be in on Friday. Francine Wells wanted to know if I'd like to look over her new stock when it came in the second week of August. Henry Bardeen had phoned from the ski lodge to tell me they had found a family of raccoons living in the little house where they stored their firewood. Did

I want a picture?

I supposed I did. Raccoons always make good pictures. I called Henry to tell him I'd send Carla up in the morning.

"I'm afraid we can't wait," said Henry, sounding unusually testy for a man whose job as resort manager required endless patience and perennial good will. "One of our guests suffers from raccoon-phobia. If we don't get those animals out of the wood house tonight Matt Tabor says he'll drive into Seattle and stay at the Four Seasons Olympic."

"Oh, for heavens' sake!" I didn't know whether to laugh or be annoyed. "Okay, Henry, I'll be up in ten minutes."

While changing into slacks and a blouse, I decided I was definitely annoyed. I didn't want to bother Vida this late, and Carla needed a good night's sleep to complete her recovery. Fortunately, I had an extra camera at home. The drive to the ski lodge would take less than five minutes, since my house was on the edge of town. But the idea of the aggressively masculine Matt Tabor being afraid of a bunch of big-eyed bandits with four legs was irksome. I wished that Henry Bardeen had at least cornered a grizzly bear.

Mama, Papa, and four babies posed graciously for my camera. Then Mama wanted to borrow the camera. I back-pedaled out of

83

the wood house and was grateful for Henry's assistance. He had brought some cooked hamburger and peeled oranges to lure the raccoon family out of its self-styled lair. A van with open back doors waited a few yards away, to transport the raccoons to the other side of Alpine.

"Having these Hollywood people here is no picnic," Henry sighed as the van headed down the road. "Oh, they're paying a pretty penny, which is always welcome in off-season; but I tell you, Emma, it's one aggravation after another." Henry Bardeen shook his head, which was topped by an artfully graying toupee.

"Like what?" I asked guilelessly.

"Like diet." Henry's thin mouth twisted. He was a slim man of medium height, with an aquiline nose and fine gray eyes. Unlike most professional men in Alpine, who tended to go in for more casual attire, Henry always wore a suit and tie. "They have the strangest eating habits. And schedules. In bed by ten, maybe even nine, then up at the crack of dawn, which means the kitchen help has to come in early. Not only to fix breakfast, but to pack up the hampers for their lunch up on Baldy. I've had to hire extra people. Tonight, Dani Marsh wanted some sort of cabbage drink sent up to her room. We had no idea how to make it, and when we finally got through to somebody in Everett, Dani was gone. Now she's a local, wouldn't you think she wouldn't be as queer as the rest of them?"

"She hasn't lived here for five years," I pointed out, wondering if there was a feature story in *The Peculiar Palates of Picture People.* Probably not, I decided. It would annoy most of the locals as much as it irked Henry Bardeen.

"She's been gone from the lodge for three hours," said Henry, looking even more aggravated. "That Hampton fellow is about to call the sheriff."

"Good," I said, hoping Reid Hampton would catch Milo Dodge in the sack with Honoria Whitman. It would serve all of them right.

"Good?" Henry stared at me. He may have possessed a gracious manner — usually — but he had absolutely no sense of humor. "What's good about having Reid Hampton roar around the lobby while Matt Tabor is cringing in a corner because some of our furry friends are living outside his window? What's good about Dani Marsh being gone for several hours? She has a wake-up call scheduled for five A.M.!"

"As you pointed out," I said in a soothing voice, "Dani *is* a native. She probably has some old friends here. And her mother, of course."

Henry's stare grew hypnotic. "Patti?" He shook his head, breaking the spell. "I know for a fact that Dani has tried to call Patti at least three times, but either she isn't in or she hangs up on Dani." Suddenly he turned sheepish. "My daughter, Heather, should be more discreet. But I'm afraid she's starstruck."

I knew Heather Bardeen, a pretty, self-contained young woman who worked for her father in various capacities, including that of PBX operator. Somehow, his description didn't sound right. "Aren't Heather and Dani the same age? They would have gone to school together."

Henry grew tight-lipped. "They did. Heather was a year behind Dani. They weren't really friends, but they knew each other. I suppose that's why Heather is so curious. In fact, Heather says that by the time Dani left Alpine, she didn't have any friends. Maybe that's why she went away."

"She'll show up," I said hopefully. "Did she take a car?"

"She may have," Henry replied, looking pessimistic. "The crew rented a whole fleet of them. They're all a white Lexus model. They got them from a dealership in Seattle, except for some custom-built job that belongs to Matt Tabor, and Reid Hampton's Cadillac. He got that here."

The Cadillac had served to take me to dinner at the Café de Flore. I gave Henry an absent nod, then glanced up at the ski lodge. Except for the main floor, most of the lights were already out. It was my understanding that the movie crew had taken up at least three of the lodge's four floors.

"You've got only a little more than a week to go," I said encouragingly. "Think of this as free promotion. It can't help but bring in more visitors next year."

"*Normal* visitors, I trust." Henry was looking very glum.

I gave up trying to cheer him, said good night, and headed for my Jaguar. Sundown had brought cooler temperatures, and a faint breeze stirred the trees. I didn't trouble to turn on the air-conditioning.

At the bottom of the road that led to the ski lodge, I noticed a white car pull up on the verge. My headlights caught a man getting out on the passenger's side. He came around to speak to the driver, who had apparently rolled down the window. As I stopped to watch for any oncoming cars from Alpine Way, I recognized Curtis Graff. And, just as I stepped on the accelerator, I realized that the woman behind the wheel was Dani Marsh.

An odd couple, I thought. Unless Francine Wells hadn't been talking off the top of her carefully coiffed head.

My intention was to tell Vida first thing about seeing Curtis Graff with Dani Marsh. Her reaction would prove interesting. But when I arrived at the office Friday morning, Vida was screaming at the top of her ample lungs and browbeating Abe Loomis. Ed Bronsky watched in dismay while Carla twittered in the vicinity of the coffeepot.

"You're crazier than a bear on a bee farm, Abe Loomis!" cried Vida, waving a sheet of paper at the shocked owner of Mugs Ahoy. "I wouldn't enter your ridiculous contest in a million years! I ought to have you horsewhipped!"

"But Vida," protested Abe, pointing a bony finger at the piece of paper, "you signed the entry form. See for yourself."

Vida glared through her glasses. Her jaw dropped. "Oooooh . . ." She yanked the glasses off and rubbed furiously at her eyes. "I couldn't have! It's a forgery!"

I took the sheet of paper from Abe. Vida's unmistakably flamboyant signature was emblazoned in the space marked for *Entrant.* Someone might have signed her name, but I doubted that anyone would go to the trouble — or have the expertise — to render such a perfect facsimile of her handwriting. It seemed to me that there was another more logical explanation. But I didn't want to mention it in front of Abe Loomis.

Finally, Vida stopped grinding her eyeballs. She sat up very straight, fists on hips, bust thrust out as if she were auditioning for Abe's contest. "All right. I'll do it. What time?"

Abe didn't exactly smile, but at least he moved his mouth. "That's wonderful, Vida. It's tonight, nine o'clock . . ."

I rolled my eyes at Ed, who was shaking his head. Carla was bouncing up and down, trying to get Vida's attention. But Vida was jotting the specifics on a notepad. At last, Abe finished relaying information, nodded to the rest of us, and left the office.

"Vida!" shrieked Carla. "You can't do this! It's demeaning! You'll give journalists a bad name!"

Vida gave Carla the gimlet eye. "A lot of journalists do that every time they get their byline on a story. Put a sock in it, Carla, I won't go back on my word. Though how my name got on that silly form, I'll never —"

I sprang around Carla to face Vida. "I think I know. You signed the entry form instead of the print order. They called from Monroe

89

Wednesday to say we didn't have an authorized signature this week, but they'd go ahead and print without one."

"Oh!" Vida blanched. "That's right! There was a lot of hubbub about then. Oh dear!" She whipped off her glasses again and started a renewed attack on her poor eyes. "Then I'm glad I gave in to that idiot Abe. I have no excuse."

In his typically lugubrious fashion, Ed had come around to Vida's desk. "It'll be just fine, Vida. We'll all come and root for you. I'll bring Shirley. Say," Ed exclaimed, showing signs of actual animation, "maybe Shirley ought to enter too. She's pretty buxom."

Buxom wasn't the word I'd have chosen to describe Ed Bronsky's wife. *Barrel* usually came to mind. I shuddered at the thought, but left the lecture to Carla. She did not disappoint me, rattling off at least a half-dozen reasons why Shirley Bronsky should not engage in such a sexist competition. For once, Ed seemed to pay attention.

By mid-morning, Carla had gone off to talk to the Chamber of Commerce about the influx of tourists, and Ed had left to confer about an ad at the Toyota dealership. Their departure gave me the chance to tell Vida about seeing Dani Marsh with Curtis Graff.

Vida turned contemplative. "How very

odd," she remarked, chewing on the tortoise-shell earpiece of her glasses.

"Why?" I inquired, perching on the edge of her desk. "Didn't Dani get along with her brother-in-law?"

Vida squinted up at me. "No, no, that isn't what I mean. Curtis and Dani were on amicable terms, as far as I know. I meant that it's strange for Curtis to show up after all these years at the same time that Dani comes back to town. This is his first trip to Alpine since he went to Alaska."

"Well," I said, as Ginny Burmeister came into the office with the morning mail, "there hasn't been much to draw him here if his parents are in the San Juans and he and Cody weren't close."

"Exactly." Vida gave a single, sharp nod of her head. "The brothers were always scrapping. But Dani makes an appearance and here comes Curtis." She snapped her fingers. "Don't you find that curious?"

"I had a crush on Curtis when I was thirteen," said Ginny, distributing stacks of mail in each of the three in-baskets in the news office. "He was almost ten years older than I was, but I used to hide behind our hedge and watch him go down the street. The Graffs lived at the other end of the block, on Cedar. I'd gotten over him by the time he went to

Alaska, but I still felt sort of sad."

"Everyone felt sad for the Graffs and the Marshes," said Vida. "That was the first case of Sudden Infant Death Syndrome in this town in several years. We've only had one SIDS tragedy since, thank heavens."

I accepted the pile of bills, news releases, and letters to the editor from Ginny. "It sounds to me as if the death of that poor baby changed a lot of lives. Dani and Cody broke up, Dani left town, the Graffs moved away, Curtis went to Alaska, and Patti Marsh doesn't want anything to do with her daughter."

"Exactly," agreed Vida, fingering a couple of wedding announcements she'd just received. "And Art Fremstad committed suicide. It was an awful year for Alpine."

I blinked at Vida, who was ripping open one of the envelopes, pink stationery with a gilded edge. "Who's Art Fremstad?" In two years, I'd never heard of the man.

Vida scanned the announcement. "Michelle Lynn Carmichael and Jeremy Allan Prescott. A have-to. Marje says she's six months along." Vida tossed the pink and gilt announcement into the box by her typewriter. "What? Oh — Art. He was a deputy sheriff, not yet thirty, and seemed to have good sense. But he was found in the river, about a mile from Alpine Falls. His family insisted it had to be an accident, but later they found a note. He was despondent, or depressed, or whatever claptrap people use to disguise the fact that they have no self-discipline."

I winced a little at Vida's harsh pronouncement. "What did Milo Dodge think?"

Vida had turned to her typewriter, obviously ready to roll. "Milo?" She gave a little shrug. "He was pretty upset. He was sure it was an accident, too, until that note turned up." The typewriter keys began to clickety-clack at about a hundred words a minute.

I looked at Ginny. "Do you remember the incident?"

Ginny ran a hand through her auburn hair. "Sure. Not that many people kill themselves in Alpine. I suppose," she added musingly, "because there aren't that many people to begin with." Her gaze was ironic.

"I suppose," I said, and wondered why I suddenly had a feeling of unease.

To my amazement, Milo Dodge called me in the late afternoon and asked if I'd like to go with him to the Mugs Ahoy wet T-shirt contest. "I heard about Vida," he said, obviously trying not to sound too amused. "You and your staff could probably use some moral support."

"Moral?" I snorted into the phone. "I don't

know whether it will help or hinder Vida to have us there. In some ways, I think we should spare her the embarrassment."

Milo laughed outright. "Vida? Embarrassed? She'll love it. What did Abe say in the ad about sticking *more* than your neck out? Vida's been doing that with her nose for years."

"We're not talking about Vida's nose," I snapped, unhappily recalling one of the changes I'd allowed Abe Loomis to make. "This whole carny show is offensive, and you know it, Milo Dodge. What does Honoria Whitman think about it?"

There was a faint pause. Apparently, Honoria had declined to attend. "She finds small towns amusing. Not that she's a big city girl," he added hastily. "She's from Carmel. She says it's getting too crowded."

"Tut," I remarked, but decided it might be prudent to drop the subjects of Honoria and the wet T-shirt contest. "Milo, why did Art Fremstad kill himself?"

This time, the pause was longer. "Jesus," breathed Milo at last, "why are you bringing that up? I was finally beginning to forget about poor Art. At least a little."

"His name was mentioned today," I said. "How was he connected with the death of Dani and Cody's baby?"

94

"Dani called Doc Dewey, who told her to send for the firemen and the sheriff," said Milo carefully. "I was out of town — it was during the time that Old Mulehide and I were wrangling over custody and all that. Art Fremstad covered for me while I was in Bellevue. He went to the trailer park where Dani and Cody were living, out there past the fish hatchery where those new townhouses went up last year. He and his wife had a new baby of their own. I think the Graff kid's death unhinged him somehow. At least that's what his note indicated."

"He was distraught, you mean? Or depressed?"

"All of the above," replied Milo, sounding very unhappy. "Muddled, too, judging from the way he wrote. Hell, Emma, it wasn't at all like Art. If we hadn't found that note, I'd have sworn it was an accident. Or worse."

Involuntarily, I pushed myself and my chair away from the desk. "What do you mean? Foul play?"

"We considered that at the time. But three days after Art was found — in fact, it was the day of his funeral — this note turned up at his home. His wife discovered it when she got back from the Lutheran church. Case closed."

And, I thought to myself, with good reason.

Art was a young man with a wife and a new baby. The trauma of finding a baby dead from the most inexplicable of causes must have shaken his very soul. Even thinking about it upset me. Art Fremstad must have been a sensitive man, as yet unhardened to the realities of the world.

"Pick me up at eight," I told Milo. There was no point in distressing him further. His recollections were obviously painful. My own emotions were unsettled.

Oddly enough, I would be very glad to see Milo Dodge.

Chapter Six

Mugs Ahoy was jammed. The noise level was deafening; the cigarette smoke weakened my resolve to abstain; the lack of air-conditioning made the interior uncomfortably warm, even at sundown; and the usually murky interior was intermittently lighted up by some sort of revolving lamp above the bar. Even Abe Loomis looked brighter than usual, his long face teetering on the edge of enthusiasm.

If I hadn't been escorted by the sheriff, I would have ended up standing by the door. But Milo pushed his way through the crowd, dragging me by the hand. We stopped at a table near the front where Carla, Ginny, and the Bronskys were already seated. Somehow, Milo commandeered two more chairs, and I squeezed in next to Shirley Bronsky while Milo draped his lanky frame in the chair beside Carla.

Our attempts at small talk failed. It was too loud for normal conversation; the jukebox was playing the Judds and Randy Travis at ear-splitting volume. Milo had ordered a pitcher and a bowl of complimentary thin pretzels. Shirley Bronsky was shoveling mixed nuts into her round mouth, and Carla was drinking white wine. If it was Abe Loomis's house vintage, I figured it probably tasted like paint thinner, but Carla was smiling all over the place. To my amazement, she leaped right out of her seat when Jack Blackwell picked up the microphone and announced that the contest was about to begin.

Jack, who had been seated in front with Patti Marsh and two couples I recognized but didn't know by name, was wearing a silk sportcoat and a string tie. For all the money he had allegedly made in the timber business, I had never seen him dressed up. He didn't exactly rival a Wall Street banker, but at least he looked presentable. Patti glowed up at him, her rhinestone earrings swinging almost to her shoulders.

Jack's first words were indecipherable, mainly because nobody had thought to turn Garth Brooks off on the jukebox. Finally, someone had the sense to pull the plug. Jack grinned at the crowd, revealing very white, if uneven, teeth.

"This is it," he began, clutching the mike to his chest as if he were about to serenade a honeymoon couple in the Poconos. "You've all been waiting for the great moment, the biggest beer bust of them all. Here we go, it's time for Mugs Ahoy's Jugs Ahoy!"

I sighed, Ed chuckled, Ginny grimaced, and Shirley giggled. Milo, thankfully, remained impassive, but to my horror, Carla clapped like crazy. It appeared that her principles had evaporated in a bottle of Yosemite Sam.

The contestants came out from the ladies' room, mounted four temporary stairs to the bar, and to the relatively subdued strains of Waylon Jennings's "Sweet Caroline," paraded above the crowd, strutting and straining in their remarkable wet T-shirts. Jack, meanwhile, shouted each contestant's name and occupation. First in line was Chaz Phipps from the ski lodge, wearing neon green with blinking earrings that must have been on batteries. I wished I'd been on drugs. The catcalls were obnoxious. But Chaz and the three young women who followed her didn't seem to mind in the least.

Milo squeezed my elbow. "You could do that," he remarked, more seriously than I would have wished. "You have a nice chest, Emma."

It was the first personal observation Milo had ever directed at me in the two years I had known him. I didn't know whether to slug him or smile in gratitude. Deciding that he meant well, but couldn't help being an inarticulate boob, I settled for a noncommittal shrug. Then I realized that *boob* was probably inappropriate. I had to stifle a laugh, lest I encourage Carla to further mayhem.

There were twelve contestants in all, and either by accident or design, Vida was last — but certainly not least. She stomped up the stairs to Johnny Cash's classic "Ring of Fire," her head held high, her glasses almost at the end of her nose. She wore a pair of dark gray slacks I'd seen fifty times at work, but her T-shirt was a sight to behold: Vida's impressive bust was adorned with the front page of *The Advocate*'s Loggerama edition, and in each hand she held a small pennant. The left said SUBSCRIBE NOW!; the right said READ BOOKS! Carla jumped onto the table and lead the applause. Naturally, I joined in. Vida sailed off the bar and down the ramp at the far end to join her fellow contestants in the men's room, which was temporarily off-limits. I noticed that Patti Marsh was no longer seated at the first-row table. Maybe she was having regrets about not having taken part in the competition.

I was never sure who the official judges were, though when I had gone in, I had assumed them to be Abe's favorite local drunks. Whoever they were, they deliberated for over five minutes before announcing that the winner was Vida Runkel. Amid a thunderous ovation, marred by only a few boos, Vida re-appeared, still waving her little flags and thrusting her bosom in various directions. Jack Blackwell shoved the microphone in her face.

"Thank you," Vida said after the crowd had begun to quiet down. "The judges' decision proves that older is better. Abe Loomis's idea to hold this contest proves that he's dumb as a rope, but we all knew that before there ever was a Loggerama." She pushed her glasses back up on her nose and gave Abe a flinty look. "The fact that you're all here proves that you're no smarter than Abe. That doesn't say much for Alpine. So two weeks from to-night, at this same time and same place, I want to see all of you back here. Your ticket in the door is a book. The drinks will be on me." Vida pasted the microphone on Jack's chest and moved majestically toward the ladies' room.

The crowd had gone very quiet, but as she made her exit, more applause began to break out. Carla had climbed down from the table-top, but was now back up on her chair, shriek-ing and clapping. "I'm going to read *War and Peace!*" she yelled after Vida. "I cheated and rented the movie for Russian lit at UW! Oh, yeah, Vida! Go, go, *go!*"

Vida went. I had hoped she'd exchange her wet T-shirt for one of her more modest —

if gaudy — blouses and join us, but she didn't. Apparently, Vida had had enough of Mugs Ahoy. I had, too, and it didn't take Milo more than half an hour to realize it, especially after I asked him four times to take me home.

Sheriff or not, Milo had been forced to park his Cherokee Chief two blocks away, in back of the Clemans Building. As we walked along Pine Street with the night air feeling like a tonic, Milo remarked that Vida had certainly been a good sport. I agreed. He said he felt that her challenge about reading books was very appropriate. I said I thought so, too. He allowed that it had been a while since he'd read anything except newspapers. I told him he was missing a lot.

"I used to read more," he said, pulling out from the curb. "Of course I have to go over loads of stuff at work. Some days I get sick of words." Stopping at the Pine Street arterial across from the Alpine Medical and Dental Clinic, Milo suddenly whistled and leaned into the steering wheel. "Look at that!"

The pearl gray car cruising past us was unlike any automobile I'd ever seen, except on a visit to Beverly Hills six years earlier. I, too, stared. "What is it?" I asked in a breathless voice.

"Damned if I know," said Milo, shaking his head as the sleek two-door coupe disappeared past the hospital. "Custom job. Did you see who was driving it?"

I'd gotten a glimpse of the profile behind the wheel. "Henry Bardeen said Matt Tabor brought a customized make to Alpine. But that wasn't Matt driving."

Milo grinned at me before making his right-hand turn. "No, it sure wasn't. That was Dani Marsh, right?"

I gave a faint nod. "Along with Patti Marsh and somebody else."

Milo and I exchanged puzzled looks.

Saturday should have been a day of rest, but journalists are never assured of having weekends off. Vida was going to cover the Miss Alpine pageant in the evening, Carla was assigned to the kiddy parade in the late morning, and I was taking on the timber sports competition in the afternoon.

The event was scheduled for the high school football field, which is less than two blocks from my home. Carrying a camera and a notebook, I walked over under the noonday sun to find a large crowd gathered in the stands. At one end zone, ALPINE was spelled out in fresh white letters; at the other was BUCKERS, the team nickname, which referred to mill-workers who specialized in the sawhorse. Or something to do with the old mill — I was

103

never quite clear; but the mascot depicted a big lug with a big grin and an even bigger saw. It seemed to fit the town's image, though there were grumbles that it was sexist. My feeling was that it was traditional, and at least the Bucker wasn't using the saw to cut a woman in two.

While Alpine's annual event is not on the official Timber Sports circuit, a number of the regular professional competitors usually show up.

Many of the Loggerama contests are not part of the usual circuit, but are steeped in local lore. One of these is Shoot the Duck, in which a decoy is perched high among the branches of a portable Douglas fir and the contestants attempt to hit the target with a catapult. Since I couldn't figure out what this event had to do with timber, logging, and other woodsy work, I questioned Vida about the connection. She informed me that her father-in-law, Rufus Runkel, was responsible. Back in 1927, his wife had promised visitors from Seattle that they would have roast duck for dinner. Armed with a shotgun, Rufus had headed into the woods, but after hiking for over three miles, he discovered he'd forgotten his buckshot. To ensure his honor as a hunter and his wife's reputation as a cook, Rufus had used a rope and a rock to fling at the unsuspecting ducks. Somehow, he bagged three of them, proudly carried them home, and earned not only the thanks of his wife, but an epigram as well:

"I figured Rufus has been shooting blanks for years, but I'm sure glad he still has rocks in his head," said Mrs. Runkel. The trophy for the event was named in his memory.

Due to my status as a member of the press, I was allowed on the sidelines. It was probably even warmer on the field than in the stands, and after the first two hours of sweating, heaving, grunting lumberjacks, I scoured the program in an effort to figure out how much longer I would have to stick around to write an adequate story. I had at least a half-dozen decent photos already and could always get the final results from Harvey Adcock, the hardware store owner who was one of the officials. There were probably close to six hundred people on hand, virtually filling both sides of the stadium. To my surprise, Dani Marsh arrived with Matt Tabor and Reid Hampton shortly after intermission. They were ushered to folding chairs just below the stands and a few yards away from my vantage point. Dani and Reid waved; Matt ignored my existence. Indeed, Matt Tabor seemed to be ignoring the entire occasion. His handsome face looked blotchy, and even at a distance, his eyes seemed unfocused. I thought again about seeing Patti Marsh in the custom-built car. If it belonged to Matt, her presence there seemed very peculiar.

Having suffered through shaving hunks of wood with an axe, log-rolling on a makeshift pond at midfield, and numerous bouts with chain saws, I decided to leave after the Standing Block Chop competition. Kneeling on the dry grass with my camera at the ready, I watched as ten contestants, including Cody Graff, confronted three-foot blocks of wood set in four-legged iron stands on blocks of concrete.

As Harvey Adcock blew his horn to start the competition, I kept my eye on Cody Graff. Like most of his rivals, he was bare to the waist. The muscles of his back and upper arms rippled as he flailed away at the block of wood. His narrow shoulders prevented him from having a physique as imposing as several of the other young men, but he seemed to wield his axe with great authority. I glanced up into the crowd to see if I could find Marje Blatt. She was probably on hand to watch her fiancé, but I couldn't pick her out in the stands.

It was while my back was turned that the axe flew past me. It sailed within two feet of my head and landed with a loud thud at the feet of Dani Marsh. The onlookers uttered a collective gasp. I let out a little cry of my own and whirled around. Cody Graff was standing with his empty hands at his side, while his malevolent expression was fixed on the trio of Hollywood visitors.

Harvey Adcock, Jack Blackwell, and Henry Bardeen were out on the field. The other contestants were still hacking away, though all eyes in the audience were glued on Cody or his axe. Matt Tabor was yelling obscenities, while Reid Hampton picked up the sharp-edged tool and shot a furious look at Cody Graff. Dani Marsh was on her feet, shifting nervously in front of her folding chair.

I moved closer to Harvey, who was now talking to Cody. Harvey seemed very earnest, but I couldn't make out his words without crossing the sideline marker. Cody was shrugging, then nodding. Jack Blackwell retrieved the axe from Reid Hampton, but he didn't give it back to Cody. Instead, Cody jogged off the field, his head down, his face impassive.

I grabbed Harvey as he came over to where I was standing. "What happened? My back was turned."

Harvey, who is no taller than I am, looked at me with troubled green eyes. "Cody says it was an accident. The axe slipped." His graying eyebrow's lifted slightly.

"What do you think?" I asked as the crowd began to settle back into the rhythm of the contest.

Harvey shook his balding head. "I can't say, Emma. It just seems odd that the axe landed right in front of Dani and her friends." With one of his typically quicksilver movements, Harvey started down the sidelines. "The heat's over. I've got to go be an official."

It seemed to me that there was more news — if you define the concept as public interest — in the flying axe than in any further description of the competition. I headed off the field and under the stands to try to find Cody. But by the time I reached the cramped, dank-smelling area that was used mostly for halftime pep talks during football season, Cody was nowhere to be seen. Having come this far, I kept going, out the back way, and into the dirt parking lot.

Cody Graff and Marje Blatt were getting into his pickup truck. They drove away without seeing me.

Two nights in a barroom were two too many for my taste, but Carla and Ginny insisted I join them at the Icicle Creek Tavern to take part in the Celebrity Bartender festivities.

"Doc Dewey's on hand for the first two hours," said Carla as we drove in my Jaguar out Mill Street to the edge of town.

At least we would avoid Fuzzy Baugh and his civic-minded libations. I pulled into the parking lot which was only half full, probably because most of the local residents were attending the Miss Alpine pageant at the high school. No doubt they would pour in later, griping about the winner's deficiencies or extolling her virtues, depending on who was related to whom.

The Icicle Creek Tavern has been controversial in the past few years, not only for its reputation as a site of weekend brawls, but because the area south of the railroad tracks has been built up with new solid middle class homes. In addition, several more expensive residences now sit just across the creek above the river. And the golf course is situated on hilly, tree-shaded grounds a few hundred yards down the road. Naturally, the neighborhood does not approve of the ramshackle old tavern with its boarded-up windows and raucous clientele. They're not even too fond of the gas station which sits next to the tavern, though they will admit it's convenient.

At one time, probably just after prohibition ended and before the loggers started pitching each other through unmarked exits, perhaps the tavern had its share of charm. The paint has faded from its shake exterior; the cedar shingles on the roof have weathered to a dull gray; and the corroded metal sign that stands in the parking lot is virtually unreadable.

The interior is even worse. So many of the chairs have been used to bash heads that in recent years the management has simply brought in apple boxes and other relatively sturdy crates as replacements. The tables are splintering, the floor is uneven, and the long mirror behind the bar has cracked in the form of a spider. Yet on this muggy Saturday night of Loggerama, there was the suggestion of a festive air. Bunting hung from the ceiling along with the cobwebs; a montage of old logging pictures had been mounted over the bar to cover up the shattered mirror; and the pool table had been turned into a display of logging tools from the early part of the century. Most of them were rusty and broken, but it was still a nice idea.

Carla insisted on sitting at the bar. Checking the stool for slivers, I sat down and greeted Doc Dewey who, surprisingly, looked as at home in his white bartender's apron as he did in his white medical coat.

"What will you girlies have?" he inquired, giving the bar a professional swipe with a wet cloth. He looked over his half glasses at Carla. "How's that sting? Any reaction?"

"Not to the antihistamine," replied Carla,

crossing her legs and swinging her feet like some barfly out of a Forties second feature. "Only to the stupid bee. Or wasp."

"Good, good," said Doc. "You're over the danger now. It can have a lot of different symptoms, though. Everything from drowsiness to heart palpitations." He patted his apron-covered chest, causing something to click in his shirt pocket. An extra set of dentures, I mused, just in case some of the patrons weren't on their best Loggerama behavior and tried to knock out his teeth.

Ginny and I both ordered beer, but Carla again opted for white wine. I shuddered, hoping it wouldn't have the same effect on her tonight as it had during the wet T-shirt contest. Taking the schooner from Doc, I swiveled on the stool to check out the rest of the customers. There were a few regulars, mostly loggers, but there was also a sprinkling of people I figured didn't usually hang out at the Icicle Creek Tavern: Cal Vickers, who owned the Texaco station on the other side of town, had come with his wife, Charlene; Heather Bardeen and her buddy, Chaz Phipps from the ski lodge; Jack Blackwell and Patti Marsh; Marje Blatt and Cody Graff.

I considered going over to Cody and asking him about the incident with the axe, but Marje seemed to be deep into a one-sided lecture and Cody was well into his cups. I decided this wasn't the time or place. Just as I was about to turn back to the bar, the door opened. Milo Dodge came in with Honoria Whitman. At least I assumed that the woman in the pale yellow painter's smock shirt and the black tights was Honoria. Her face was a perfect oval, with short ash blond hair and wide-set gray eyes. She had an air of serenity about her, as if nothing could go wrong in her world as long as she was on hand to prevent it.

Except that something obviously had: To my dismay, Honoria Whitman was in a wheelchair. I tried not to let my jaw drop.

Milo nodded in my direction. A bit awkwardly, I descended from the bar stool and went over to greet him and his companion. Milo made the introductions. Honoria extended her hand. It was long, slim, and milk white. She did not fit my preconceived notions of a transplanted Californian in the least.

"Milo speaks so well of you," she said in a cultured, husky voice. "He says you're every inch the professional, a real addition to this community."

"Oh — that's kind of him." I glanced up at Milo, who was flushing. So was I.

More people were coming into the tavern, including Al Driggers, the undertaker, and his spunky wife, Janet. Right behind them, a contingent from the high school faculty trooped in. I recognized Steve Wickstrom, who taught math, and his wife, Donna, along with Coach Rip Ridley and Mrs. Ridley, whose first name I seemed to remember was Dixie. Schoolteachers who drank in public were frowned upon in Alpine, but Loggerama was obviously an exception. The faculty could get as drunk and stupid as the rest of the residents without being hauled up before the school board.

Milo pushed Honoria's chair over to an empty table near the rest room doors. I returned to the bar, where Carla and Ginny were head-to-head, obviously speculating about Milo and Honoria.

"The sheriff has a *girlfriend?*" Carla shook me by the arm. "Emma, I thought you and Milo Dodge were —"

"We weren't," I cut in tersely. "Milo and I are friends, period. Honoria seems quite charming." It was, I thought, unfortunately true. Swiftly, I changed the subject, trying to draw Doc Dewey into a conversation about Art Fremstad's suicide. But Doc had suddenly become very busy. He didn't have time for chitchat. I nursed my beer and sat back to listen to Carla exchange gossip with Ginny about the latest Alpine romances. Since most of the people involved were young enough to be my children — though I was awfully glad

113

they weren't — I didn't pay much attention. Instead, I studied the growing crowd, watching an animated Janet Driggers use lots of hand gestures to describe something to Charlene Vickers. Patti Marsh and Jack Blackwell were snuggling near the pool table. The Wickstroms and the Ridleys were still trying to find some vacant boxes to use for seats. Milo Dodge was demonstrating concern for Honoria Whitman's comfort. I sighed. If it had been me instead of Honoria, I could have been sitting on a six-inch spike and Milo wouldn't have noticed.

Another dozen people had entered the tavern in the past half hour. Jack Blackwell had abandoned Patti Marsh to help Doc behind the bar. I had no idea who the regular bartender was, but the owner was an old curmudgeon who lived way up on Icicle Creek not far from the ranger station. I debated about ordering another beer, but before I could get Doc's attention Dani Marsh came in with Reid Hampton and Matt Tabor. A hush fell over the gathering, then scattered applause broke out. Dani bobbed a curtsy and flashed her beautiful smile. Across the room, her mother curled her lip. I couldn't see Cody Graff from my angle on the bar stool, but I suddenly felt uneasy. If the axe incident had been unintentional, would Cody apologize to

Dani and her coworkers? Or had he done so already? Somehow, I doubted it.

And I was right. While Dani Marsh and Reid Hampton moved straight for the bar, Matt Tabor angled over to Cody and Marje's table. I twisted around for a better view. The crowd had quieted down. There probably wasn't a person in the room who didn't know about that axe.

Carla was nudging me in the ribs. "Emma — are you going to write up what Cody did at the stadium? How close did that axe come to Dani?"

"Within inches," I replied soberly. "He was just damned lucky he missed all three of them. And me, for that matter. It flew within a couple of feet of my head."

Carla's dark eyes grew very wide. "Wow! I didn't know that! Everybody's been talking about what a close call Dani had! I wonder what Marje Blatt thinks. Hey," she went on, giving me another jab, "I've got a headline for you — CODY GRAFF AND MOVIE STAR EX-WIFE: WAS IT REALLY AN AXE-CIDENT?" Carla let loose with her high-pitched giggle.

I didn't bother to tell Carla that headline writing wasn't her strong suit. Come to think of it, I wasn't sure what was. Carla was deficient in a lot of areas, except for enthusiasm.

The conversation between Matt Tabor and

115

Cody Graff was getting heated. Cody had gotten to his feet, despite Marje's efforts to restrain him. By now, all of the customers were staring, and except for the blur of background music over the tavern's antiquated sound system, silence dominated the room like an unwanted guest.

Cody was unsteady on his feet. Matt braced himself against the table with his knees. "You ever pull a stunt like that again and I'll kill you, you son of a bitch!" roared Matt in his trained movie voice.

"Go screw yourself!" shouted Cody though the words weren't quite as distinct as he'd intended. He lunged across the table, but Matt Tabor was too quick for him. Matt's fist struck Cody square on the jaw, sending him slumping against the wall. The apple box beneath him crashed to one side. Marje and several others screamed. Milo Dodge was on his feet, wrestling his way around Honoria's wheelchair.

Matt backed off, while Cody wallowed around on the floor. Marje, having made sure her beloved was still alive sprang at Matt. "Listen, you two-bit Hollywood jerk, we don't need your type around this town! Why don't you take yourself and that hotshot movie star tramp of yours back to California where you belong?"

Milo had a hand on Matt's arm, but his

116

words were directed at Marje. "Sit down, Marje. Or better yet, take Cody home. I think he's had enough already. In a lot of ways."

Marje shot Milo an outraged look. "He's had two crummy beers! Big deal! If he were really drunk, would Doc serve him again? Hey, Sheriff, is this Loggerama or what?"

Matt was trying to shake loose of Milo, but the sheriff was holding fast. "Then you'd better drive, Marje. And keep Cody under control, okay?" He shook a warning finger at her, then pulled Matt Tabor back to a safe distance.

"Watch it, Badge Man," said Matt in a surly tone, as Milo finally let go. "I'm under contract to Gemini Productions. You want to get your butt sued?"

"My butt's covered, buster," retorted Milo, wheeling around to lope back to Honoria. He stopped short as he realized that war had broken out on yet another front at the Icicle Creek Tavern. Jack Blackwell was refusing to serve Reid Hampton.

"This is the bastard that cut down my trees! To hell with him!" He hurled the bar towel onto the floor and spit into the nut dish. "He owes me eighty grand! He's outta here, or else I am!"

Reid Hampton, who was wearing a snake-skin vest and an array of Indian jewelry, threw

117

his fawn-colored felt hat across the bar. "Don't be a jackass, Blackwell! We've got an iron-clad contract and you know it!"

"And you've got iron-clad pants!" roared Blackwell. "Just show me where it says in that freaking contract that you got any right to saw up my valuable timber."

From three stools down, I watched Dani Marsh watch Hampton and Blackwell. She looked vaguely alarmed, but not exactly upset. More to my surprise, she had made no move to console Matt Tabor, who was drinking thirstily from a mug poured by Doc Dewey. It was only when Patti Marsh charged up to the bar that Dani shrank back.

"Look here, Doc," yelled Patti in her hoarse voice as she elbowed Reid Hampton out of the way, "have you got a right to serve or not serve whoever you want in this dump or not?" Before Doc could answer, she pointed a painted fingernail at her daughter. "Let's start with her. She doesn't have a right to mix with decent people like the rest of us! How about dumping her out in the gutter where she belongs?"

Doc's mouth set in a rigid line, the type of expression he used on patients who wouldn't take their medicine. "Button it up, Patti. You don't know your backside from a hole in the ground."

"Yes, she does," said Janet Driggers, who had come up to the bar to get a new pitcher and some snacks. "It's the one on the left, obviously."

Doc broke into a grin, and Patti whirled around, her anger diverted. But Janet was so outrageously blunt that only the most mean-minded Alpiner could be annoyed by her. Patti started to say something, then saw that Reid Hampton was heading back to his table. "Hey, you!" shouted Patti. "Come here! I want a word with you, Mr. so-called-movie-producer-director-whatever-the-hell-you-are!"

But Reid Hampton ignored her. Patti started after him, but Milo again resorted to his strong-arm technique. "Come on, Patti, sit down, go eat some of that popcorn with the Driggers. Let's not turn Loggerama into a war zone. I had more peaceful evenings in Nam."

Patti glared at Milo, then realized that his hand was on her waist and gave him a co-quettish look. "Hey, sheriff," she cooed in a sudden shift of gears, "did anybody ever tell you you got terrific eyes? Soulful, or something like that."

Milo didn't flush this time, but he steered Patti away from the bar and into the care of a bemused Al and Janet Driggers. If Al was at a loss, his wife wasn't: "Sit down, Patti. Tell us if it's true about you and Jack doing it on the donkey engine up at Carroll Creek."

Cody was back on his box, looking like a floppy doll. Marje fussed over him, checking his bruised chin and offering him a fresh beer. Dani Marsh had finally joined Matt Tabor at the other end of the bar. Reid Hampton was allowing Doc Dewey to pour him a beer while a fuming Jack Blackwell served Milo. Patti had settled in with Al and Janet Driggers. I had to wonder why Patti and Dani had been driving around in Matt Tabor's fancy car Thursday night. How had they not managed to gouge out each other's eyes? I gave myself a shake, feeling as if I'd been involved in an old-fashioned Hollywood Western barroom brawl.

Back at the sheriff's table, Honoria looked composed, her head moving on her graceful neck as her serene gray eyes surveyed the aftermath of the mayhem. She caught me looking at her and gave me a conspiratorial smile. *Drat,* I thought, *I might get to like this woman.*

"This is fun," exclaimed Carla to Ginny. "We should come here more often. It's a lot more exciting than the Venison Inn."

"So is gang warfare," I remarked, wondering how much longer I could hold out.

Luckily, Ginny wasn't as taken with the Icicle Creek Tavern's floor show. "Frankly, I've got a headache from all this noise. Why don't we grab a pizza and then head home?"

Carla's face fell, but she rebounded quickly. "Double cheese, pepperoni, mushrooms, anchovies, and onions? Okay, we can eat it at my place. Want to get a video or catch the end of the Miss Alpine pageant? Emma?"

I shook my head. "Count me out. I've got a whole weekend to cram into half of tomorrow. Don't forget the parade and the banquet and the fireworks." Fortunately, my presence was required only at the banquet. Carla would cover the parade; Ed had volunteered to take pictures of the fireworks.

Carla finished her wine, and Ginny took a last sip of beer. My schooner had been empty for a long time. I asked Doc for our tab and insisted on treating my employees.

"Quite a night, eh, girlies?" asked Doc with a shake of his head. He was looking extremely tired, and I couldn't say that I blamed him. "I wonder when the loggers will start trying to kill each other?"

"I thought they signed a truce for Loggerama," I said with a grin. "When do you get done with your shift?"

He looked above the bar at the old clock featuring the Hamm's beer bear. "Ten minutes," he said with a grateful expression. "This seems like the longest two hours of my life. It wears me down, girlie. I'd rather do surgery. Dr. Starr should be along any minute." His lined face became unwontedly grim.

I led the way to the door, but halfway across the room I paused to greet the Driggers and the Vickers. Patti Marsh had returned to her table where she sat alone, sending malevolent glances in her daughter's direction. After an exchange of pleasantries, I began to pick my way through the tables again. I saw Cody and Marje leaving just ahead of us, about a minute after Curtis Graff had come into the tavern. The brothers ignored each other. Or, more likely, Cody was too bleary-eyed to recognize Curtis. Marje had her fiancé by the arm, propping him up. Milo had been right: Cody Graff hadn't needed a third beer. He looked as if he could barely make it to the parking lot.

It was fortunate that Marje Blatt was going to do the driving. At least Cody would get home alive and in one piece.

I couldn't guess that I was only half right.

I allowed myself the luxury of sleeping in until nine-fifteen on Sunday morning. Mass at St. Mildred's was at ten, and I could shower, dress, grab a cup of coffee, and get to church in under three-quarters of an hour. I was just about to struggle out of bed when the phone rang. Shielding my eyes against the bright morning sun, I groped for the receiver. It was Milo Dodge.

"Emma," he said, sounding tense. "I've got some bad news."

My brain wasn't quite on track yet. "What?"

Outside, I could hear the blare of trumpets. The high school band was assembling just a block and a half away, practicing for the big parade.

"There's been an accident," said Milo, with the sound of male voices in the background. "Durwood Parker ran over Cody Graff last night. Cody's dead and Durwood's back in jail."

I fell back on the bed, one hand on my head. Sunday wasn't going to be a day of rest, either. Except, of course, for Cody Graff.

Chapter Seven

Cody Graff had been struck down out on Mill Street, just west of the turnoff for Burl Creek Road. A weeping Durwood had turned himself in shortly after six A.M. He knew he wasn't supposed to drive, he told Milo, but he figured that if he took just a little spin on a quiet Sunday morning, nobody would be out on the road.

"We'll have to charge him with vehicular manslaughter," Milo told me after I got to the sheriff's office two blocks up from *The Advocate* on Front Street. I'd gone straight from mass, which Father Fitzgerald had cut short due to Loggerama.

"You know the prayers," he'd announced from the pulpit, "so it's at home ye'll be saying them." His parishioners were grateful, since the little wooden church was already unmercifully hot. We were also spared Father Fitz's meandering sermon of the week, which frequently came out of a time warp and often featured The Hun and The Red Menace.

"Poor Durwood," I sighed. "How's his wife doing?"

Milo shrugged. "Dot's pretty upset. She

124

said she knew this would happen some day. I told her to get a good lawyer, somebody from Seattle maybe."

"Can't you release him on his own recognizance?"

Milo sat down heavily in his imitation leather chair. "It's Sunday. He can't post bail until tomorrow. What can I do?" He gave a helpless lift of his shoulders.

A silence fell between us. I was the first to break it, suddenly aware that we seemed to have forgotten about the dead man. "What on earth was Cody Graff doing out by Burl Creek Road at six in the morning? The last time I saw him, he looked as if he'd sleep for a week."

"Beats me." Milo gazed at the ceiling of his small no-nonsense office. As usual, his desk was cluttered and his in-basket piled high. He was in uniform, because he was due to ride in the parade with a couple of his deputies. "Cody lived in those apartments between Pine and Cedar, across from the medical-dental clinic. How he ended up out at the edge of town at that time of day, I don't know. Maybe Marje Blatt could tell us."

"Have you told Curtis?" I asked.

"I don't know where he is," replied Milo, taking a roll of mints out of his pocket and offering me one. "We called up to the San

Juans to let Cody's parents know. They're coming down this afternoon, if they can get on a ferry. You know what traffic is like between the islands and the mainland this time of year on a Sunday."

I did. Despite the frequent ferry runs, car passengers were often forced to wait in line overnight on summer weekends. "Maybe Curtis is staying in a motel," I suggested, tasting spearmint on my tongue.

"We're checking," said Milo. "Damn, this is a hell of a thing to happen during Loggerama. And I've got an election coming up." He gave a rueful shake of his head.

"It's not your fault," I said in what I hoped was an encouraging tone. "Durwood shouldn't have been driving. And the thought of Cody wandering along on a country road at dawn is pretty bizarre. In fact, it's just plain inexplicable." I gazed straight into Milo's hazel eyes, waiting for him to agree with me.

But Milo's thoughts were going off in another direction. He stood up. "I've got to go get my horse from the Dithers sisters' farm. Fuzzy Baugh insisted we ride like some Wild West posse, instead of in our squad cars. Jeez!" He made a disparaging gesture with his hand. "I haven't been on a horse in ten years."

I wished Milo well and headed for my car.

126

I had no desire to watch the parade, which was scheduled for one o'clock. It was now after eleven-thirty, and I hadn't had any breakfast. The Venison Inn and the Burger Barn both looked crowded. I stopped by the office to call Vida and asked if she'd like to drive with me down to Index, where we could get some brunch.

"Do you want to eat or have a powwow?" Vida demanded. "What's this gruesome business with Cody Graff? Marje has been bleating in my ear for the last hour." Vida didn't sound too sympathetic toward her niece.

We agreed that we could eat and discuss Cody's demise in Index as well as we could in Alpine. Five minutes later, I picked Vida up at her neat white frame cottage on Cascade Street, and we headed for the main highway. The town of Index is located some twenty-five miles down Stevens Pass on the north fork of the Skykomish River. The Bush House Country Inn is old, architecturally interesting, and serves an exceptional buffet brunch. We had to wait fifteen minutes for a table, but at last, with our plates piled high, we seated ourselves and tackled not only our food, but also Cody Graff's death.

"You're right," Vida agreed, buttering a fluffy blueberry muffin. "Durwood's an old fool, but Cody shouldn't have been out on that road so early in the morning. Marje says she dropped him off at his apartment right after she took him home from the Icicle Creek Tavern. She took his pickup to her place. So how did he get to the Burl Creek Road?"

"You mean she's still got Cody's truck?"

Vida gave a jerky nod. "That's right. It's parked in front of her house. Or rather her parents' house, but then you know what I think of her mother and father. Nincompoops, both of them, even if Ennis is my own brother. But Marje is sensible, all things considered. I just never thought Cody was suitable for her. Still," she added virtuously, "I kept out of it. Now, I can't say I'm sorry she won't be marrying him. It's a shame he's dead, but it may save Marje a lot of grief later on."

How Vida managed to say all this while consuming two link sausages, half a muffin, and a great quantity of scrambled eggs, I'll never know. But she did. "This is beginning to sound stranger by the minute. I didn't ask Milo — was Doc Dewey called in to do his medical examiner's act?"

Vida attacked a small container of marionberry jam. "Doc and Mrs. Dewey headed for Seattle early this morning. Young Doc Dewey was in emergency, setting some fool of a tourist's broken leg. I suppose he was going to view the body after he got done, but Marje

128

says he's pretty busy with all the visitors in town. They don't have enough sense not to keep hurting themselves while they're trying to have fun. One idiot from Idaho fell out the window of the Tall Timber Inn last night."

Visions of lawsuits and tricky news stories danced through my head. But that lay in the future. Cody Graff's death had occurred in the last few hours. "There's something about this whole thing that bothers me," I confessed. "I saw Cody leave the tavern around ten o'clock last night with Marje. I know how drunk he was. He probably passed out as soon as he got back to his apartment. So he wakes up at five or even earlier this morning and *walks* two miles out to the Burl Creek Road? It doesn't make sense."

Vida didn't seem at all unsettled by my pronouncement. Indeed, it was obvious she'd already come to the same conclusion. After waiting for a busboy to clear the table next to us, she leaned closer: "Of course it doesn't, Emma. That's why I don't think Durwood killed Cody."

I hadn't gotten quite that far in my thinking. I gaped at Vida over a forkful of ham. "You mean he was already dead when Durwood hit him?"

Vida's gaze was steady. "That's right. Dot told me on the phone that Durwood swore he didn't see Cody. Now Durwood couldn't see an elephant on an escalator, but it *is* fairly light at six in the morning this time of year, and according to Dot, Durwood was just going around that little bend by the Overholt farm. The road dips down. If Cody had been walking on the pavement — or even close to it, Durwood doesn't exactly keep to the road — he would have seen *something*. But if Cody had been lying there, not moving, that might explain it." She waved a spoon at me. "So we're back to the original question. Dead or alive, what was Cody Graff doing out there in the early morning dew?"

I stared at her thoughtfully for some moments. "I suppose we'll have to wait for young Doc Dewey to tell us what really happened."

"Of course." Vida poured a lavish dose of syrup over her stack of pancakes. "I told Dot to insist on an autopsy. I'm not for letting Durwood loose in that rattletrap of his, but I'd hate to see the poor old fool get sent to prison for something he really didn't do."

As ever, I marveled at Vida's communication network. Already, she'd been in touch with two of the major figures involved in Cody Graff's death, Marje Blatt and Dot Parker. For all I knew, she'd been receiving messages from Durwood in a bottle sent floating down the Skykomish River.

130

For the rest of the lengthy meal — Vida went back for seconds and thirds — we discussed some of the other incidents of the past twenty-four hours, including the flying axe at the timber sports competition, the row between Cody Graff and Matt Tabor, the face-off featuring Jack Blackwell and Reid Hampton, and Patti Marsh's defamation of her daughter's character in front of the Icicle Creek Tavern patrons — even though Milo and I had seen the two of them drive off in Matt Tabor's custom-built car the previous night. It was only when we were paying the bill that I remembered to tell her about seeing Curtis Graff show up at the tavern just before Cody and Marje left.

"Do you know where Curtis is staying?" I asked.

But for once, Vida had to confess ignorance. She had not seen Curtis since he returned to Alpine. "A nice boy," she allowed. "Much more character than Cody. Smart, too, but not terribly quick." She tapped her temple.

We returned to Alpine just as the parade was ending. For the first time since I'd moved to town, I became embroiled in a genuine traffic jam. As soon as we turned off the main highway, we found ourselves backed up on the bridge over the Skykomish River. Some of the parade participants had taken the wrong route after leaving Front Street, and a float featuring a giant fried egg, as well as a girls' drill team from Monroe, had ended up on the bridge instead of going in the opposite direction on Alpine Way to the football field. It was after three o'clock when I got Vida home. I decided to drive back downtown and see if Milo had survived his horseback ride.

He had — barely. Looking as if he were in pain, Milo was sitting gingerly in his chair, sipping ice water. I commiserated briefly, then asked if Dot Parker had requested an autopsy on Cody Graff. Milo eyed me curiously.

"Yes, she has. How'd you know that, Emma?"

I tried to look enigmatic. "It's my job to know all things."

Milo pulled a face, enlightenment dawning. "Vida." He sighed wearily. "We'll have to get somebody from Snohomish County to do it. Young Doc Dewey is all tied up. You heard what happened to the Three Little Pigs?"

I wasn't sure I wanted to, but Milo told me anyway. The Three Little Pigs, whose job it was to promote homeowners' insurance for the local independent agent, had been the victim of the Big Bad Wolf, who had huffed and puffed so energetically that he'd gone right through the flooring of the float, sending the driver into a Skykomish Public Utility District

132

pole at the corner of Fifth and Front. The Big Bad Wolf had managed to keep his balance, but the Three Little Pigs had tumbled into the crowd, causing several lacerations, abrasions, and contusions. No one was seriously hurt, but the mending, patching, and stitching would keep young Doc Dewey busy for the next few hours. It was a driving mishap that would have made Durwood proud — if he could have seen it from his jail cell.

"When will the autopsy be done?" I asked, after I had emitted the appropriate chuckles and expressed the suitable regrets.

"Tomorrow, maybe. It depends," said Milo, once again showing signs of discomfort. "They'll be doing us a favor in Everett, so we can't push them. It's a bunch of bull, but I suppose the Parkers have their rights. As I said, this was bound to happen to Durwood eventually."

I decided not to let Milo in on Vida's theory. He would dismiss it out of hand. But if the autopsy proved that Cody was already dead when Durwood's car hit him, then Milo would have to consider other uglier possibilities.

I was on my feet, wishing Milo would install air-conditioning in his office. "I'll see you at the banquet tonight. Are you bringing Honoria?" I tried to keep my voice light.

"No," he said with a laconic shake of his

head. "She's going to some gallery deal in Seattle." He looked up. "You want a lift?"

The Loggerama banquet was going to be held in the Lutheran Church hall, the only adequate facility for such a large gathering. The Lutherans also owned the retirement home in the same block. Due to Alpine's large Scandinavian population, the members of their faith outnumbered any other flock by at least a two-to-one ratio.

"Sure," I said, wanting to be a good sport. "By the way, I thought Honoria seemed like a lovely person."

For a brief moment, Milo's face lighted up. "Really? Well, yes, she's pretty nice. Determined, too. She drives — she's got a specially rigged car — and goes everywhere on her own. But then she's had a lot of practice."

I leaned on Milo's desk. "What happened?" I wasn't going to pry unless Milo gave me an opportunity. Now he had.

Milo's face tightened. "She married very young. Her husband beat the crap out of her. On her twenty-first birthday, he threw her down a flight of stairs."

I winced. "That's awful! Did she leave him?"

Again, Milo gave a mournful shake of his head. "Her brother shot him. And got ten years for it. He should have had a medal."

I didn't argue.

To my relief, the banquet had gone off without incident. Pastor Nielsen had asked us to bow our heads in memory of Cody Graff. Fuzzy Baugh had introduced the new Miss Alpine, a shy redhead who was a checker at the Grocery Basket. Dani Marsh had been invited, but had bowed out of both the parade and the banquet, apparently owing to the death of her ex-husband. Harvey Adcock, as the current Chamber of Commerce president, read a brief note from Dani, expressing her regrets for not attending. I wondered if she had some other regrets as well.

Monday was a wild day at work. We were going to have another jam-packed issue, but this week we wouldn't have the extra Loggerama ads to support so many pages. I decided to hold off writing the story about Cody's death until we got the autopsy report. I hoped it would come in before our late Tuesday deadline. I also chose not to run anything about the axe incident. Now that Cody was dead and couldn't defend himself, it didn't seem right to carry an article that would, by its very existence, imply that he'd been trying to injure his ex-wife or her companions.

Meanwhile, Durwood no longer languished

in jail. Dot had posted bond and taken him home in the early afternoon. I didn't talk to Milo all day, since I was too busy putting the paper together. Vida, however, had stopped in at the sheriff's office and said that he had told her he hoped the autopsy would be completed before five o'clock. Meanwhile, Cody's parents were at the Lumberjack Motel, waiting for the body to be released. Curtis Graff was with them.

Out on Front Street, a small crew of city employees and several merchants were dismantling the Loggerama decorations. Down came the bunting, the banners, and the bigger-than-life-sized model of a woodsman that Fuzzy Baugh insisted on referring to as "an erection." I don't think the mayor ever stops to listen to what he's saying, but I suppose that's all right, because none of the rest of us do either. Fuzzy, in his native New Orleans fashion, does tend to run on.

Hot, tired, and feeling a headache coming on, I drove home shortly before six. This time, the mail held no surprises. But it reminded me that I had yet to deal with Tom Cavanaugh's letter. Tomorrow night, perhaps, I told myself as I fell onto the sofa and kicked off my shoes. I needed one more day to recover from the rigors of Loggerama.

I was in the kitchen cleaning up from my

meager supper of creamed shrimp on toast when the phone rang. It was Milo Dodge.

"We got the autopsy report from Everett about an hour ago," he said, sounding as weary as I felt. "It's the damnedest thing you ever heard."

"So what am I hearing?" My voice was a little breathless.

Milo cleared his throat. "Cody Graff had been dead for several hours by the time Durwood hit him. The extent of rigor —" He stopped, obviously reading his notes. "Anyway, we'll have to dismiss the charges against Durwood." Milo sounded almost sorry. I'm sure he had visions of Durwood immediately leaping into his old beater and wiping out a whole herd of cows.

"Go on," I urged. "Who did run over him?"

"Nobody," replied Milo. "The medical examiner says he didn't die from getting hit by a car. Cody Graff was murdered. Somebody poisoned the poor bastard. What do you think of that?"

Chapter Eight

Milo and I were having drinks at the Venison Eat Inn and Take Out. We were both relieved to note that most of the tourists had departed from Alpine, leaving our streets and restaurants and shops back under our control. Even though Pacific Northwest politicians and Chamber of Commerce types may work hard to promote tourism and thus beef up the economy, the truth is that most people, merchants included, aren't fond of visitors. Worse yet, some of the tourists may decide to move in. Growth is not good. Money is suspect. Space is much better.

"What kind of poison?" I asked after the cocktail waitress had glided away. I didn't want her to think I was talking about the Venison Inn's beverages.

"Haloperidol," said Milo, emphasizing each syllable. "A central nervous system depressant. It's especially lethal with alcohol. It also produces symptoms that are very similar to drunkenness. Marje Blatt insisted that Cody had only two beers when I told him he ought to go home. They'd had an early supper at the Loggerama fast food stand in Old Mill

Park because Cody was hungry from all that action with the axe at the high school field. Then they went to see some of the Miss Alpine competition. They got to the Icicle Creek Tavern about half an hour or forty-five minutes before I did."

"So how did he ingest this stuff?" I asked, reconstructing Marje's account of their evening to see if it made sense. As far as I could tell, it did. If she wasn't lying.

"The M.E. in Everett says it was probably in the beer. Marje says they ate around five-thirty. If it had been in Cody's food or his coffee, it would have started to act much sooner, maybe even by six o'clock. There's no sign that he had anything to eat or drink after he left the Icicle Creek Tavern shortly before ten. Maybe Marje was right about how much — or how little — he had to drink. I just thought she was covering for him."

"How long does this stuff usually take to act?" I asked, unable to keep from looking at my bourbon without a certain amount of suspicion.

"That depends, according to the M.E. If Cody had been some old guy in poor health and was drinking shots of gin, he could have been a goner within fifteen minutes. But Cody was young and in good shape. He'd only had a couple of beers. The M.E. says it might take up to two hours before he died."

I shuddered. "Poor Cody. But how on earth did he end up dead by the Burl Creek Road?"

Milo lifted his shoulders and hoisted his Scotch. "Nobody's come forward to say they carted him off. What I'm trying to figure out is why somebody would poison him, then drive him off and dump him on the road. It's crazy."

"Marje doesn't know anything, I take it?"

"No. She said it was just after ten when they got to his apartment. There's no elevator, so she had to help him up the stairs to the second floor. She left him on the couch."

"Had he passed out?" I asked.

"No. She said he was muttering about his brother Curtis, and Dani, and Matt Tabor. He was sort of incoherent, but still conscious." Milo nodded to a young couple I knew only from seeing them at church. They sat down at a table near the unlighted fireplace. I gave a little wave. It wouldn't hurt for me to help Milo woo his constituents.

"Where would anybody get that . . ." I reached down for my purse and took out a notepad. "Spell it, will you Milo?"

He did, and I jotted the unfamiliar word down. Haloperidol. I'd never heard of it. I repeated my question.

Milo gave a wry little laugh. "Five, six years

ago, Durwood would have been the prime suspect, being a pharmacist. But nowadays, who knows where drugs, legal and otherwise, come from around here? The only thing I can say for sure is that somebody planned ahead."

"Premeditated," I murmured. It was an ugly thought. "Why? Who? And how?"

Milo's smile became more genuine. "Ever the reporter, huh, Emma? I sure as hell don't know who or why. But how? If it was in his beer, somebody slipped it to him when nobody was looking. Even Marje couldn't be watching every minute. Unless," he added, the smile fading, "it was Marje who did it."

My eyes widened at Milo. "Marje? No, that's crazy. If she wanted to get rid of Cody, all she had to do was break the engagement. Besides, I think she genuinely loved the guy."

Milo nodded. "Could be. But there was so much commotion going on that anybody could have dumped this stuff into his schooner. It can come in several forms, including a syrup. Cody wasn't the sharpest tool in the shed. He liked to guzzle. And frankly, if something tasted funny at the Icicle Creek Tavern, I'm not sure I'd notice. I'd half expect to find a trace of ugly in my brew."

Milo was only half-kidding. I mulled over his words, then had a sudden flashback. "Hey, Milo — Cody had *three* beers the other night.

He got another one after you warned him off. Would that make the poison work faster?"

Milo said it probably would. But he cautioned that the M.E. was cagey about fixing the time of death. "Somewhere between ten and midnight is as close as he'll come."

Somebody had seen Cody during those two hours. But it suddenly dawned on me that that mysterious blank face didn't necessarily belong to the killer.

Selfishly, I wished the autopsy hadn't been concluded so soon. The old-fashioned concept of a newspaper *scoop* had all but died out with the advent of the electronic media. In a small town like Alpine, a scoop had never had a chance: the grapevine was always faster and more effective. Everybody from Burl Creek to Stump Hill would know that Cody Graff had been poisoned before we could get the paper to Monroe to be printed.

I spent most of Tuesday tying up loose ends. I wrote the story of Cody's death, careful to stick to the facts and quote strictly from Milo and the Snohomish County Medical Examiner. For the time being, I avoided contacting Cody's parents, his brother, or his ex-wife. Their comments could come later, for next week's edition, when I had more room and the sheriff had more results.

Vida did the obituary, noting that the

funeral was set for Thursday. It would not be held in Alpine, but up at Friday Harbor, with burial in the cemetery on the San Juan Islands.

"Marje thinks that's a shame," said Vida, yanking the article out of her typewriter. "She said she thought Cody would want to be buried here, next to his baby. But I suppose his folks have a plot up at Friday Harbor."

I looked up from the headline Carla had written about the wet T-shirt contest. I hadn't seen it until just now and was dismayed: NO FALSE FRONT FOR *ADVOCATE* ENTRY; RUNKEL BUSTS UP COMPETITION. It wouldn't do. What had become of Carla's high-minded principles?

RUNKEL WINS T-SHIRT CONTEST; ASKS BOOKS FOR BEER. My revision was deadly dull, but it would keep Vida from blowing up — and prevent a stack of letters from irate readers.

"Is Marje going to attend the funeral?" I inquired.

"She doesn't know yet," Vida replied, looking up from the finished version of her House & Home page. "With Doc Dewey Senior gone, there's not as much for her to do, but young Doc has been so busy she may have to help cover. They only have the two nurses and Marje at the clinic, you know."

I did. But it seemed strange that Marje

143

wouldn't attend Cody's services. Of course, it wasn't easy to get up to the San Juans this time of year. "How's she taking it?" I asked.

Vida handed her completed page over to me. "Oh — she's upset, of course. But Marje isn't an emotional type. Crying her eyes out won't bring Cody back. Maybe she hasn't taken it all in yet. She certainly refuses to consider that Cody was murdered."

"Really?" Milo had officially announced that Cody Graff's death had been caused by foul play. Luckily, the sheriff hadn't made a formal announcement of accidental death. Otherwise, he would have to go through all the legal rigmarole regarding corpus delicti. Perhaps he had also saved himself from getting sued by Durwood Parker. Milo had a right to throw Durwood in jail just for breaking the thirty-day ban on driving.

Vida was pushing up the window above her desk. The midday heat was bringing unwelcome humidity. "Marje insists that nobody would want to kill Cody." Vida brushed tendrils of damp gray hair off her high forehead. "I suppose she has a point. I have to admit I'm flummoxed over this whole mess."

So was I. Worse yet, I had the feeling that Milo Dodge was as baffled as we were. If Cody Graff had been poisoned at the Icicle Creek

Tavern, Milo and I had both been eye-witnesses. Yet neither of us had seen anything suspicious. Milo probably would question everybody he could find who had been in the tavern Saturday night, but it was doubtful that they would be able to shed any light on the matter. Not only had there been too much confusion, but many of the patrons probably had been too far gone with drink to be observant or reliable witnesses.

Vida was sorting through some handouts on late summer garden care. She uttered a contemptuous snort and dumped the whole batch into her wastebasket. "What do these promotional people think we are, *idiots?* Who wouldn't know when to cut back old growth and prune fruit trees?" Vida wasn't the best gardener in town; she worked only in spurts, but with great energy. Still, she was knowledgeable. I was about to ask her when I should put in my spring bulbs, but she had already moved on to another topic: "You never told me about your date." There was a hint of reproof in her tone.

"Some date." I made a deprecating gesture. "At least the food was good."

"Reid Hampton's not your type. Shallow. Pretentious. Stuck on himself." Vida was dead-on.

I decided to get her opinion of Milo's new

friend. "What did you think of Honoria Whitman?"

"Pleasant. Smart. Dull. Milo needs somebody with more pep."

"She's very gutsy," I pointed out.

Vida pushed her glasses back on her nose and frowned at me. "What has courage got to do with *pep?* Milo does his job well enough, but he's on cruise control when it comes to his personal life. If you ask me, that's what went wrong with his first marriage. It's too bad you're so hung up on Tommy."

I winced for various reasons: Vida had met Tom Cavanaugh on his visit to Alpine the previous autumn. She had liked him a lot. She also knew the rest of the story, and passed no judgment on either of us. But she was the only person I knew who ever called him Tommy.

I was going to tell her about Tom's letter when Marje Blatt walked into the newsroom. Marje's piquant face was sunburned, yet somehow lifeless. Her white uniform didn't seem quite so crisp. The bright blue eyes had lost their luster. Yet there was no indication she had been crying. Marje said hello to me, then went straight to the point:

"Aunt Vida, have you had lunch?"

Aunt Vida had, varying her customary diet lunch with Rye Krisp instead of cottage

146

cheese. "Yes, it's after one. But if you want company . . ." Vida was already springing toward the door.

I wanted to talk to Marje, too, but I couldn't intrude. Besides, the fish and chips basket I'd brought over from the Burger Barn would do me until dinner. Unlike Vida, I wouldn't be able to sit down and consume an entire meal with all the trimmings.

Instead, I finished working on the paper, then gave Milo a call, using the need to find out if there had been any further developments as my excuse for bothering him. We wouldn't want to send *The Advocate* off to Monroe without the latest news.

"There's nothing new," admitted Milo, unhappily. "Our forensics guy is checking fibers and such. We've been talking to some of the other customers who were at the tavern Saturday night. Janet Driggers says Cody probably poisoned himself, but that's only because she and Al are miffed that the funeral is being held up at Friday Harbor — Al won't get his usual fat undertaking fee. Cal Vickers said something kind of interesting, though."

"Such as?" I asked, wondering what the owner of Cal's Texaco & Body Shop might have to add.

"Well, he and Charlene stayed on for about an hour. It was their twenty-fourth wedding anniversary, so I guess they got sort of sentimental and decided to drive out to Burl Creek, where he proposed. They were coming back down around midnight when they saw a strange-looking car parked across from the Overholt farm. Cal had seen it around town this past week and said it was a Zimmer. You know how interested he is in unusual cars."

"Was it the same one we saw the other night?" I inquired.

"Sounds like it. It's definitely Matt Tabor's car — he drove it up from California, but he had it made out south of Seattle, in Des Moines. They're only three places in the country that hand-build these things. They must cost a shitload, but they sure are beautiful."

I wasn't paying much attention to Milo's car commentary, which had no doubt been inspired by Cal Vickers. I was more interested in why the custom-built Zimmer had been parked in the vicinity of Cody Graff's body. "Did Cal or Charlene notice if anyone was in the car?"

Milo sighed. "No, they were either too moonstruck or concentrating just on the car itself. The Zimmer's headlights were off, though. Cal did notice that."

"Hmmmm." I mulled over Milo's information while one of his deputies asked him a question in the background. "We know it wasn't necessarily Matt Tabor driving, don't we?" I finally remarked after Milo had finished talking to his subordinate.

"I'm going to ask Dani — or Matt — about that," said Milo. "If I had a car like that, I sure wouldn't let just anybody drive it."

I agreed. But Dani and Matt were hardly strangers; they were engaged to be married. Still, I wondered what the Zimmer was doing parked out by the Burl Creek Road at midnight on Saturday. It was such a conspicuous vehicle — somebody was bound to see it.

And somebody had. But the real question was whether or not the murderer was at the wheel.

As I drove up to the ski lodge after dinner, I had to scrutinize my motives. Was I going to see Dani Marsh because I thought there was a real news story in her reaction to Cody Graff's death? Or was I insinuating myself into her life because I wanted to help Milo find her ex-husband's killer?

Or, I asked myself with a grimace, was I trying to put off replying to Tom Cavanaugh's letter?

I couldn't answer any of my own questions. I'm a great one for rationalizing my actions, and rarely will one clear-cut explanation serve. I must have at least two or more reasons for anything I do that might be on shaky ethical ground. By the time I reached the lodge, I'd convinced myself that I was also calling on Dani to offer my condolences. Judging from a lot of comments about her return, she might not have a local shoulder to cry on. Certainly not her mother's.

Henry Bardeen informed me that Dani was in her room, but that all visitors had to be screened by some flunky who was eating dinner at the Venison Inn.

"Half the town has tried to get in here in the past few days to see the movie stars," Henry said crossly. "Fortunately, the company makes its own rules. We're off the hook. But it's been a real nuisance all the same. Even Patti Marsh came storming in here this afternoon."

"She did? To see Dani?"

Henry shook his head. "No — Reid Hampton. I had to get very firm with her. Patti has no manners."

Apparently, Henry Bardeen was going to be very firm with me as well. He had the grace to look ill-at-ease, however, as he suggested I call the Venison Inn and ask for the flunky to come to the phone. I was considering just that when Reid Hampton strolled through the lobby.

Hampton greeted me heartily, practically

squeezing the blood out of my hand. Relieved to have someone from the film company present, Henry slipped away toward his office. I informed the movie director that I would like to see Dani.

Hampton's hearty manner changed instantly, shifting into appropriately mournful gear. He gazed up into the vast ceiling of the lodge with its rough-hewn rafters and knotty pine walls. "Dani's really distraught," he said at last, lowering his booming voice to a mere rumble. "She and Cody . . . what was his name? Grass?" He seemed to be reading from a cue card on the Indian blanket suspended from a crossbeam. "Graff, that's it. They may have been divorced, but it's still a shock."

"It must have been a shock when Cody threw that axe and practically chopped off her feet," I remarked.

Reid Hampton's gaze deigned to drop down to earth and meet mine. "That was strange," he admitted. "An accident, though, I'm sure. Would you like to have a drink in the bar, Emma?"

I considered my options: I could decline the invitation and renew my efforts to see Dani. But Reid Hampton would probably refuse permission, and I might not fare any better with the flunky who was eating chicken-fried steak at the Venison Inn. If I accepted Reid's offer, he might mellow and let me talk to his star.

"Sure," I responded, with a smile meant to flatter.

Hampton nodded, then swaggered off toward the bar on the other side of the lobby. The Aprés-Ski Room had recently been remodeled, a tasteful job that featured the best appointments of the original hole-in-the-wall watering place. More warm wood, rustic lamps with cedar bark bases, and some handsome sketches by Pacific Northwest Indian artists gave the room a comfortable native flavor.

After ordering us each a brandy, Reid Hampton leaned across the polished pine table and gave me a seductive smile, capped teeth flashing in his tawny beard. The man must be close to fifty and there wasn't a gray hair in sight. I suspected that not only did Reid Hampton dye his hair — and beard — but that the lionlike shade wasn't natural. It certainly didn't match the darker hairs on his arms and chest.

"I've been meaning to tell you I had a wonderful time at dinner the other night," said Hampton, at his most suave. "I hope we can do it again before I leave town, Emma."

I don't think I managed to hide my surprise. Reid Hampton had to be kidding. I was certain he'd had as crummy an outing as I had. But maybe he felt compelled to say otherwise. Accepting his gallantry at face value, I stopped looking startled and smiled politely.

"Thanks, Reid. When do you wind up the shoot?"

"Early next week." He twirled the brandy snifter under his nose and inhaled. "We finish up at Baldy Wednesday. Are you ready for the paint job?"

Again, I was evasive. Surely Reid Hampton really didn't want to colorize Front Street. "Has Dani been able to work the past couple of days?"

"She's a trooper. I was afraid she might want to go up to the San Juans for the funeral, but she hasn't insisted. That relieves my mind — it would have put us off schedule. We can't shoot around her with the way the script is written." He took a sip of brandy and savored it slowly. "It's lucky she's had Cody's brother to lean on."

"Curtis?" Again, I had to guard my reaction. "I didn't realize they were close. I've only lived in Alpine a couple of years."

Hampton lifted one of his broad shoulders. "He came to see her as soon as he heard Cody was dead. Say, Emma," he continued in a different, more intimate tone, "you aren't going to play this as a homicide, are you? In the

153

newspaper, I mean?"

"But that's what it is," I replied, dumbfounded.

Hampton lifted his hands in an expressive gesture. "Crazy! Who knows what that guy was taking? He has a lot of beer and then he overdoses. It happens all the time in L.A. Nobody goes around shouting, 'Help, Murder!' Your sheriff must be very naive."

Cody Graff had his faults, but taking drugs wasn't one of them, as far as I knew. If he had been a user, Marje would have known, and thus so would Vida. I gave a definite shake of my head. "Sorry, Reid, the sheriff is right. Somebody deliberately poisoned Cody Graff. Have you got any ideas who?"

The question was off the top of my head, and Reid Hampton looked as if I were out of my mind. "Hell! That's rot, Emma! No, I don't have — Why would I know who'd kill some small-town loser?" He looked genuinely offended. He also looked as if he'd define anybody who lived in a small town as a loser. Including me.

I began to feel irritated. "You certainly made Jack Blackwell angry by cutting down those trees. Cody worked for Blackwell. If you want to start scratching for motives, I could count you in." I gave him my most ingenuous smile.

Hampton was not amused. "More rot," he muttered. "My lawyers are better than Blackwell's lawyers. I don't need to waste some punk over a pile of logs. All this poison crap is ridiculous."

I realized it was useless to argue with Reid Hampton. It was also counter-productive. I had probably already ruined my chances of using him to get to Dani Marsh. I drank some brandy and tried to think of a different, more conciliatory approach.

But I didn't need it. Dani Marsh floated into the bar at that moment, smiling sweetly at a middle-aged couple in the corner and a couple of men I recognized as grips or gaffers or some such technical workers from the movie location. She headed straight for us. Reid Hampton grimaced.

"Dani," he began, standing up, "Emma and I were just leaving. I'll see you upstairs in half an hour, okay?"

Dani had already sat down in the chair next to me. "Oh — Reid, I don't want to drink alone. In fact, I only want some mineral water. Don't rush off." Her limpid brown eyes appealed to both of us.

"That's okay, Reid," I said, with a little wave. "You go do whatever a big director has to do, and I'll keep Dani company. I haven't finished my brandy yet."

Reid Hampton did not look pleased. He gave Dani a glance that might have been a warning, tossed a ten dollar bill on the table, and left the bar. Dani gave me a conspiratorial smile.

"Reid can be a twit, but he's wonderful to work with," she said with a wave to the cocktail waitress. Dani ordered a gin and tonic. I wondered what had happened to the cabbage extract.

After Dani was served, I offered my condolences on Cody's death. She assumed a mournful expression which seemed genuine enough, though I reminded myself she was an actress. "It's terrible," she said with a sigh. "When somebody dies young, it's such a waste. Even with Cody."

I wasn't precisely sure how to take her qualifying remark. Instead, I asked about Curtis. "Was he very upset?"

Dani turned thoughtful. "Yes, I think so. Curtis won't miss Cody, since they hadn't seen each other in almost five years. I don't think Cody had seen his parents since they moved up to the San Juans. Still, they've got to be feeling blue."

Unbridled grief wasn't the watchword of the week. I said as much. "I take it Cody didn't have a lot of other family or a wide circle of friends."

156

"There were some relatives in Spokane," Dani said. "Cousins, aunt and uncle. But I don't think they kept in touch. He had his beer-drinking buddies. And of course there was that girl he was going to marry."

I thought of Marje Blatt as I had seen her earlier in the day. Maybe she was still in shock, and great gushes of grief would come later. "Reid Hampton doesn't think Cody was murdered," I said, watching closely for Dani's reaction.

"I don't think so either," said Dani Marsh flatly. "Why would anyone kill Cody? He didn't have any money. He wasn't involved in a triangle, at least that I know of. And I doubt that he'd turn to blackmail. What other motives are there besides monetary gain, jealousy, and fear?"

"Knowledge," I replied promptly. "People have been killed for knowing too much."

Dani emitted a lame little laugh. "Knowledge doesn't suit Cody. He wasn't exactly stupid, but he wouldn't be interested enough in anybody to invite their secrets. No, Ms. Lord, I don't buy into this murder business either. It's so . . . so melodramatic. Oh, Cody may have ingested some strange drug, but he probably did it himself."

My eyes widened. "You mean suicide?"

Maybe Janet Driggers's idea wasn't so wild after all.

"No, no," replied Dani, after a gulp of her gin and tonic. "He'd never do that. But he might have been experimenting, or taking some kind of medication. Surely the sheriff has checked into that?"

Surely Milo had, I thought. As the Deweys' medical receptionist, Marje was in a position to know if Cody was taking prescription drugs. If so, she would have told the sheriff. Or Vida. I had to wonder why Dani and Reid were so determined on insisting that Cody had not been murdered. Maybe they didn't want the adverse publicity.

"As far as I know, Cody wasn't on this stuff." I wished I could pronounce the name of the drug more easily. "If I may be blunt, Cody Graff struck me as the kind of person who might incite someone to violence. He appeared to be a very sulky, perhaps even selfish young man."

Dani Marsh threw back her head and laughed, that rarified musical sound that reminded me of tinkling crystal chandeliers. "If every sulking, selfish man I know in the movie business got killed, Hollywood would have to fold."

I was faintly miffed by her dismissal of my theory. "You couldn't get along with him,"

I pointed out. "At least that's why I assume you got divorced."

Dani's gaze wandered around the Aprés-Ski Room. "Oh — I don't know. We were so young, immature, impatient. I wanted more out of life than Alpine could offer. I think we both saw that we'd made a mistake. After the baby died, we realized there wasn't any future for us." She still wasn't looking at me, but rather at the totem pole that stood between the tall windows at the far end of the bar.

Dani didn't seem to be helping me much in terms of information. I'd finally finished my brandy and she was over halfway through her gin and tonic. "You've got Matt Tabor now," I said, hoping to sound more congenial. "You can make a fresh start."

Dani took another swallow from her tall glass. "Right. Matt's a good guy." Her eyes were still wandering around the bar.

"When's the wedding?" I felt as if I were prying. Was it because Dani was a celebrity? Yet the question was as natural as asking a chicken farmer how his eggs were doing.

Dani finally met my gaze. "We haven't set a date. Next summer, maybe. We both have commitments through June."

I decided it was time to throw in the towel. Getting to my feet, I started to make my fare-well, but had a sudden thought. "I understand you've seen your mother." The statement tripped off my tongue, and I waited for Dani to look startled.

"Mom's such a hard-nosed person," she said, then laughed again. "Honestly, she has never forgiven me for getting crummy grades in high school. Somehow, going to Hollywood and breaking into the movie business doesn't make up for it. I think she hates me because I didn't enroll in the University of Washington and get a degree in education." She ran a hand through her honey blond hair. "I shouldn't say that. She doesn't hate me, she's just resentful. And I understand why. Some day, I hope she'll get over it. We used to be great pals."

"The two of you must have made up enough that she'd let you drive her around in Matt's Zimmer," I remarked, hoisting my handbag over my shoulder. "I saw you the other night in that gorgeous car."

For just an instant, a strange look passed over Dani Marsh's beautiful face. Surprise? Fear? Anger? I couldn't tell. She composed herself quickly and gave a little shrug. "Matt likes to show off that Zimmer. He let me drive it to go see Mom. She couldn't resist taking a spin around town. I suppose nobody up here has ever seen a car like that. There aren't that many even in L.A., not at all like sighting a Rolls or a Lamborghini — *they're* a dime a dozen."

Not on my salary they weren't. But I merely smiled and left Dani to lap up her gin and tonic. She might look like an angel, but she acted like a clam. My trip to the ski lodge had been a washout.

It was only later that I realized Dani — and Reid Hampton — had told me almost everything I needed to know.

Chapter Nine

Having flunked with Dani Marsh, I decided to make a complete fool of myself and call on her mother. Patti Marsh lived in a small frame house above the cemetery, between Spruce and Tyee Streets. It was almost dark when I arrived, but I could see that the yard was overgrown, the lawn needed mowing, and the house itself begged for fresh paint. I assumed this was where Dani Marsh had been raised. It was a far cry from Benedict Canyon.

Patti came to the door in tight black pants and a green halter top. She had a drink in one hand and a cigarette in the other. "What do you want?" she asked in her hoarse, hostile voice.

I gave her my most winning smile. "I just wanted to make sure that our article didn't cause you any problems. The more I thought about it, the more I realized that you had a right to be upset." The truth was, I hadn't thought about it at all. But I needed some excuse to get my foot in the door.

Patti gave a little snort. "You're damned lucky so much other crap was going on around here. Otherwise, half the town would have

162

been sniping behind my back. No, I got no problem with it. Now."

"Good." I tried to look relieved. And lied some more. "It occurred to me after you left that we hadn't told the whole story. After all, we never got your feelings about what it's like to have a famous movie star for a daughter. Let's face it: Dani is what you made her."

Obviously, that idea had never occurred to Patti. She threw back her shoulders, looking like a candidate for Abe Loomis's next wet T-shirt contest. "Well now," she said with a toss of her bleached hair, "when you put it like that . . . Sure, I did what I could for the kid. Role model, isn't that what they call it?" She seemed to realize that we were conducting our conversation both inside and outside her house. "Come in, Mrs. Lord. Want a drink?"

I calculated: I was five blocks from home and not feeling much effect from the brandy. "Sure," I said, following her into the living room. It was small, with aging Italian provincial furniture that would have made a gypsy wince. Reds, greens, and yellows predominated. The sagging drapes were drawn, making the house not only too warm, but oppressive. Half-naked gods and goddesses stood on the mantel, skin-by-fin with several carved trout. The walls boasted Harlequin-

163

masks, a watercolor of Mount Baldy, and a bas-relief of Bacchus doing what looked like the hop with a lot of unclothed nymphs.

Anxiously, I searched for a place to sit down. The green and gold sofa was covered with celebrity magazines and tabloids; the chairs were piled high with old *TV Guides* and *Soap Opera Digests*.

"Here," said Patti, whisking a foot-high stack of tabloids topped by *The Globe* from the end of the sofa. "What'll you have?"

"Bourbon? Canadian?" I sat down gingerly, putting my feet under the big coffee table that covered most of the floor space between the sofa and the TV across the room. More magazines, several romance novels, three dirty glasses, and a full ashtray shaped like a big leaf stared back at me. The house smelled of smoke, onions, and a perfume I'd once been trapped with in a Portland high-rise elevator. I'd almost gotten carsick.

Patti was at the bar, which was actually a counter between the living room and kitchen. "I was a bit of an actress myself," she said, shoveling ice out of a mock leather covered bucket. "In high school, we did *Our Town* and something about a bunch of Pilgrims."

"Oh?" I was wondering if the change in Patti Marsh's attitude had been engendered by my soft soap or her previous highballs. She wasn't drunk, but she wasn't exactly sober. I tried to pay attention. "Pilgrims?"

"Yeah, right." She handed me a hefty bourbon on the rocks. Her own drink was fresh, either vodka or gin. "They had this thing about witches. All the women were called Goody something-or-other. They ganged up on people." Patti sat down in the faded red cut-velvet chair next to the TV. "Imagine, saying all this guff about innocent men and women! What kind of a small town was that, I wonder?" Patti rolled her eyes.

"The Crucible?" I offered, thinking that Salem, Massachusetts could easily be substituted for Alpine, Washington any day.

"Right!" Patti laughed and held out her glass as if toasting me for my fabulous wit. "I wanted to say *Cubicle*. Oh, well. Cheers."

"Cheers." I sipped slowly. "So you encouraged Dani with her acting?"

"Oh — no." Patti seemed to have gulped a fourth of her drink already. She set the glass down long enough to light another cigarette. "Dani wasn't interested in acting back then. I just sort of set the stage, if you know what I mean." She clapped a hand to her cleavage. "The stage! That's good! Get it?"

I smiled appreciatively. Patti kept going. "Dani was more interested in boys and clothes and boys and hair and boys and makeup —

165

and boys." She stopped to see if I'd gotten the point. "So she got married right out of high school to Cody, and I could have told her it wouldn't work. Just a couple of kids, playing house. I should have told them to live together for a while. Everybody does that nowadays, no harm, no foul. But she wanted a wedding with a long white dress and a veil, so off they went to the Methodist Church and tied the knot." Patti puffed and guzzled. I waited for her to continue. "Then along came the baby. A little girl, named Scarlett. Dani'd just seen *Gone with the Wind*. If they'd had a boy, he would have been Rhett."

Patti was losing steam. She stared into her glass while the cigarette burned down in the overflowing ashtray. "Of course she didn't look like Scarlett. She was blond, blue-eyed, so sweet." Tears welled up in Patti's eyes. "Then she was gone." She made an ineffectual snap of her fingers. "Like that. Dani was a rotten mother."

"But SIDS isn't caused by anything," I protested. "At least that they know of. It just happens."

Patti didn't seem to hear me. She was crying noisily, her face on her forearm. "Dani wanted to go dancing and do the malls and party. She didn't give a damn about taking care of that baby! I couldn't even get her to use cloth diapers! No wonder Scarlett died! She was neglected!"

I waited for the storm to pass. Patti had my sympathy, a grandmother robbed of her grandchild. But somehow I had the feeling she was being too hard on Dani. Her tears seemed to flow out of an excess, either from a pent-up reserve of self-pity or too many glasses of vodka. It was quite possible that at nineteen, Dani Marsh Graff hadn't wanted the responsibility of parenthood. Still, the infant's death could not be blamed on Dani's desire to have a good time. After five years, I figured I didn't have a prayer of getting through to Patti Marsh.

"Dani's older now," I finally said when Patti showed signs of composing herself. "She and Matt Tabor will probably have children of their own. They'll be able to afford nannies and the best of care. You'll have another grandchild, maybe soon."

Patti made a slashing movement with her hand. "Bull! Dani won't sacrifice her career for a kid! And I wouldn't want Matt to be the father if she did!" Another wild gesture, this time almost toppling her half-filled glass.

"You've met Matt?" It was a guess; there had been a third person in the Zimmer last Friday night.

Patti wiped her eyes with her hand. She sniffed several times, then put out her cigarette and picked up her drink. "Naw. I seen him, at the tavern. Another loser. Dani don't know how to pick 'em. If I want to meet a drunk, I can go down to Mugs Ahoy and pick out somebody I know."

I didn't argue. In fact, Patti was getting to the point that she could meet a drunk by staggering to her feet and walking over to the gilded mirror above the fireplace. I took another sip of bourbon and decided to take my leave. but before I could say anything, the doorbell rang.

"Who's that?" asked Patti, as if I should know.

"I can get it," I volunteered.

But Patti yelled for her visitor to come in. A moment later, Jack Blackwell was in the living room, looking surprised at my presence, but undismayed by Patti's efforts to drink herself under the coffee table.

"What's this?" he asked in a contentious manner. "You being grilled by the press, Pats? You don't know anything about Cody. Or so you told me."

" 'Course I don't," growled Patti. "Get a drink. Lord here and me are talking about how I made Dani a star."

Suddenly I had the feeling I'd taken the

168

wrong tack with Patti Marsh. Or at least a detour. "A lot of people don't think Cody was poisoned," I said calmly. "How do you two feel about it?"

Blackwell turned away from the makeshift bar to scowl at me. "It doesn't matter one way or the other. Cody hadn't worked for me long enough to get vested. He missed death benefits by six months."

"Timely of him, wasn't it?" I smiled sweetly. Probably sappily, too, but the irony was lost on Jack Blackwell, who was making himself a powerful Scotch, no ice, a splash of soda.

"Cody came on with us right after he split with Dani," Blackwell said, turning around and looking not at me, but at Patti, who was studying her empty glass. At least she still had enough sense to realize there was a decision to make about a refill. "He was a decent worker. Loading and hauling, mostly. At the rate things are going in this crazy business, I'd probably have had to lay him off anyway. If it isn't the weather, it's the chicken-shit environment experts." Blackwell looked fit to spit.

Patti leaned forward in the red chair and held her glass out to Jack. "Gimme half," she muttered. "I'm gettin' sleepy."

Blackwell took the glass but made no move

to fill it. "I thought you wanted to go down to Skykomish and do some dancing."

Patti slumped in the chair, her head resting against a crooked antimacassar. "Naw. Not tonight, Jack. I'm beat."

Blackwell put the glass on the counter. Apparently he had made Patti's decision for her. "Poison is a weird way to go. I mean, for a murderer. How can you be sure it'll work?" Blackwell belched.

"You've got to know what you're doing," I said. "Whoever killed Cody must have planned his death very carefully."

Blackwell raised his dark eyebrows. "That right? Jeez!" He seemed more bemused than dismayed. "With all the ruckus going on at Icicle Creek, the wrong bastard might have got poisoned."

Patti's eyes were slits. "Maybe he did." The words were almost incoherent. But that didn't make them any less credible. I was about to ask her why she thought so when I realized that she'd passed out.

"I'd better go," I said, resolutely getting up.

Blackwell followed me to the door. "Patti's smashed," he said. "It was Cody, all right. Milo Dodge won't have to look far to find the killer."

I gazed up at Blackwell, who was looking

faintly smug and drinking his Scotch. There was a saturnine quality about the man that made me feel uncomfortable. "What do you mean?"

Jack Blackwell took a package of long thin cigars out of his shirt pocket. "That actor guy — Matt Tabor. Who else?" He shrugged, jiggled the packet, and caught a cigar in his mouth. "Bad blood between them. You saw what happened with the axe, you were at the tavern. Maybe this Tabor guy figured Dani still had the hots for Cody." Blackwell produced a slim silver lighter and touched off his cigar. The little flame made shadows on his face, emphasizing the hollows under his cheekbones, the sharp angle of his nose, the thin line of his lips.

"Could be," I said lightly, not wanting to argue with Jack Blackwell. Avoiding his gaze, my eyes traveled to the chipped Bombay chest that stood in the narrow entry hall. A wilted bouquet drooped in a green glass vase. Tiger lilies, gladioli, and asparagus ferns: the same arrangement I'd seen Curtis Graff carrying when he'd stopped by *The Advocate*. Had he brought them to Patti? I hadn't noticed the flowers when I'd come in.

I sketched a wave at Blackwell and started down the three steps that led from the tiny porch. From inside the house, a hoarse, strangled voice followed me onto the over-grown walk:

"Could not!" growled Patti Marsh. "Jack, you don't know the half of it!"

Apparently, neither did I.

Milo Dodge was sitting on my doorstep, looking like a rejected suitor. It was almost nine o'clock, and I couldn't imagine what he was doing. I was so surprised to see him that I almost nicked his Cherokee Chief with my Jaguar as I made the turn into the driveway.

"You got a beer?" he asked, unfolding him-self and standing up.

"I think so," I said. "If Adam didn't drink it all the last time he was home."

He waited for me to open the door, then trooped along behind me into the blessedly cool living room. My log house smelled like pine needles and sink cleanser. It was a definite improvement over the atmosphere at Patti Marsh's place.

"What's up?" I asked, handing Milo his beer and opening a Pepsi for me.

Milo loped out of the kitchen and planted his long shambling frame on the sofa. "This is the damnedest homicide case. If that's what it is." He let out a weary sigh, then drank thirstily.

I waited as patiently as possible. Milo was

gazing at the fireplace, which had accumulated a lot of trash in the past few days. Maybe I could set it off tonight if the house stayed cool.

"Billy Blatt talked to Marje today," he finally said, referring to one of his deputies who also happened to be Marje's first cousin. "She told him Cody was taking that stuff, Haloperidol. It's a tranquilizer, and he was having some weird mood swings."

"Oh." I felt deflated, and wasn't sure why. Was it disappointment that Cody's death had been an accident after all? Or did I get a thrill out of homicide? If so, my only consolation was that Milo was looking as dejected as I felt. "Well, Marje would know," I said. "She works for the Deweys."

Milo's hazel eyes were still troubled. "Right, except that when we checked the prescription out with Garth Wesley at the drug store, he couldn't find one. So Billy went back to Marje, and she said that was because she'd been able to give him some pharmaceutical samples." Milo gave me an inquiring look.

I, too, grew puzzled. "Hmmmm. That's probably not ethical. Do you know if either of the Deweys had treated Cody for his mood swings?"

Having unburdened himself, Milo stretched out his long legs under my coffee table and

173

relaxed a bit. "Marje told Billy that Cody hadn't seen a doctor. She'd noticed how moody he was and had told him he ought to make an appointment, but he wouldn't, so she got him the samples."

"Of syrup?" I asked.

Milo stared at me. "That's right. It wasn't pills." He sat up straight, pounding his fist into his palm. "Damn! Marje Blatt is lying! Why?"

"No," I said slowly, "she may not be lying. Perhaps she just doesn't know the whole truth. Cody might have gotten hooked on the stuff and got it from somebody else in another form. Or someone knew he was taking Haloperidol" — I uttered the word carefully — "and slipped him an extra dose."

Milo was shaking his head. "I don't see how we'll ever figure this one out. I can't get a handle on it. None of it seems quite real to me."

I was forced to agree. We sat in silence for a few moments, Milo drinking his beer while I sipped my Pepsi. "Any report from your forensics fellow?" I asked.

Milo gave a little jump. "Yeah, I almost forgot. He found some fibers that match the upholstery in Matt Tabor's Zimmer."

That seemed like big — if not unexpected — news to me. Milo, however, wasn't exactly

174

elated. "So? Cody rode out to the Burl Creek Road in Matt Tabor's car," I mused. "Who drove him? Was Cody dead or alive at the time?"

"I don't know the answers to either of your questions," Milo replied glumly. "Matt Tabor says he didn't take his car out at all Saturday night. He rode with Dani and Reid Hampton to the tavern. Henry Bardeen isn't sure if the Zimmer left the ski lodge that night because he was up at the high school, helping judge the Miss Alpine contest. But we know somebody had that car out by the Burl Creek Road, and we know that Cody was in it."

I was sitting in the easy chair across from the sofa, my chin resting on my hands. "You're right, Milo — this is a real mess. On the one hand, we've got several people who refuse to accept the fact that Cody was murdered. Then we've got some others — some of them the same ones — who refuse to tell us anything helpful."

"*Us?*" Milo gave me a crooked grin. "Jeez, Emma, when did I slap a badge on your chest?"

"Let's leave my chest out of this," I snapped, recalling his comment at Mugs Ahoy. "Don't you want me to help? It seems you could use a little assistance." To strengthen my case, I told him about my visits to the ski lodge and Patti Marsh's house. Milo didn't look terribly impressed, but at least he seemed mildly interested.

"Dani insists there's no motive to kill Cody," I pointed out. "On the face of it, she's right. But I think Cody knew something about somebody. I don't mean he was a blackmailer, but I'll bet he had some knowledge that was dangerous. And it can't be a coincidence that he was killed right after Dani and the rest of the movie people came to town."

Milo's expression was skeptical. "I don't see it that way. The only one of those people that Cody knew was Dani. I've got another angle on the timing — it was Loggerama, and emotions were running high, they always do. Whatever it was that spurred the killer into action was probably triggered by all the excitement."

I suppose I haven't experienced enough of small-town life yet to go gaga over a three-day celebration of tree-chopping. Still, I had to allow for the differences in background. Loggerama definitely changed the ebb and flow of Alpine's life. It wasn't every day that we had an erection, as our mayor would put it, in the middle of Front Street. At least I hoped not.

"I don't know, Milo . . ." I began, but he was crushing his empty beer can in his hands and shaking his head at me.

"Look at all the tourists and locals who got themselves banged up over the weekend," he said with uncharacteristic heat. "Look at the hordes of people who crowded into town. Look at Cody himself, throwing that axe at Dani and her friends. I wasn't there, you were, but now that Cody's been killed, I'll bet my boots he did it on purpose."

"If he did, it was a dumb stunt," I said. "Even if he'd actually hurt one of them, there were several hundred witnesses."

"And he could claim it was an accident." Milo was still wringing the beer can. I gathered he wanted a new one.

"He hated Dani," I remarked, heading into the kitchen. "He said some awful things about her the day she came to town. Oddly enough, Dani doesn't seem to hate Cody. Or else she hides it better. I have to keep telling myself she *is* an actress." I returned to the living room and gave Milo his fresh beer.

He took a deep swig, feet now flat on the floor, arms resting on his knees. "Hell, Emma, this isn't getting us anywhere."

Somewhere between the refrigerator and Milo's outstretched hand, I'd had a thought: "Milo, if somebody brought that Haloperidol to the Icicle Creek Tavern, what was it in?" I noted the sheriff's blank look and clarified

177

my question. "If it was a syrup, it had to come in some kind of container A bottle, a vial, a ten-gallon jug. Did your deputies go through the tavern's trash?"

"Hell, no," replied Milo, faintly belligerent. "By the time we got the autopsy report, everything had been hauled away. Shoot, Emma, whoever brought the stuff — assuming somebody did — could have walked right out the door with the bottles or whatever. It took two days before we realized Cody had been poisoned."

Milo was right. "I suppose the risk was minimal," I allowed, now back in the easy chair, with my legs tucked under me. "Your forensics guy must have found something in the Zimmer. Who else has been driving it besides Matt Tabor and Patti Marsh?"

"Patti's hair, Dani's hair, Hampton's hair, lots of stuff," said Milo with another sigh. "You'd think they'd all gone bald in that car."

They hadn't, of course. But Cody Graff might have lost more than his hair in the Zimmer. In the elegant, handcrafted, meticulously detailed setting of the custom-built automobile, he very likely had lost his life.

Chapter Ten

"Marje is *not* liar." Vida was emphatic. She tipped the straw hat over one eye and gave me a cold stare. "She may be confused, but she wouldn't lie. In fact, I find it hard to believe she admitted passing out purloined pills to Cody. She certainly never told *me* he was on medication."

"They were samples," I reminded her. "I had a friend in Portland who was a nurse. She was always handing out free samples. What else can they do with them?"

Vida wasn't appeased. She was, however, disturbed. It appeared that her own arguments had created misgivings. "There's something very wrong here," she pointed out. "I had lunch with Marje yesterday. She hadn't talked to Billy yet. She was upset, mostly about Cody, and the fact that she couldn't believe anyone would have a reason to kill him. Marje actually got quite inarticulate — most unlike her. But she never once mentioned that he was taking that Haloperidol. And even though Cody had a bad temper and could be mean as cat dirt, she didn't complain about him being moody. Now why did she suddenly give her cousin all this blather?"

If Vida didn't know, I couldn't even guess. We were in the news office, waiting for the paper to come back from Monroe. Vida was at her desk, and I had borrowed Ed's chair.

"I suppose," I ventured, "because Billy is a deputy sheriff and Marje felt she had to be candid with him. Let's face it, Vida, we're not out of the Dark Ages yet when it comes to attitudes on mental problems. Would Marie want to go around town telling everybody that her fiancé was taking tranquilizers because he couldn't control his moods?"

Vida shook her head so hard that she had to hold onto her hat. "I'm not talking about telling *everybody*. I'm talking about telling *me*. Marje and I are very close. Her mother, Mary Lou, is a pinhead."

Ed lumbered into the office just then, with Curtis Graff in tow. I hid my surprise and gave Curtis a pleasant smile. He was leaving in a few hours for the San Juans, and wanted to clip Cody's obituary. Did we have copies of the newspaper yet?

We didn't, but I told Curtis he could wait for Kip MacDuff who ought to be getting in from Monroe very soon. Curtis sat down at Carla's desk, I vacated Ed's chair, and Vida fixed our visitor with a shrewd gaze.

"Curtis," she began without any bothersome preamble, "who do you think killed your brother? Or do you think he may have accidentally killed himself?"

Curtis did not return Vida's gaze. "I haven't had anything to do with Cody for five years. Don't ask me how he died. I just wish I hadn't been around when it happened."

"But you were," Vida noted, never one to let a squirming fish off the hook. "Didn't you talk to Cody before he died?"

"I sure didn't," said Curtis with fervor. He was now looking at Vida, matching stare for stare. "Why would I want to talk to that jerk?"

Ed looked up from his clip art and I gave a little jump from my place by the coffeepot, but Vida was unmoved. "I never did know what you and Cody had your falling-out over," she said, implying that someone had been remiss by not telling her. "But it must have been a pip. What was it, Curtis — a girl?"

Curtis stood up abruptly, glaring at Vida. Then he uttered a lame little laugh, and shoved his hands into his pockets. "Yeah — you could say that. A girl." He made a half-hearted effort to kick Carla's desk. "I'm heading out. I don't want to miss the Anacortes ferry. I'll pick up those papers when I get back to Alpine in a couple of days." He moved swiftly to the door and let it swing shut with a loud bang.

Vida was bristling. "Well! I was right. The Graff boys did have a real set-to. Now I wonder why?"

We all did. But at the time, we couldn't begin to understand what had caused the rift. And we certainly didn't see the connection with Cody's death. Given the circumstances, we couldn't blame ourselves.

When I got home that evening, there was a call from Adam on my machine. He had a few more items for Curtis Graff to bring back to Alaska. His fleece-lined denim jacket. His navy blue ribbed knit sweater. His leather driving gloves. His ten-speed bike. And, if I had time to go shopping, could I throw in some crew socks, a half-dozen boxer shorts, a pair of Nikes, and olive green Dockers with one-inch belt loops? Oh — and a seven-eighths of an inch woven black belt?

Grimly, I dialed the cannery's dormitory. But Adam wasn't there. He had a couple of days off and was on an overnight rock climbing expedition. My son had neglected to tell me about that, obviously being too caught up in the size of his belt — which was considerably larger than the size of his brain.

Or so I decided as I banged down the phone. It rang under my hand, and I answered in a vexed voice.

"Emma, you sound as if some outraged reader put a bomb under your desk," said Tom Cavanaugh, in that easy, resonant voice that always made me tingle. "What's wrong?"

I was about to say "My son," then realized that would get us off on the wrong foot. "We had another homicide. I don't suppose it was in the San Francisco papers."

"No, we have too many of our own," said Tom. "Who got killed?"

I explained, as briefly as possible. The account gave me time to catch my breath and regain my temper. It also allowed me to recover from the surprise of hearing Tom's voice. Even though I'd spoken with him as recently as early June, I had the feeling that he could call me every day and I'd still get a little breathless. *Sap,* I chided myself and concluded my recitation with Milo's frustration over the complexities of the case.

"Dodge is a good man," said Tom, "but he's not much for subtleties. I agree with you, I don't think this Loggerama business is what set the killer off. Assuming there *is* a killer. Your theory about Dani Marsh's return makes more sense. Given that, though, it would work better if Dani, not Cody, had been the victim."

"Well, she wasn't," I said. "Cody was a bit of a drip, but he wasn't worth murdering. If you know what I mean," I added hastily, aware that I sounded crass.

"Right." Tom spoke absently. "Did you get my letter?"

I bit my lip. "Yes. I was going to answer it . . . tonight. I just got home. We've been so busy with Loggerama and then Cody's death . . ."

"And you didn't know how to fob me off." Tom chuckled. "Emma, I'm going to do *something* for Adam, and that's that. But it would be better if we agreed on what it would be."

"Okay," I said. "Pay for his tuition to the University of Alaska. Throw in room and board." I smirked into the phone, figuring I'd hoisted Tom on his own petard.

I was wrong. "Fine, when does he have to register? Are they on a quarter or a semester system? Has he declared a major?"

I was virtually speechless. "Tom —"

He trampled my protest. "I don't know much about the state university system up there, but he ought to make sure his courses are transferable to the lower forty-eight. How many credits does he have from Hawaii?"

Tom had to stop asking me questions I couldn't answer. Adam's transcripts looked like Egyptian hieroglyphics. "Adam has saved up to go to school. That's why he's working in Ketchikan. I think he needs the responsibility of earning most of his own money.

184

But you could give him the price of an airline ticket to Fairbanks."

Tom was silent for a moment. "Stanford would be closer."

"To who? You?" The words tumbled out unbidden.

"Emma." Tom was a patient man, but he sounded faintly exasperated. "To both of us, if you put it like that. But I was only thinking in terms of Stanford because of its reputation. What does Adam want to do with his life?"

I laughed. "Adam has planned his life only as far as his next party. Give me a break, Tom, do your kids know what they're doing?"

"My *other* kids?" Tom with the needle was a new experience for me. "Graham still likes taking cinema at USC, but he doesn't know if he wants to be a director, a cinematographer, or sell Milk Duds at the Tenplex in Beverly Center. Kelsey says she's not going back to Mills. She wants to see Europe and meet Alberto Tomba on the ski slopes." He paused, but not long enough to let me interrupt. "Okay, airline tickets it is. I'll send enough so Adam can come home for the holidays."

I was about to ask how his mentally unstable wife, Sandra, was doing when he turned away from the phone. "Terrific," I heard him say. "I always said green was your color."

A woman's voice answered in the background. Sandra's voice. She sounded almost normal, which meant she wasn't cackling like a chicken or howling like a loon. I glanced at my watch — it was almost six-thirty. I guessed that they were going out to dinner. Together. I put my hand to my head and fought down a terrible urge to cry.

"Thanks, Chuck," Tom said into the phone. "I'll get back to you in a few days. Good-bye."

Chuck. Chuck who? Chuck what? I felt my mouth twist into a bitter little smile. I should have chucked my emotions out the window a long time ago. Unfortunately, feelings aren't as easy to dump as old clothes.

But, I thought, getting up off the sofa and moving briskly into the kitchen, I'd just saved the price of an airline ticket.

I tried out Tom's theory on Vida. She didn't discount the idea. "Tommy's no dope," she said. "So where does it lead us? Back to Dani and Cody five years ago?"

"Maybe." We were driving in my Jag out to the Burl Creek Road. It was a muggy Thursday morning, and we wanted to have a look at the spot where Durwood had mistakenly thought he'd run down Cody Graff. "Vida, what do you remember about Cody and Dani?"

Vida leaned back against the leather upholstery, her flower-strewn fedora slipping down almost to the rim of her glasses. "Not much," she admitted. "That was the year my three daughters insisted I go to Europe. They'd been nagging me to use their father's insurance money for a long time, and after they were all married and settled down, I finally gave in. I was gone three months, so I missed the wedding."

I stopped for the arterial onto Alpine Way. Across the street, I could see Old Mill Park with its statue of Carl Clemans, the town's official founder, and despite the discrepancy in spelling, kin to Samuel Clemens. A family of tourists was going into the museum that housed logging memorabilia. On the tennis courts, a half-dozen people were energetically lobbing balls back and forth across the nets. It was too early in the day for the picnickers to show up with their jugs of Kool-Aid and containers of potato salad and raw hamburger patties. In my mind's eye, I tried to recreate the original mill, which had stood next to the railroad tracks. Old photographs usually showed it under a lot of snow, with lumber piled high on the loading dock and great puffs of smoke pouring out of slim steel stacks.

"They had a baby shower for Dani at Darlene Adcock's," Vida went on. "I didn't go, but I wrote a little story about it. Darlene said Dani was very excited, thrilled to pieces over every gift she got. Then the baby came — and went." Vida shook her head, tipping the fedora even farther down on her forehead.

"Patti told me Dani was a rotten mother," I remarked, following the railroad tracks past the sign advertising the new Safeway.

Vida adjusted her hat. "I don't think that's true. I saw Dani a couple of times downtown with little Scarlett — what a terrible name to give a child, no wonder she died, probably of mortification — but Dani was proud as punch. She had the baby all dressed up in the sweetest little things — which is a lot more than I can say for Patti when Dani was a baby. She just threw a bunch of hand-me-downs on her and stuffed her into a stroller."

"I take it Dani never knew her father?"

"Ray Marsh? No. Patti couldn't track him down to get any child support, which made her wild. I think he went to California. They often do," Vida said, as if there were big signs at the Agricultural Inspection Stations on the state line that read WELCOME IRRESPONSIBLE MEN OF THE WEST.

At the little dip in the road, I applied the brake. "It must have been right about here," I noted. The Burl Creek Road was to our left, the Overholt farm just across the intersection. Vine maple, cottonwoods, and a few firs lined the other side of the road, concealing the train tracks and the river. We pulled over and got out of the car. "The Zimmer must have been parked where we are, at least according to Cal and Charlene Vickers."

"Yes," said Vida, walking slowly around the Jaguar. "I suppose Milo and his deputies scoured this area thoroughly."

"No doubt." I watched Vida bend down, her lack of confidence in Milo and his men apparent. "Do you think they missed something?"

Vida shot me a wry look. "Did you ever know a man who didn't? Remember, Emma, men aren't like other people. My late husband could never find his hunting shirt, right there in front of him in the closet. It was *red plaid.* Imagine!"

I joined Vida in her search. Three full days had passed since Milo had decided that Cody Graff had been murdered. Maybe. Careless passersby had already littered the roadside with the usual beer cans, gum wrappers, and Styrofoam cups. Vida clucked at the vandals' leavings, even as she checked each item to make sure it couldn't possibly be a clue. She was well off into the brush now, up to her knees in fiddlehead ferns.

"Ah!" she cried, holding up an object that looked like a pen. "See this!" Triumphantly, she charged up through the ferns and presented me with an eyeliner pencil. "It's almost new, obviously expensive. What do you bet it belongs to Dani Marsh?"

I turned the eyeliner over in my hand. It was a brand I'd seen only in high fashion magazine advertisements. No store in Alpine carried the line, and it would probably be hard to find even in Seattle. "Could be," I said. "So what?"

Vida was gesturing in the vicinity of my car. "Let's say the Zimmer was parked the way we are now, heading out of town. The driver's side is next to the road. Dani has Cody with her, he passes out, maybe dies right there, she panics and pushes him out of the car. The eyeliner rolls out, too, and goes down that little bank. Got it?"

I wasn't sure. "Then how did Cody get onto the road? If he'd been on that side of the car, he would have gone down the bank, too. And Durwood would never have thought he'd hit him."

Vida frowned. "If Cody acted so tipsy, there's no way he could have driven. So to put him on the passenger side next to the road, they had to be coming *from* somewhere. But where? And why?"

"We can't be sure Dani was driving," I objected. "An expensive eyeliner doesn't prove

190

she was in the Zimmer."

"It does if it's hers." Vida was once again combing the underbrush, without much success this time. "Let's return it. Are they still up on Baldy?"

"I don't think so. They were going to film on Front Street today, remember?"

Vida did, but pointed out that the movie company hadn't been in evidence when we left the *Advocate* office at eight-thirty. "There was some action down by the taco place, but no lights or cameras," she informed me, tramping back to the Jag.

We decided to head for the ski lodge, which could be reached by taking the Burl Creek Road. Henry Bardeen's attempt to enforce the film personnel's screening process fell flat with Vida.

"Who started this lodge, Henry?" she demanded, using her height and her hat to tower over the unfortunate manager. "Rufus Runkel, my father-in-law, that's who. Where did your most glowing reference come from when you applied for this job, Henry? This old girl, that's who. Now turn your back and pretend you never saw us. We're going upstairs."

"Wait," I hissed, trotting after Vida, who was already inside the small elevator. "How do you know which room Dani is in?"

Vida gave me a patronizing look. "The FDR suite, what else? The old fool stayed here back in 'forty-two when he came West for the Grand Coulee Dam opening. Then that busybody wife of his came here in 'forty-three. What a pair! It's a wonder this country didn't lose the war. Or maybe it did." She tromped out of the elevator on the fourth floor and headed down the hall to the last door, which was set in an alcove. Vida's knock was anything but timid: It could have raised FDR's ghost. If he'd had the nerve.

But Dani Marsh didn't respond. Vida tried again, then pressed her ear to the pine door. "It's quiet," she whispered. "Oh, well. We can wait." She retracing her steps down the hall.

"We can't wait forever," I said to her back. "I've got to get to work. So do you."

Vida stopped so unexpectedly that I almost fell over her. She froze, then pointed to the room on our right. The words ALPINE SUITE were burnt into a slab of cedar. We could hear voices on the other side of the door. Or one voice, at least. Matt Tabor sounded very loud and extremely angry. Though the walls were thick and sturdy, we could catch snatches of his furious words:

". . . faithless as they come . . . You used me! . . . You don't know the meaning of love! To think I cared about you so damned much. . . ."

Vida and I exchanged startled glances. Down the hall, the elevator opened. The young woman I'd seen with the script up at the location on Baldy now emerged carrying a big manila envelope. She gave us a curious glance.

Undaunted, Vida yanked at the collar of my cotton blouse. "There! Now you're presentable. Let's go see Henry Bardeen."

The ruse apparently worked. The young woman walked off in the opposite direction. Vida and I made for the elevator. We were in luck, catching it before the doors closed all the way.

"My, my," said Vida, leaning against the frosted glass at the rear of the car, "true love isn't running smoothly. Maybe it's a mercy that Matt and Dani haven't set a date for the wedding."

"Hollywood romances must be especially rough," I remarked, though I would be willing to match my own little love against any of them. "All those egos and temptations and ambition."

"Ambition." Vida breathed the word and gave me a puzzled look as we got out of the elevator. "Now that's something I would never connect with Dani. Whatever else she was when she was growing up, ambition played no part in it."

We were in the lobby, where several guests were checking out at the front desk. Heather Bardeen was looking very professional this morning in her desk clerk's navy blazer and silk crimson scarf.

"We can check with Dani about the eyeliner later," I said, looking at my watch. "It's going on ten. The mail will be in any minute and Ginny will wonder what happened to us. If they're going to film on Front Street, we may be able to catch Dani this afternoon."

Reluctantly, Vida agreed. But in the parking lot, she grabbed my arm. "We can catch Dani now," she whispered in my ear. "Look!"

In a specially reserved slot next to the lodge, Dani Marsh was getting out of a brand-new Lexus. She had obviously just arrived. My jaw dropped; Vida stared over the rims of her glasses. Then she charged after her prey.

"Dani! Yoo-hoo! Over here!" Vida waved her fedora.

Dani squinted at us against the sun, then smiled pleasantly. "Yes?" She was obviously in a hurry.

Vida whipped around the other parked cars like a half-back breaking tackles. "Here, Dani," she said, handing over the eyeliner. "We found this."

Dani glanced down at the proffered object. "Oh! Thank you. I was wondering what I'd done with it." She gave Vida her dazzling smile.

I had moved a few steps so that I could see both of the women's profiles. Vida was gazing down at Dani, the tortoiseshell glasses catching the sun. "You lost it out by the turn-off to the Burl Creek Road."

Dani blinked a couple of times. "Oh? That's odd — I thought I lent it to my mother." She took the eyeliner and dropped it in her Sharif handbag. "I'm glad to get it back. I always prefer using my own cosmetics, rather than the makeup crew's." The smile remained fixed as she turned to head into the ski lodge.

Vida was standing with her hands on her hips. "Well, if that doesn't beat all!"

I had sidled up next to her. "Yes?"

Vida looked down her nose at me. "Dani and Patti trading makeup? Punches would be more like it. And who was Matt Tabor quarreling with, if not Dani Marsh? What's going on here?"

I hadn't the slightest idea. My only hope was that Milo Dodge had a better grasp of the investigation than we did.

But, unfortunately, that was not so.

Chapter Eleven

Carla had gone in to see young Doc Dewey and find out if she needed a refill on her antihistamine. She didn't, but when she got back from the clinic, her dark eyes were huge and her cheeks were flushed.

"Patti Marsh was there, all black and blue," gasped Carla, leaning on Vida's desk. "She said she'd fallen off her porch."

I was standing in the doorway to my office, holding the mail that Ginny Burmeister had just brought in. "Porch or perch?" I responded. "Or neither one?"

Carla nodded vigorously. Vida sniffed. "Jack Blackwell. He probably beat her up. I'd guess it wasn't the first time."

"Creep," remarked Ginny, who was dumping Ed's mail in his already overflowing in-basket. "Maybe that's why his first wife left him."

Irrationally, I felt a twinge of guilt. "It must have happened last night, after I left Patti's. Jack seemed okay, and Patti was practically on her ear."

But Carla shook her head, long black hair swinging over her shoulders. "No, it was this morning, I'm sure. She had a cut over her eye, and it was still bleeding."

"Men!" huffed Vida, glancing at Ed's vacant chair as if he were responsible for the entire sex. "I've been tempted to deck Patti a few times myself, but that's different. I'm a woman."

"Now Vida," Ginny began, "violence doesn't have a gender. You really shouldn't say things like that."

Vida had turned back to her typewriter. She veered around in her chair, giving Ginny a vexed look. "Hush! I'm old enough to be your grandmother! Do you want to get *spanked?*" The typewriter rattled and shook as Vida launched into her latest article. Before any of the rest of us could say anything further, a knob flew off, a couple of screws clattered to the floor, and Vida's typewriter was dead in the water. "Oh, blast!" she cried. "Now what?"

"Vida," I began, tossing the mail onto my desk and reentering the news office, "it's time to upgrade yourself. Let's go buy you a word processor."

"No!" Vida recoiled as if I'd threatened to burn her at the stake. "It just needs fixing, that's all!" She groped with one foot, retrieving the knob. "Get me a screwdriver. I can do it myself."

"Ed borrowed it to fix his front door," said Ginny. "That was three weeks ago."

"Great," I muttered. Ed had a habit of borrowing items from the office and never returning them. "I'll run over to the hardware store and get another one."

"I can go," offered Ginny.

"You need to answer the phones," I said, already halfway to the door. "It's Thursday. I don't want to talk to every crackpot with a complaint about the latest edition of the paper."

Harvey Adcock's Hardware and Sporting Goods Store was only a block and a half away, and coincidentally in the same building as the local florist. I hurried up Front Street, trying to pretend that at eleven o'clock in the morning it wasn't already stifling. Compared with the previous week, the tempo of the town seemed to have slowed to a snail's pace.

Across the street, a middle-aged couple looked longingly at the Whistling Marmot movie theatre's air-conditioning sign. In the next block, three teenagers stood close together in the shade of the Venison Inn's entrance. At the corner of Fifth Street, the bookstore's cat had decamped from its usual place in the front window to sit among the leafy greenery of a sidewalk planter. The air, which in other seasons smells of evergreens and damp and woodsmoke, was tinged with gasoline fumes and cooking grease. The smokestacks at the mill were moribund; the ski lodge catered only to the traveler. In summer, there was a fallow feeling to Alpine, despite the number of tourists and the presence of the movie company. It was as if we were on hold, waiting for the rain and the real business of the community to begin anew.

Harvey's store, with its high ceilings and two separate showrooms, seemed cool by comparison to the outdoors. He was behind the counter, sorting faucets. His pixie-like face brightened when he saw me.

"Emma! What broke?"

I explained, asking him for a cordless screwdriver, just like the one I had at home. Ed would probably walk off with it eventually, but I might as well facilitate matters for now.

"Regular or bendable?" asked Harvey, coming around the counter to a display rack on the other side of the store.

"They bend now, too?" I was impressed. "Sure, why not?"

Harvey sprinted back behind the counter, ringing up the sale. "That's $43.27, with tax."

My jaw dropped. I had only twenty-five dollars in cash, about twice that much in my checking account, which hadn't been balanced in two weeks, and payday wasn't until tomorrow. I dug into my wallet for my emergency fund, a hundred dollar bill I kept tucked away for dire necessities. Like bendable cordless screwdrivers.

"Can you change this?" I asked, almost hoping Harvey couldn't and thus I would be let off the hook. An ordinary screwdriver probably went for under five bucks.

"Sure can," said Harvey cheerfully. "I went to the bank when they opened at nine-thirty." He took my hundred; I hoped he didn't notice how my hand lingered on the bill. "There I was waiting for them to open up, and who comes along but Patti Marsh, sassy as you please." The cash register jingled and Harvey made change. "She must have won the lottery."

I frowned at Harvey as he counted the money into my hand. "What do you mean?"

Harvey's pointed little ears seemed to move up and down. "What? I mean she was pleased with herself. She had a big deposit, or so I gathered standing next to her in the bank. You should have heard her and that MacAvoy kid carry on! 'Shall I get a gunny sack for it, Mrs. Marsh?' he asked her. They were laughing themselves sick. Of course Richie MacAvoy is new at the teller's job and probably should he a mite more discreet."

"Wait a minute, Harvey," I said, leaning

on the counter and lowering my voice as an elderly man I didn't recognize ambled into the store. "Patti Marsh was just treated by young Doc Dewey for . . . cuts and abrasions," I said quickly, not sure I should spread gossip any faster than the rest of Alpine. "How did she look?"

Harvey gave a shrug of his slender shoulders. "Fine. You know Patti — lots of goo on her face, even in the morning. I suppose she was on break from work."

From work at Blackwell Timber, I thought to myself. "Well." I tried to act unconcerned. "She must have taken that spill after she went to the bank."

"Maybe so." Harvey was handing me the paper bag with the screwdriver, but he was looking at the elderly man who was bringing a box of washers up to the counter. "Hi, Marco. What've you got?"

Thanking Harvey Adcock, I left the store and scooted around the corner to Posies Unlimited. The owner, Delphine Corson, was a flabby blonde of fifty with high color and a low neckline. She greeted me with a throaty laugh.

"You're too late," she announced, slapping the empty plant stand next to the refrigerated case. "I can't get any more flowers up to the San Juans in time for the funeral, not even by wire or phone."

To my dismay, I realized that while Cody Graff's death was never far from my mind, I had completely forgotten about his services, which were scheduled for today. Hastily, I explained that I didn't know the family and had only met Cody a couple of times.

Delphine moved with a graceless tread to the bench, where she was aging red and yellow roses in a wicker basket. "It's mostly friends of his parents who've sent flowers," she said. "I don't think Cody had a lot of pals." She picked up a handful of maidenhair fern and clipped an inch off the stems. "Funny, though — you'd think his fiancée would have had me do a spray for his casket."

"Marje?" I fanned myself with my hand. It was very warm in the small shop, and the heady scent of flowers was almost overpowering. "Maybe she had something sent from Friday Harbor."

"Oh, no," said Delphine with certainty. "The Blatts always use me. Marje had already been in to discuss the flowers for her wedding. That's off now, so there goes a nice chunk of change. She wanted four hundred gardenias."

I didn't comment on the canceled ceremony or Delphine's unrealized profits. Instead, I steered the conversation back to the Graffs.

"I gather Curtis was in the other day. Those tiger lilies were gorgeous."

Delphine plucked out a red rose that wasn't up to snuff and put it in her cleavage. "Curtis? The older Graff kid? Oh, right, he's back from Alaska. He sure had lousy timing. Isn't your kid in Ketchikan, too?"

"Yes," I said, trying not to get sidetracked. "I couldn't figure out why Curtis was taking flowers to Patti Marsh. What's the connection?"

My blatant probing didn't seem to bother Delphine. That's one advantage of being a journalist: other people figure you have a right to know. It rarely occurs to them that you may be just plain nosy.

Delphine gazed at me with cornflower blue eyes. "It was July 30."

My face must have been a blank. "So?"

"Oh, that's right," said Delphine with a little grimace. "I forgot. You're a newcomer."

I had the feeling that I would still be a newcomer if I stayed in Alpine until I died. Native Alpiners were not only wary of strangers, but were loath to embrace anyone who hadn't spent at least a couple of decades in their town.

Delphine had finished with the arrangement and was gathering up leftover leaves and stems. "Five years ago on July 30, the Graff baby died. Curtis was taking a bouquet to

203

Grandma Patti. Nice of him, considering."

"Considering what?"

Delphine shrugged. "Considering that he's been gone for so long. And that he and Cody were on the outs. As for Dani, I don't know — it seems to me he should have taken her a bouquet, too. I suggested it, but he didn't seem to hear me. So I lost a fifteen dollar sale on that one." She looked disappointed.

"What about Cody? Did he buy flowers, too?"

"He never has, not in all the years since little Scarlett died." Disapproval was etched on Delphine's face, though I couldn't tell whether it was motivated by Cody's lack of sentiment or the loss of another order.

"Say, Delphine," I said, suddenly reminded of another tragedy, "do you remember when Art Fremstad killed himself?"

Delphine's heavy jowls sagged. "You bet. What a nice guy. Talk about flowers! I made enough off of that one to send myself to Palm Springs for a week! I even had to hire extra help to deliver. Poor Art. Poor Donna."

I assumed Donna was Art's widow. "Did she remarry?"

"Yeah, about two years ago. You know Steve Wickstrom from the high school? Trig and geometry teacher."

I remembered seeing Steve and Donna

Wickstrom at the Icicle Creek Tavern with Coach Ridley and his wife. In the spring, Carla had done a piece about Steve's contribution to a math text. She'd called him *Stove*. Carla's proofreading wasn't any better than her typing.

Thanking Delphine for her time, I started to leave but felt her blue eyes boring into my back. "Oh," I said a trifle giddily, "I forgot. I wanted to get a bouquet." I cast around the flower shop. Everything looked as if it would cost at least twenty dollars a dozen. "Or maybe a plant. Yes, how about a nice cyclamen?"

With a grunt, Delphine bent down and picked up a bright pink specimen. "This is a beauty. "That'll be $17.58 with tax. After it finishes blooming, keep it in the dark."

That figured, I thought to myself. We all seemed to be in the dark when it came to Cody Graff's death. But I was the only one who was going broke. If I hurried, maybe I could still get back to the office while I had enough money for lunch.

But as I carted the plant and the cordless screwdriver over to *The Advocate*, I decided I could put the cyclamen to good use. The Jaguar was parked around the corner. I jumped in and drove the five blocks down Railroad Avenue to Blackwell Timber.

Patti Marsh wasn't there. The fresh-faced

young woman at the receptionist's desk said Ms. Marsh had gone home early. Sick, she gathered. Maybe the heat. It was really too warm for Alpine.

It was almost noon. Maybe it was just as well if I skipped lunch. I got back in the car and drove up to Patti's house. In the midday sun, the tired little house didn't look any more hospitable than it had last night. Although Patti's black compact car was in the drive, the door was closed and the drapes were still drawn. I hesitated, then knocked loudly.

On my second effort, Patti called from inside, asking my identity. I told her. Warily, she opened the door a couple of inches.

"I heard you'd had an accident," I said, feeling a bit foolish as I tried to wedge the cyclamen inside the door. "Isn't this a pretty shade of pink?"

"What is it?" she asked, opening the door all the way. "Some kind of orchid?"

"It's a cyclamen, from Posies Unlimited." I had a fixed smile on my face as I crossed the threshold. The bouquet on the Bombay chest was shedding petals. Patti looked as if she'd lost all her bloom, too. Her face was swollen, and there was a small bandage above her right eye. "How do you feel?"

Patti took the plant and limped into the living room. The house was still dreary and airless. She went over to the TV and turned off a soap opera.

"I feel like crap," said Patti, indicating that I should sit down on the cluttered sofa. "I decided to take the rest of the day off."

"How'd it happen?" I asked in what I hoped was a guileless voice.

Patti eased herself into the cut-velvet chair and lighted a cigarette. She still wore a wary expression. "Hey, Mrs. Lord, cut the bullshit. Since when were we buddies? What do you really want?"

I allowed the smile to die. "Okay. I don't like seeing women get knocked around. You didn't fall off your front porch, Patti. You looked just fine when Harvey Adcock saw you at the bank this morning. If somebody's beating you up, why don't you file a complaint?"

"Sheesh!" Patti rolled her brown eyes and looked at me as if I were the original babe in the woods. "Where'd you grow up, in a bird cage? Hey, people — like men — get pissed off. They start swinging. That's how they handle stuff. They don't mean anything by it, they just don't know what else to do. Then they're sorry, and they come crawling back, full of apologies, and maybe a present or two. It's the way of the world, honey."

"Not my world." I spoke firmly, perhaps

even primly, judging from the amused expression on Patti's face. Before she could contradict me, I leaned toward her, careful not to knock any of the items off the coffee table with my knees. "Beating up women is a coward's way of dealing with problems. It's also stupid, and men who do it are stupid. What kind of woman wants to hang out with a stupid coward? I can't think of any present that's worth the price, and that includes a terrific night in the sack."

No longer amused, Patti stiffened, apparently surprised at my candor. Maybe she didn't expect it from me. "So how do you change a man?" she asked with a sneer.

"I'm not sure you can change a man. But you can change men. Find somebody who doesn't think with his fists. They don't all go around beating women senseless. Jeez, Patti, that can get out of hand pretty fast. You could end up dead." I stared straight into her eyes, which were so like Dani's, except for being bloodshot and a bit puffy.

Patti recoiled as if I'd decided to use her for a punching bag. "Shut your mouth!" she gasped, clearly shaken. "Here!" She struggled to her feet and grabbed the plant from on top of the TV set. "Take this cycling thing and get out!"

I didn't budge. "No, I won't." If Patti

needed a lesson in being firm, I was about to give it. "I'm not done." I waited for her to sit down, pitch a fit, or throw the cyclamen at my head. Instead, she cradled the plant against her bosom and narrowed her eyes.

"You're nervy," she said. The anger still sparked in her eyes, but she also looked frightened. "What now?"

I had been sure of my moral ground when I'd lectured Patti about allowing herself to be beaten. But I had absolutely no reason to inquire about her bank deposit. Not even my credentials as a journalist gave me the right to ask such a question.

I stuck with candor as my best weapon. "I heard you had some good luck today. Then I heard you were at the clinic, all banged up. It didn't make sense, and maybe I thought there was a story in it, especially since Cody Graff was murdered. Violence breeds violence. I was following my reporter's instincts, I guess." My attitude was self-deprecating; I was relying on Patti's sympathy. If she had any. "After all, we've got a murderer loose in this town."

Her response startled me. Patti Marsh threw back her head and laughed, a hoarse, unsettling sound that turned into a cough. She stubbed out her cigarette, wiped her mouth, and leaned against the back of the cut-velvet chair. "No we don't. Stick to your movie star stories and your raccoon pictures, Emma Lord. You don't know siccum."

I left the cyclamen, convinced that it, too, would wither and die in the sunless, stifling atmosphere of Patti's house. I didn't understand a woman like Patti, who seemed content to live off the leavings of an ill-tempered man like Jack Blackwell. Then again, I didn't understand myself, hanging on to a twenty-year-old dream. Maybe Patti and I weren't so different after all.

"Well," said Vida, when I returned to the office, "you look like a dying duck in a thunderstorm. What happened? I thought you went out for a screwdriver."

I recounted my adventures of the last hour and a half while Vida sipped iced tea. "I'm only guessing it was Jack who beat her up," I said in conclusion, "but I can't figure out why she hooted with laughter when I told her there was a murderer on the loose."

Vida was looking thoughtful, her floppy pink linen hat shoved back on her head. "Why do so many people not want to believe Cody was killed? Isn't that what it comes to?" Vida peered at me through her glasses.

"Is it?" I was sitting in Ed's vacant chair.

He had gone to a Rotary Club luncheon; Carla was out getting a story at the fish hatchery. "Vida, do you know Donna Fremstad Wickstrom?"

"Of course." Vida looked at me as if I were losing my mind, which I felt wasn't far from the truth. "Donna Erlandson Fremstad Wickstrom. A four-point student in high school, two years at Skagit Valley Community College, Associate Arts degree, worked in the library, married Art Fremstad, one child, a girl, widowed, remarried Steve Wickstrom about three years ago. She runs a day care in their home, has another baby, a boy, ten months, she jogs, belongs to the Alpine Book Club, is an excellent baker, does their own plumbing. What else do you want to know?"

I was about to say I couldn't possibly imagine when I saw an odd movement outside the window above Vida's desk. Somebody was putting a ladder against the building. "What's that?"

"What?" Vida eyed me curiously, then followed my startled gaze. "Oh! Good grief! Public Utility District workers? No — there's no PUD truck. I've no idea."

We both went outside. Three men in coveralls were hooking up a spray painter. One of them, a short stocky youth with black eyes and dark brown hair, smiled broadly.

"I hear you like yellow," he said, revealing lots of white teeth.

"Says who?" I gaped as one of the other men began to assault *The Advocate*'s outer walls with a blast of sunbright color. "Hey! Stop that!"

The stocky young man was still grinning. "We've got permission. It'll look great on film. You'll love it."

"The hell I will!" I glanced up Front Street. Half the buildings, from Francine's Fine Apparel to Adcock's Hardware, wore new coats of paint. I had returned to the newspaper office from the other direction and hadn't noticed the change. "Oh, damn! Is this for the movie?"

It was. I asked who in the name of heaven and earth had given permission to turn *The Advocate* the color of a giant canary.

The stocky young man gestured at the entrance to the newspaper. "Your advertising guy. Burnski? Bronsti? We gave him a check for five hundred bucks."

I held my head. Vida was standing with her hands on her hips, watching *The Advocate* take on a jaundiced hue. Ed Bronsky had sold me out for five bills. If somebody had offered to buy that much advertising, he would have fought them tooth and toenail. I didn't know whether to throttle Ed — or Reid Hampton.

212

As I took another look down Front Street, I could see not only the newly painted red, blue, and green facades, but a barricade at the corner of Fifth, by the Venison Inn and the Whistling Marmot Theatre. Ironically, the Marmot needed some work, as its owner, Oscar Nyquist, hadn't fixed up the exterior since 1967, when an outraged member of a Pentecostal sect had set fire to a life-size cutout of Mrs. Robinson's stocking-clad leg in a promotion for *The Graduate*. Further along Front, cameras were perched on big dollies and bright lights shown down on the main drag. As far as *The Advocate* was concerned, it was too late to do more than groan.

"This is hopeless," I muttered to Vida. "Let's go see Donna Wickstrom."

Vida had screwed up her face, observing the paint job in process. "Donna? What for?"

I was already heading for my car. If nothing else, I wanted to keep its green exterior from getting splattered with yellow dots. "We need to stop another murder," I yelled over the sound of the spraying machine.

Vida, with her flat-footed step, hurried to join me. "Who?" she asked, startled.

I opened the door for her on the passenger's side. "Ed. If I don't get out of here, I think I'm going to strangle him."

Chapter Twelve

Vida's further lack of curiosity about my insistence on seeing Donna Fremstad Wickstrom puzzled me. As we made a detour to avoid the film company's barricade, she was unusually quiet. At last, as we approached the Wickstrom home in the Icicle Creek Development, I asked her what she was thinking.

"I'm thinking about what you're thinking about," she said very soberly. "You're trying to tie Cody's murder into something that happened between him and Dani, that something being little Scarlett and the effect of her death. At least that's the only incident we know about. And somehow, Art Fremstad fits into it. Maybe."

I was trying to concentrate on finding Wickstrom's address while listening to Vida. "That's right." I remarked. "The only common topic in regard to Dani and Cody is their baby. They haven't been in touch for five years. Curtis has been gone for five years. His parents moved away five years ago. Art Fremstad has been dead for five years. Everything points backwards. If there's any link between Cody's death and Dani's return, it has to be the baby. I don't know if Milo is on the same wavelength."

"Milo is doing fibers and fingerprints and tire tracks," said Vida, with a shake of her head. "That's how he works."

"Well?" I had turned into Dogwood Lane. "Do you think Art Fremstad was a suicidal type?"

Vida had taken off her floppy hat and was mopping her brow. "No. He had too much sense. But I'm not a mind reader. If there's one facet of human behavior I've learned in over sixty years, it's that you can never be completely certain what anyhody else is thinking."

I spotted the address on my right. Donna and Steve Wickstrom lived in one of the more modest homes in the new development, a two-story version of a Swiss chalet with a single-car garage. There were no goats on the lawn, but there was a tricycle, a sandbox, and a plastic wading pool.

Donna Wickstrom came to the front door with three small children attached to her legs. She was a pretty young woman with short brown hair and long curling eyelashes. Her unruffled expression indicated that not only was she unfazed by our unexpected arrival, but that there was very little in life that amazed her.

"Mrs. Runkel," she said, extending a hand. "How nice! I haven't seen you since the shower for Angie Fairbanks last May."

Vida introduced me to Donna, who somehow managed to lead us into the living room without disengaging herself from the trio of toddlers. Two more children were playing on the floor, pounding colored pegs into a sturdy wooden bench. The room was filled with sunshine, bright colors, and soft furniture. Donna Wickstrom was only a mile from Patti Marsh, but their dwellings were worlds apart.

I allowed Vida to broach the subject of our visit. She did so with remarkable tact — at least for Vida.

"This town is in a mess," she said, after we refused Donna's offer of tea or coffee. "First Cody Graff's baby dies. Now Cody is dead, too. Nobody, including the sheriff, knows why. I'm wondering, Donna, do you think Art would know if he were still alive?"

If Vida's words upset our hostess, she gave no sign. Donna Fremstad Wickstrom looked very grave, but didn't seem to find Vida's line of inquiry peculiar. She glanced into the dining room, where all of the children, including a girl of about five who looked remarkably like Donna, were dumping a pile of toys out of a big cardboard box.

"Do you mean that Art knew something so

216

awful he killed himself?" she asked in a low voice.

"Exactly." Vida, as ever, was brisk. "Has that thought ever occurred to you?"

Again, Donna appeared undismayed. "Frankly, yes." She gave a quick look into the dining room to make sure that all was well, then folded her hands in her lap. "I was visiting my sister in Seattle when the Graff baby died. I came back to Alpine three days later, and Art was very upset. *Upset,* not distraught." She gave us each a hard look to make sure we understood. "For a long time, I kicked myself for being so caught up in restoring order after my visit out of town. You know how it is when you're gone, even for a short time. It takes forever to get everything back on track. Anyway, when Art disappeared two days later, I was stunned." For the first time, emotion showed in Donna's hazel eyes.

"Where did you think he'd gone?" Vida asked, giving Donna a chance to collect herself.

"He was on the night shift, five to midnight. It was just this time of year, and at first I figured he'd arrested some tourist or picked up a drunk driver. But about two in the morning, Jack Mullins called and asked if Art had come home instead of checking in at the sheriff's office. Of course he hadn't. That was when Jack and Milo and Sam Heppner went looking for him." She turned away, not toward the dining room this time, but to the front door, as if she still expected Art Fremstad to come home.

Vida, who was sitting next to Donna on the sectional sofa, placed a hand on the younger woman's arm. "They found him in the late morning, down past the falls. I remember that very well. His patrol car was parked off the highway on a dead-end logging road, about a hundred yards from the river." Vida glanced over at me. "We were all sure it was an accident. Especially Milo."

Donna's head jerked up. "And me. There was no way I would ever have thought Art would kill himself. I still wouldn't believe it if he hadn't left that note." In her fervor, she had raised her voice. Donna turned swiftly to see if the children were listening. They weren't. Toys were sailing in various directions, and several squeals erupted from small lungs.

I decided it was my turn to ask a question: "What did the note say, Donna?"

But Donna was on her feet, moving swiftly to intervene with the squabbling youngsters. Gently but firmly, she set matters straight and returned to the living room. "It said . . ." She paused to swallow hard. " 'Life is too tough. I hate being a deputy and arresting people. I can't go on.' Then he signed his name — 'Art.' That was it." She raised a limp hand, as if her late husband's last words had not only summed up his suicide, but a lifetime of events that had led up to it.

We were silent for a moment, as if acting out our own commemoration. Then Vida tapped Donna's wrist. "Wait a minute — he *signed* his name? I never heard that part. Do you mean he typed the note itself?"

Donna nodded. "We had an electric typewriter then. Steve and I have a word processor now — he uses it for school."

Under her floppy pink hat, Vida was frowning. "Art typed a note that ran about four lines? Donna, does that make sense to you?"

"He must have been under a lot of stress. People behave strangely." Donna smoothed the wrinkles in her olive walking shorts.

"Was he under stress? Did he seem depressed?" Vida wasn't giving up.

"No, not really. I told you, he was upset by that Graff baby's death." Donna ran a hand through her short brown hair. "Art didn't talk a lot about his feelings. I wish he had. You know how most men are. They keep their emotions bottled up."

I looked at Vida. "Did Art talk to Milo?"

Vida was chewing her lower lip. "No. Not

that I know of." She turned back to Donna. "Where did you find the note?"

"Under the telephone. I'd invited everyone back here after the funeral, and I noticed this piece of paper sticking out when I went to call Delphine Corson and ask who sent the big basket of begonias while we were gone. There wasn't any card. Then I read the note . . ." She stopped, her shoulders slumping. "I showed it to Sheriff Dodge. He couldn't believe it, either. But of course we had to. It was a terrible shock."

Again we were silent, the little ones providing a background of innocent vigor. Vida's next question surprised me as well as Donna.

"Who did send the begonias?"

Donna stared at Vida. "Why — I don't know. I was so stunned by the note that I never called Delphine." She shook herself. "Isn't that awful of me — somebody didn't get a thank-you note."

I looked at Vida. Judging from the flash of her eyes, she was thinking about something far more dreadful than a lapse of etiquette. But she didn't say so to Donna. Maybe that was just as well.

There was a story in the dispute over the movie company's alleged unauthorized cutting of Jack Blackwell's trees. It wasn't the kind of article I usually ran before formal charges or lawsuits were filed, but it gave me an excuse to talk to Blackwell. After taking care of the most urgent messages that had accumulated on my desk, I returned to the timber company. Filming was underway in the vicinity of the Lumberjack Motel. The bright lights seemed blinding in the middle of the afternoon. Even from a distance, they looked hot. As for *The Advocate*, its bright new coat of yellow paint was drying quickly in the August sun.

The same young woman who had told me Patti Marsh wasn't in led the way into Jack Blackwell's office. His desk was an oval of mahogany, highly polished and fairly tidy. A salmon, in the neighborhood of sixty pounds, was mounted on one paneled wall, and a moose head stared blankly above a glass-fronted bookcase. The decor didn't suit my taste, but in general, the room had more class than its owner.

Jack looked up from a computer printout. "No, I haven't any idea when the logging ban will be lifted. The fire danger is still higher than a kite. I'm losing money hand over fist. And in the meantime, all those do-gooders in D.C. work overtime trying to figure out how to screw me and the rest of the timber industry."

I sat down in a curved chair that matched

the desk. "Actually, that isn't why I'm here. I wanted to find out if you're going to file a civil suit against the movie company for chopping down your trees."

Blackwell's forehead creased, and his thin mouth formed a firm, tight line. "I will if I have to, but I'm thinking criminal, not civil, charges. How'd you get wind of this?"

"I was at the Icicle Creek Tavern the other night," I explained, feeling somewhat puzzled. "You and Reid Hampton had words, practically under my nose."

Jack Blackwell made an angry gesture with one hand, sweeping the computer printout onto the floor. "I don't mean that crap. I mean about the payoff. Has Patti been shooting her face off?"

Enlightenment was beginning to dawn. I decided to play it close to my chest. "It's hard for her say much of anything, with her face so swollen." It wasn't exactly the truth, but I took the chance that Blackwell wouldn't know any better. "She sure made the people at the bank happy, though."

"Goddamn!" Blackwell pounded his fist on the desk, rattling pens, a stapler, an ashtray. "That bitch! What kind of games is she playing now?"

Although I knew the question wasn't meant for me, I hazarded an answer: "Why would

222

the movie people make a check out to Patti and not to you or Blackwell Timber?"

Jack Blackwell turned an angry, baffled face on me. "That's what I want to know. That Hampton is one real dumb bastard. Patti's not an officer of this company; she's a secretary. And then she lies about it, the cheating little tramp!" He jackknifed out of his chair, whirling around and looking as if he were about to assault the stuffed salmon. " 'Get your own money, Jack,' she told me, laughing in my face! 'I got mine.' Bullshit! Why does Reid Hampton owe *her* money? Those were *my* goddamned trees!"

"So you smacked her," I said calmly. "I don't imagine that got any money out of her."

Blackwell was facing me again, his saturnine face dark with rage and frustration. It dawned on me that I might get smacked, too. "So what? She's a thief!"

I got to my feet, forcing myself to remain casual. "Then you ought to tell Milo Dodge. Maybe you can get Patti *and* Reid Hampton arrested."

Blackwell's mouth twisted, not so much in anger, as in confusion. Maybe the idea hadn't occurred to him. He stared at me as if I had become an ally. "You think so? Ah hell, I don't want to put Patti in the slammer. She'll pony up. I just don't like her laughing in my face."

"That can be annoying," I allowed, inching toward the door. "Have you ever heard of friendly persuasion?"

Blackwell wasn't impressed by the suggestion. "Patti's already friendly enough. She can wear a man out. Are you saying she's too friendly with that Hampton prick?"

I wasn't, but it was a thought. Yet it didn't ring true. Or did it? Vida was right — you never really knew what went on in other people's heads. "She hardly knows him," I said, aware that the remark didn't necessarily exonerate Patti.

"Oh, yeah?" countered Blackwell. "He's been over to her place a couple of times. And she sure as hell knows him well enough to get fifty grand out of him."

That, I thought, was well enough for me.

Milo was going to bring Honoria Whitman over for a drink after dinner. I had issued the invitation when I checked in with Milo before I left the office. There was nothing new to report on the investigation, he told me, but they were working on the source of the Haloperidol. They were also trying to prove that Dani Marsh and Cody Graff were in the Zimmer at the time of his death. Dani had been unreachable all afternoon, because she was filming on Front Street. Milo would try to see her before he brought Honoria to my place.

But Milo showed up alone. Honoria had unexpected company from Carmel, old friends touring Washington State. I had to smirk. A recent arrival, and already Honoria was suffering from a virulent Pacific Northwest disease: the surprise guest with a complete ignorance of the motel and hotel industry. I hadn't had anybody drop in for three months, except for my brother, who had spent a week with me in June. Ben had come to visit before going on to his new assignment as a parish priest in northern Arizona. After over twenty years in the home missions of Mississippi, he was feeling both sad about leaving the people he loved and excited at the prospect of working with the Navajos. Ben wasn't company; he was my other self.

Milo entered my house looking downhearted. "Honoria asked me to drive down and have dinner with her and this other couple, but I was too beat to go all the way into Startup. You got any Scotch, Emma?"

"You're the only one who drinks it here," I said, going to the bottom shelf of the bookcase where I kept my limited liquor supply. "Why don't you just strap it to your leg?"

Milo didn't respond to my feeble effort at humor. "I might as well resign," he said in a doleful voice. "If I don't arrest somebody pretty soon, my chances of getting reelected are down the drain."

"Oh, shut up, Milo," I said testily. "Here, have a drink. Shall I make some popcorn?"

Milo brightened. I was heading for the kitchen when a voice trumpeted from the porch. It was Vida. "Well." She stalked into the living room, wearing her gardening clothes, which consisted of red culottes and a white blouse. "Here you are. Where's Delphine?"

Milo and I both stared. "Delphine Corson?" I finally said, sounding stupid.

Vida threw her floppy pink hat onto the sofa. "Yes, yes, Delphine Corson. She was going to come over and tell us who delivered those blasted begonias. She had to go through her records. The woman isn't computerized."

"Neither are you, Vida." I couldn't resist the barb.

"Never mind," said Vida, going to the phone and punching in a series of numbers.

Milo clutched his Scotch as if it were an antidote. "What's all this about?"

I explained while Vida talked to Delphine. Vida finished first. "She just found it. I was right — Cody Graff delivered those flowers to the Fremstad house. He volunteered. In fact, he paid for them."

"How did he get in?" I asked.

Vida plopped down on the sofa next to Milo, narrowly missing her hat. "The door wasn't locked, I suppose. This isn't the big city, Emma. Especially five years ago." She looked very smug.

Milo, however, was still looking mystified. "Will you two please tell me —"

"Yes, yes, just pay attention," said Vida. "Really, Milo, you ought to have been more aware five years ago. Do you want some idiot like Averill Fairbanks to beat you when the primary election comes 'round next month?"

Milo groaned. Vida ignored him and continued: "I'm betting dollars to doughnuts that Art Fremstad didn't commit suicide. Nobody ever thought he did. Cody Graff brought those begonias over to Art and Donna's house during the funeral, when he knew no one would be around. He also left a phony suicide note. It was typewritten, badly worded, not up to Art's style, in my opinion. And how hard is it to sign a name like *Art?*"

Milo's face was working in an effort at comprehension. "But . . . Vida, why?"

"Oh, Milo!" Vida gave him a little kick with her blue canvas shoes. "Because Cody killed Art, that's why!"

It took another Scotch and a lot of fast talking by Vida to convince Milo that Art Fremstad had died at the hands of Cody Graff.

"Of course you can't prove it," huffed Vida. "And what good would it do if you could? Cody's dead, too. The important thing is to figure out *why* Cody killed your deputy."

In his usual deliberate, thorough manner, Milo was sifting through the possibilities. "Cody must have asked Art to meet him near Alpine Falls. Somehow, he must have caught him by surprise — hit him over the head maybe. There was a blow to the skull, but at the time we figured it was from jumping off the cliff and hitting those big rocks. We checked for tire tracks, but there were too many — plenty of tourists stop there in the summer." With a somber expression, Milo made some notes on a little pad. "Damn it! This is really terrible. Why would Cody kill poor Art?"

Vida took a big gulp of her ice water. "If we knew why Cody killed Art, we might know who killed Cody." Her eyes were hard, like those of a canny gray wolf catching the scent. "Get up," she snapped at Milo. "We've got things to do and people to see."

Milo looked up at Vida, abashed by her command. "It's after eight o'clock, I've had two drinks, I don't want to go around smelling like a distillery. I'm running for office."

"Ooooooh!" Vida waved her floppy hat. "You're running away from a five-year crime wave, you idiot! All right, all right." She turned to me. "We'll go, Emma. Get your shoes on. Really, how you girls can go around barefoot without ruining your arches . . . ."

Having both been chastened by Vida, Milo and I decided he should take his Scotch-tainted breath to his office and look up the official reports of Art Fremstad's death while Vida and I called on Dani Marsh.

But Dani wasn't at the ski lodge. Henry Bardeen claimed he didn't know where she'd gone, but that Reid Hampton did. Hampton, however, wasn't around either, having driven over to Lake Wenatchee for dinner at the Cougar Inn.

Vida announced that we were stuck with Patti Marsh. "There's nobody else," she explained as we headed back into town. "Curtis Graff is still up in the San Juans, Doc Dewey is in Seattle, and no Dani." She sighed. "Poor Marje."

The remark caught me off guard. "Marje?"

"Of course. She almost married a murderer. And I thought she had more sense." Vida shook her head sadly. "Well, she's out of it now."

Is she? I wondered. But I wasn't sure what I meant. It wouldn't be tactful to mention to

Vida that her niece was embroiled in an ugly murder investigation. But Vida, of all people, knew that. At the arterial on Alpine Way, I shot Vida a sidelong glance. Her expression was inscrutable. That wasn't like Vida.

To my relief, there was no sign of Jack Blackwell's presence at Patti Marsh's house. I steeled myself for another foray into that stuffy, dismal dwelling, which seemed so rife with bitterness.

But Patti wasn't home. Her car was parked in the driveway, but the house was dark. We figured she might be watching TV with the lights off, since the sun had set only a few minutes earlier. I fought down an ominous feeling as Vida and I descended the three steps from the front porch.

"She may be with Dani," Vida said in an uncharacteristically uncertain voice.

"Should we get Milo to check?"

Vida stood in the middle of the overgrown cement path. "Yes. Let's do that." She turned around, once again animated. "We'll help him."

"Vida, he'd need a warrant for us to go snooping through Patti's place."

Vida wasn't concerned with the niceties of a warrant. We drove downtown, where we found Milo in his office, drinking instant coffee and going through a file folder. We expressed our apprehension about Patti. To Vida's chagrin, Milo said he'd send his deputy, Jack Mullins, to check out the situation.

"She's probably out drinking with Jack Blackwell," said Milo. "Let's piece this together. Vida, you've got a memory like an elephant. Help me out."

The one window in Milo's office was open halfway, its screen dotted with moths seeking the light. The overhead tube fixtures made all three of us look as if we had jaundice. A big fan stood on the floor, whirring around at low speed. Vida and I sat down in front of Milo's desk. He picked up a sheet of paper on which he'd made some notes.

"There's not much from the reports on Art's death that we don't already know," said Milo. "Everything here is consistent with suicide or homicide. Did Donna Fremstad keep Art's note?"

"*Alleged* note," corrected Vida. "I've no idea. She repeated it from memory, I'm sure. But you might ask her."

Milo nodded. "Okay — so I've made a chronology of what happened, going back to Art's disappearance."

"No, no," interrupted Vida. "Go back to little Scarlett's death. Really, Milo, if Art was killed by Cody, then we have to tie the two of them into the event that brought them together in the first place."

Milo regarded Vida with skepticism. "You don't know that it had anything to do with the baby."

Vida, who had taken off her hat, ran her fingers through her short gray hair in an impatient manner. "Of course I don't *know* it. But it's the obvious situation. It's the one event we *do* know that ties Cody, Dani, Curtis, and Art together. Where's your file on that?"

"There isn't one." Milo gave a shrug. "Dani called the sheriff because Doc Dewey told her to. And the fire department. But there was no criminal activity, so Art didn't file a report, except for the log."

Vida cocked her head to one side, her thick curls looking more disheveled than usual. "I did the story. Not that I put anything in it except that little Scarlett died of SIDS, survivors blah-blah, services set for etcetera, memorials to Alpine Volunteer Firefighters — Oh!" She clapped a hand to her cheek. "How very strange! Why didn't I think of that before?"

"Before what?" asked Milo dryly.

Vida gave Milo a severe look. "The firefighters. Why didn't Dani and Cody ask that the memorials be sent to the SIDS foundation?"

Milo had flipped to an empty page in his

legal-sized tablet. "In shock, probably. People don't think straight. Okay, so what happened?"

Vida appeared to be lost in thought. She gave a little jump, then rallied. "Dani had been out somewhere — the grocery store maybe. Cody was with the baby. Dani came home and went to check because it was time for a feeding, or whatever. Little Scarlett was dead. Dani called Doc Dewey who said he'd be over, but to call the sheriff and the fire department. They came first, I have no idea in which order. Then Doc came and Al Driggers was sent for, and they took the baby away to the funeral parlor." She lifted her hands in a helpless gesture. "That was that. The funeral was three days later, the same day Art Fremstad disappeared. Dani was gone by the end of the week. It turned out she'd filed divorce papers at Simon Doukas's law office before leaving town."

I stared at Vida. "That fast?"

"Yes. There was trouble from the start," said Vida. "Nobody expected it to last. The death of little Scarlett merely sealed the fate of the marriage."

Milo was laboriously writing everything down. "A week after the baby died?" He was also having trouble keeping up with Vida's rapid-fire delivery.

"That's right," said Vida. "Dani left the day of Art's funeral. Oh, dear." She took off her glasses and rubbed her eyes. "So many tragedies all at once. Life's like that. But could they really be a coincidence?"

I knew Vida didn't think so, and I was beginning to agree with her. "So when did Curtis and his parents go away?"

"Well, now," mused Vida, putting her glasses back on and blinking several times, "my guess is a week or two later. I know he left Alpine before his parents did, and they moved out over the Labor Day weekend. Curtis said — or so I was told — he wanted to get in on the late summer salmon run in Alaska. We thought he was going for just a few weeks. But he never came back. Until now." She looked first at me, then at Milo. "That's what I mean — everybody suddenly shows up. And Cody Graff dies. Why?"

Chapter Thirteen

It was unspeakable, but not unthinkable. Indeed, I couldn't keep it out of my mind. Had Cody Graff killed his tiny daughter? If he had, why didn't Dani turn him in? Perhaps the answer lay not with Dani Marsh, but Patti Marsh: the inexplicable mixture of fear and acceptance at the hands of a violent man. Like mother, like daughter, I thought as I undressed for bed. Dani had taken the easy way out. She'd run away. But she'd left behind a legacy of hate, much of it directed toward herself.

Unless, of course, it was not Cody who had killed that little baby. I pictured Dani Marsh, with her beautiful face and dazzling smile, acting out a scene of violence more tragic than any part she had ever played on the screen. It didn't fit. But Dani was an actress. I felt as if I were immersed in a drama where the script made no effort to search for truth.

I didn't sleep well and I awoke to bright sunlight and more heat. While the rest of the world may welcome cloudless skies and rainless days, unrelieved sunshine depresses the true Pacific Northwest native. Like the Douglas fir and the wild rhododendron, we too need our roots watered. After about two weeks of hot weather, tempers grow testy and dispositions turn glum. My soul was beginning to feel parched, my brain withered. I drank three cups of coffee, choked down a piece of toast, and drove to work.

Carla, being young and therefore resilient, had not lost her edge on enthusiasm. But she did feel that the atmosphere was getting dreary.

"All that stuff on Loggerama was okay," she announced, hopping around my office, "but I'll bet anything that what readers remember most about that issue was Cody Graff dying. *Downer*. I've got this terrific idea to get a really romantic piece about Dani Marsh and Matt Tabor. Pictures, quotes, the whole nine yards. It'll be like an antidote to death." She looked suddenly wistful. "Gee, I wish I could call it that."

"Gee, I'm glad you can't." I gave her a baleful look. "But go ahead, see if you can get Dani and Matt to talk about their love life. They probably wouldn't mind some positive publicity."

"I'm sure Mr. Hampton would like it," said Carla, hopping around some more. "I just read in *Premiere* magazine that he's financially troubled." She stopped long enough to arch her thick black eyebrows at me.

"Who isn't?" I responded as the phone rang. Carla danced away, presumably to line up Dani and Matt with a cutout of Cupid. Putting the receiver to my ear, I was half-relieved, half-annoyed to hear Patti Marsh yelling at me.

"Can't you keep your mouth shut? Why don't you just run my frigging bankbook in the paper? Everybody in town knows how much I put in my account yesterday! It's nobody's goddamned business, and I can't even walk into the 7-Eleven without four people asking me how I struck it rich!"

I waited for her to run down. "It wasn't me, Patti. Hey, you've lived here all your life — you know how gossip travels around this town. Start with the teller, the bank manager, the rest of the customers who were there. And don't forget Jack Blackwell. How do you feel today?"

"Fine. And leave Jack out of this." She had stopped shouting, but still sounded angry. "If I had any sense, I'd take that money and blow this town. Seattle, maybe, or some place on the Oregon Coast. I went there once with Ray. He liked the ocean."

It took me a minute to recall Ray Marsh, Patti's ex-husband. "Is that where he ended up?"

"Huh?" She sounded surprised at the question. "No." Patti laughed, a harsh sound that jangled in my ear. "Ray. That's funny." She hung up.

In the outer office, Ed Bronsky was trying to find a picture of a chicken in his clip art. "Whole-bodied fryers, eighty-nine cents a pound," he said into the phone. "What about lettuce? I got a picture of lettuce."

Vida was late, and when she came in the door five minutes later I realized why: she had her grandson Roger in tow. I shuddered. The last time she had allowed Roger to spend the day with her at work he had sat on Ginny's copy machine and made a Xerox of his rear end. It was a wonder Ed hadn't tried to include it in his clip-art.

"Roger's going to help me today," Vida said with a big smile for her grandson, who was eyeing me as if I ought to be wearing a tall pointy hat and straddling a broom. "He's going to organize my files."

I was speechless. Vida's files consisted of five drawers stuffed with wedding invitations, birth and graduation announcements, death notices, recipes, gardening tips, household hints, and all manner of articles culled from other publications. She almost never referred to these wrinkled bits and pieces, but carried everything she — and her readers —

needed to know inside her head.

"Amy and Ted had to go to Vancouver for the weekend," Vida explained, yanking out a drawer bulging with paper. "They left Roger with me. He has an eleven o'clock appointment with Doc Dewey, so we'll be gone for about an hour. In fact," she beamed at Roger, who had discovered my new cordless screwdriver and was trying to take Carla's desk apart, "I'm treating him to lunch so we won't be back until after one."

Two hours of peace, I reflected, then asked Roger to give me the screwdriver. To my amazement, he did. He even smiled. "Young Doc Dewey?" I asked as an afterthought.

"No," replied Vida, putting the drawer on the floor. "Doc Dewey Senior. He got back from Seattle late last night." She gave me a meaningful glance. Obviously, Vida had some questions for Doc.

Roger was ignoring Vida's so-called file drawer. Instead, he had crawled under Ed's desk. Ed was still on the phone, now trying to talk the Grocery Basket out of a double-truck ad. "Why go two pages when you've always done just one? People around here aren't going to change to Safeway overnight. Alpiners are loyal. Hey!" Ed jumped, almost dropping the phone. He ducked under the desk. "Knock it off, Roger! I don't want paste

239

all over the floor. I'll get stuck."

"Right," said Roger, emerging on all fours. "Hey, Grams, can I go down to the 7-Eleven and get a Slurpee? I'm bored."

Roger, with money in hand, went out the door just as Carla came in. There was a blight on her bounce. "They won't do it," she pouted. "They're too busy *filming*." She made it sound illegal.

"Maybe later," I soothed. "They're supposed to wind up shooting in a few days. What about tonight?"

Carla collapsed into her chair, sinking her elbows onto the desk. Something clattered to the floor. "Hey — the knob fell off my drawer! How'd that happen?"

Vida didn't look up from her typewriter, where she was now ripping away at a story. I took the cordless screwdriver over to Carla's desk, searched for the screw, and put it back in. "Never mind," I sighed, keeping one eye on Ed who, judging from the puce color of his face, was giving in to the Grocery Basket's wild whim to go to two pages. "Carla, talk to Reid Hampton. If he needs publicity for this picture, he may be able to get Dani and Matt's cooperation. You could get a wire story out of it. Hampton would have to like that."

Carla, however, was still pouting. "No. Dani was very obstinate. In fact, she was almost rude. Matt Tabor sneered. I think they're both stuck up. And Dani seemed so nice! She's a two-faced Hollywood snot!"

Carla's original idea had struck me as good copy, though I hadn't been foaming at the mouth over it. Now, in the face of adversity, and with a building painted the color of egg yolk, I felt *The Advocate* should be treated with more respect.

"I'll see Reid Hampton," I said. "They're right down the street." Putting on my publisher's face, I headed out into the bright overbearing morning sun. The camera crew had advanced up Front Street to the Venison Inn, where the sidewalk was covered with fake snow. I had a frantic desire to cross the barricade and wallow in it. Instead I paused, watching Matt Tabor, in parka and ski goggles, approach the restaurant's entrance.

"Cut!" yelled Reid Hampton, who was aloft on a crane. "Matt, you're not out for a morning stroll! The woman you love is inside with another man! Purpose, purpose, *purpose!* She's yours! Claim her!"

It took six more takes before Matt appeared to be full of purpose and ready to claim his ladylove. The shot, which couldn't have lasted more than five seconds, was pronounced ready to go into the can. Several onlookers applauded. Feeling hot and sweaty, I waited for

Reid Hampton to come down off his perch.

"Emma! I was going to call you," he said, ventilating his wide-open denim shirt with tugs of his hands. "How about dinner before we leave town?"

I hesitated. "Saturday?" I suggested.

"Damn!" He smacked a fist into his palm. "I can't. I'm going into Seattle tomorrow to meet with some film lab people. I was thinking maybe Monday, if everything goes along on schedule."

I was about as anxious for a rematch with Reid Hampton as I was to get a tetanus shot, but I realized he might have some pieces of the murder puzzle tucked away inside his tawny mane. At the very least, there was probably a story in it. I should have taken notes the night we ate at the Café de Flore.

Agreeing to the possibility of Monday, I tried to exhibit enthusiasm. I also tried to put the arm on him for Carla's sake. "She's been very much entranced by Dani and Matt," I gushed. "I'm sure she'd do a wonderful article on them. She takes pretty good pictures, too." That much was true, as long as she remembered to put film in the camera. And remove the lens cap.

Hampton, momentarily distracted by a query from his assistant director, ran a hand through his thick tawny hair. "It *sounds* good," he said in his deep voice which was tinged with regret, "but Dani and Matt are very private people. This business with Dani's ex, Dody? Tody? Cody, right?" He gave me a quick, brilliant smile. "It's made her skittish. Understandably. Besides, I think she's committed to *People* or *Good Housekeeping* or *Esquire*. Tell your little reporter we'll send her some stills from this picture. Steamy clinches. Then she can do a memory piece, you know, 'I Watched Dani and Matt Make Love in Alpine.' That approach. Your readers will go nuts."

I had the impression that he thought they already were. Frustrated, I tried to think of an argument that would sway Reid Hampton. Glancing around the street, I realized that Dani wasn't present. "Where's your star?" I asked.

Hampton looked puzzled, then nodded at Matt Tabor, who was complaining volubly to the assistant director about his ski boots. I gathered they hurt. "Matt's right there. Isn't he something? If only he could act!" Hampton caught himself. "I mean, if he'd only had formal training. He could be an American Olivier. You wait; he'll bigger than Gibson, Costner, Schwarzenegger."

"And Dani?" I spoke quietly, not quite sure what motivated me to ask.

Reid Hampton stared, then broke into a huge smile that didn't quite reach his eyes. "Oh, Dani! She's luminous! I've been in her corner all along. Major talent, major star. This is a breakthrough picture for both of them. If *Blood* doesn't encourage Dani to go on, nothing ever will."

He turned away abruptly, his attention drawn by his cinematographer, who appeared to be verging on an aneurism. I waited for at least two minutes; then, as Matt Tabor started shouting about the inadequacies of wardrobe and the assistant director announced that the stunt man was missing, I gave up and headed back to *The Advocate*.

I was startled to find Dani Marsh waiting for me, her cheeks stained with tears. Closing the door to my office, I sat down and offered Dani coffee. She declined.

"I'm being persecuted," she sniffed, using a Kleenex to wipe her eyes. "My mother warned me not to come back to Alpine. I should have listened."

"Who's doing the persecuting?" I asked, noting that even with smeared makeup and reddened eyes, Dani still looked beautiful.

"The sheriff. He came to see me this morning at the ski lodge, but I'd already gone down to Front Street to start shooting. Reid didn't need me for a while, so I went over to Dodge's office." She gestured in the direction of Milo's headquarters, two blocks away from *The Advocate.* "Why is he raking up the past? What has that got to do with Cody overdosing?" She was perilously close to shedding more tears.

My initial reaction was to utter a disclaimer on her theory about Cody's manner of death, but I didn't see any point in arguing. Yet. "Did Sheriff Dodge ask you about Art Fremstad?"

Dani shifted in the chair, obviously trying to compose herself. "Yes. I don't know anything about Art. I mean, I knew him, I'd seen him around town, but he graduated from high school before I got there. The first time I really talked to him was . . . when . . . when he came to our place after I called for help." The thick lashes dipped over the big brown eyes. Dani didn't seem to be able to say the words out loud: *when my baby died.* I didn't blame her.

"Did the sheriff ask what Art did or said while he was at your house?"

"It was a trailer, out where those new town houses are now. I don't remember a thing," Dani asserted, her voice cracking. "How could I? It was all so horrible!"

Posing tough questions is part of my job. But I either lack the nerve or am too soft-

245

hearted to always go for the jugular. My editor on *The Oregonian* used to tell me I was gutless. I preferred to think of myself as kind. But this was one of those nasty situations where I knew I had to seize the moment or very likely never know the truth.

"Dani," I began, keeping my voice firm and determined, "are you absolutely certain your baby died from SIDS?"

Her head jerked up, the honey blond hair floating like a soft cloud around her shoulders. "Of course! What are you saying?" The agony was back in her eyes, her voice, every fiber of her body. "Why? Why? You, the sheriff, everybody . . . I can't take this!" To prove her point, she flew out of the chair and ran from my office.

Vida gaped from behind her desk, Ed stumbled on his way back from the coffeemaker, and Roger put the straw from his Slurpee up his nose.

"What was that all about?" demanded Vida.

I started to explain, but Vida suddenly noted the time. "Oh! It's five to! We're going to be late. Come along, Roger."

Roger expelled the straw into the coffee mug Carla had left on her desk. After grandmother and grandson left, I took the mug out to Ginny Burmeister who was in charge of coffee.

"Roger's a caution," she remarked, finishing up the particulars for a new classified ad.

"Actually, he seemed a little subdued today," I said. "He hasn't tried to set any fires or blow anybody up. For Roger, that's good." I paused, glancing at the list of classifieds Ginny had taken for the next issue. It wasn't impressive, but that was typical for early August. Many people were on vacation, it was too soon for end-of-summer garage sales, and the housing market wouldn't move for at least another week. "Say, Ginny, you don't recall talking to Curtis Graff before he left Alpine five years ago, do you?"

Ginny, in her conscientious manner, frowned in recollection. "I did, as a matter of fact. I ran into him one morning on my way to the Burger Barn. I bused tables there that summer. He said he was going to Ketchikan and get rich fishing."

"That's it?"

Ginny was still frowning. "I think so. He seemed kind of nervous. No, not nervous, just ill at ease. I remember, because I'd had that crush on him and he'd been broken up with Laurie Vickers for a while. So I suddenly thought, hey, what if after all this time Curtis has a crush on *me?* But he didn't. I suppose he was just in a hurry, getting everything ready to leave for Alaska. He took off kind of quick. I mean, one day he was here, and the next day, he was gone. Almost."

"He didn't mention anything about Cody and Dani Graff's baby?"

"No." Ginny slowly shook her head. "No, though it had to be on his mind. It was certainly on everybody else's since it had just happened."

"Did he bring up his brother?" I marveled at the lack of curiosity Ginny displayed at my questioning. But Ginny has absolutely no imagination.

"No. All he said was what I told you. At least that's all I remember." She looked faintly apologetic.

I was considering a tactful explanation for my inquisitiveness when Vida stormed into the front office. Her car wouldn't start; could I drive them up to the clinic?

Doc Dewey's office was only four blocks away. Vida was a notorious walker. She saw the puzzlement on my face and made an exasperated gesture. "Roger doesn't feel like hoofing it. Please, Emma, we're going to be late."

I didn't argue, though I knew that Roger had already hiked twice the distance and back to the 7-Eleven to get his Slurpee. But Roger was looking mulish and Vida was growing frantic. We hurried to the Jaguar, which

Roger appraised with an expert eye.

"Buff," he said, presumably in approval, and scrambled into the backseat.

Ten minutes later I returned to the office, having agreed to collect Vida and Roger at eleven-thirty. I called Milo to ask about his interview with Dani Marsh, but he was out. For a long time, I sat with my arms folded on my desk, trying to figure out why so many people were still denying that Cody Graff had been murdered. And why Dani Marsh had become so distraught over my suggestion that her baby hadn't died of SIDS.

My reverie was broken by the telephone. It was Milo. Curtis Graff had returned to Alpine. He was staying with Patti Marsh.

"I think he stayed with her before," said Milo. "Hey, Emma, why do I feel as if I'm running around like a hamster in a big maze?"

"Swell," I responded. "You're supposed to know all the tricks of the homicide trade. I already feel as if I've got the second female lead in a B movie. Milo, do you or do you not think Cody Graff may have killed little Scarlett?"

I heard Milo suck in his breath before he answered. "Why don't you ask his brother? Curtis is just pulling up in front of your cute yellow building. I saw him drive by in Patti's car."

But Curtis wasn't calling on me. When I got outside, he was at the barricade, talking to Matt Tabor. Neither man looked very happy, and before I could make up my mind about approaching them, they disappeared inside the Venison Inn.

Just as well, I thought: it was smack on eleven-thirty. I drove up to the clinic and parked across the street by the gift shop. Marje Blatt was behind the desk, her face thinner and her uniform less crisp.

"Doc's running late," she said without preamble. "Aunt Vida and Roger will be out in a few minutes."

I sat down in one of the venerable chairs that had served two generations of Dewey patients. The only other person in the waiting room was an elderly man with a cane who was reading a well-thumbed copy of *Business Week*.

"How are you doing, Marje?" I asked infusing my voice with sympathy.

Marje looked up from her appointment book. "Okay. How are you?"

Somehow, it didn't seem an appropriate rejoinder. "Have you talked to Cody's parents?" I wasn't letting Marje off the hook, though I knew she must have already been thoroughly grilled by Vida.

"Only on Sunday." She set the appointment

book aside and scooted her chair over to a tall metal filing cabinet. "Curtis says they're doing okay. Considering."

The elderly man wore a hearing aid. I wondered if it was turned off; he didn't seem to be paying any attention to us. I got up and walked over to the reception desk, lowering my voice.

"Marje, did you have any premonition about Cody?"

She glanced up from the open file drawer. It was as neat as her aunt's was untidy. "No. Why should I?" Marje flipped through the folders, pulling a chart. "Look," she said, meeting my gaze head-on, "you and Aunt Vida get a kick out of playing detective. Cody had his faults, like everybody else. Maybe he had more than I knew about — we never lived together. He was moody, he could fly off the handle. I don't like ups and downs. So I thought some medication might make him more steady That's what you really want in a husband, isn't it?"

How would I know? I thought. "Wasn't that a little risky?"

Marje shrugged. "I know what both Deweys prescribe for people with Cody's problems. I only gave Cody a couple of sample packets."

251

"But they were pills, not syrup," I pointed out.

A flicker of emotion passed over Marje's face, then she gave another shrug. "I suppose he got the syrup somewhere else. It's terrible how easy it is for people to get hold of drugs these days. Young Doc Dewey is going to start a drug education class at the high school this fall. Really, it amazes me how even a small town like Alpine can have so many people who are hooked on something. I wish big cities like Seattle would keep their vices to themselves." She had grown quite heated, causing the elderly man to look up from his magazine. He nodded once, then resumed reading.

I was about to say that I knew Alpine had its share of drug-related problems, though I wasn't aware of any epidemic. But the words never came out. Vida and Roger emerged from the examining room area with Doc Dewey bringing up the rear.

"You're not keeping pace, Vida," warned Doc Dewey. "You know darned well I'm a cautious man. Too cautious, my son would say, and he's the one who should be seeing Roger today. But we're doing right by your grandson, believe me."

"It's ridiculous," Vida declared, her hand on Roger's shoulder. "I expected better of you than of Gerry — your son never did have as much sense as he should have. But you're as pigheaded as he is. I'm telling you once and for all, I won't take this prescription into the pharmacy." She waved a white slip of paper in Doc Dewey's face.

"Amy and Ted will when they get back." Doc spoke matter-of-factly, though his expression indicated he wished Vida would shut up and go away. Indeed, he brightened a bit when he recognized me. "Hello there, girlie. How's your little reporter doing with her allergy reaction?"

"Carla's fine," I assured him. Doc was looking less haggard than when I'd seen him at the Icicle Creek Tavern almost a week earlier. But the fragile air remained. Perhaps he'd earned it. The man must be over seventy, and he'd devoted a half-century to healing Alpine's sick. "How was your trip?"

"Hot," replied Doc, turning to greet the elderly man who was struggling to his feet with the aid of the cane. "The air-conditioning doesn't work most of the time. Well, young man," he said to his next patient, "how's that knee?"

Vida and I bade Marje farewell, then let Roger lead the way outside. "Doc's daffy," said Vida. "It's bad enough that his son's pouring medicine down Roger's throat, but after only a week, they're changing the prescription. If you ask me, the Deweys are experimenting on poor Roger. You'd think the child was a gerbil."

Since Roger was now climbing onto the roof of my Jaguar, I wasn't inclined to argue. "What's he taking?" I asked, trying to show an interest in Roger's problems, which seemed to stem from a complete lack of discipline rather than any chemical cause. But I didn't dare say so. Besides, I had to assume that Doc knew what he was doing. Or, it dawned on me, he'd gotten absolutely nowhere with a diagnosis similar to mine.

Vida glanced at the slip of paper while I gave Roger a frozen smile which I hoped would coax him off the car roof. "Thorazine. Roger can't drink juice with it. Doesn't that beat all?" She crushed the prescription and threw it into her purse. "Three freshly squeezed oranges a day is what he gets for breakfast when he stays with me. If Amy and Ted want to be such silly fools, that's up to them."

Roger finally dismounted, badgering his grandmother about what he wanted for lunch, which sounded like great quantities of deep-fried grease. Inside the car, I asked Vida if she knew why Doc had gone to Seattle.

"I never got a chance to ask," she said, still grumpy. "I was too busy trying to talk sense

254

into the old fool. But he told Marje it was for a tune-up. Every year or so I guess he checks himself into the Mason Clinic or one of those places and gets an overhaul. If you ask me, he should have his brain replaced. Maybe I should take Roger into Seattle myself and see what they think. I'll bet they'd find out he's just too bright for his age."

I glanced in the rearview mirror at Roger. His eyes were rolled back in his head and he was drooling. "Hey, Grams," he said in a gurgling voice, "I'm having a fit. Double fries'll cure me."

Vida smiled fondly at Roger, then turned to me. "You see, Emma, the boy knows what he needs. Maybe he'll grow up to be a doctor."

Maybe, I thought to myself, he'll grow up. *Maybe*.

I'd assigned myself the task of taking a picture of the new baseball diamond, which was being put in at the high school field now that Loggerama was over. Coming down Seventh Street, between Spruce and Tyee, I saw Patti Marsh's house. The front door was open and the drapes were pulled back. A white Lexus stood in the driveway, looking as out of place as a tiara on a bag lady.

I stopped and got out. Sure enough, Dani Marsh came to the door. I expected her to be annoyed by my unannounced arrival, but instead, she looked embarrassed.

"Ms. Lord! Are you here to see my mother? She's at work."

In the golden glow of afternoon, Dani looked very different than she had in the harsh morning sun. Her eyes were no longer red; her hair was pulled back and tucked into a knot at the nape of her neck; and she wore a mint green leotard that suggested she'd been working out.

"You're not shooting?" I inquired.

"I finished for the day about an hour ago. Do you want to come in?"

I did, if only to get out of the sun that was beating down on the little porch. Entering the house, I noticed that someone had finally removed the wilted bouquet from the hall. My cyclamen reposed there and looked as if it had been recently watered. Indeed, the whole house looked different, more welcoming. Not only were the drapes open, but so were two of the windows, bringing in badly needed fresh air. Some of the clutter had been cleaned away, and the ashtray on the coffee table was empty. Was this Dani's handiwork, or had Patti used her day off to clean house? It didn't seem right to ask.

"I'm sorry I was so upset this morning," Dani said, giving me a penitent smile. "Sometimes I can't seem to separate my emotions off and on the set. I realize that Sheriff Dodge was only trying to do his job. But it seems to me that he's going off on a tangent. Poor Cody simply made a terrible mistake. It happens all the time, mixing drugs and alcohol."

"You really think that's what happened?"

"Yes, I do." Her voice was firm, but she avoided my eyes. "Two more days, then I'm done with this stupid picture," Dani said, going over to the makeshift bar. "Would you like something to drink?"

I requested pop, which she produced from the refrigerator along with a seltzer for herself. "You don't like the movie?" I asked, sitting on the sofa, which was marred only by a cookbook and a *TV Guide*. It seemed as useless to pursue the manner of Cody's death with Dani Marsh as it had been with Marje Blatt.

"It's trash," she said simply. "They should have brought in a script doctor, but Reid's too cheap. Oh, it'll have big grosses the first week or so, but word of mouth will kill it. Still, Reid should make money with all the ancillary rights. It's hard not to these days, as long as your budget isn't out of control."

I marveled at her candor. Didn't she realize she was talking to a newspaper person? "I thought stars were supposed to ballyhoo all their movies, no matter how lousy."

Dani sat down, not in the cut-velvet chair her mother favored, but in a blue-and-green-striped lounger that looked as if a cat had used it for a scratching post. "We are. *They* are," she amended. "I'm thinking of changing careers. I'd rather dance."

I was startled. "Can't you do both? I mean, act and dance? Like musicals?"

"Musicals aren't really in," said Dani, sipping at her seltzer. "Reid told me that. He thinks I'm crazy. To quit acting, I mean." The brown eyes caught and held mine, as if she expected me to side with her director.

I was, in fact, tempted to agree with Hampton. Dani Marsh was just beginning to emerge as a bona fide star. At twenty-four, she seemed too old to start a dance career. But it was none of my business. "What does Matt think?"

Dani's wide-eyed gaze glistened with amusement. "Matt? I've no idea. I haven't asked him."

I may never have been a wife, but I've certainly been a mother. My maternal instincts took over, suddenly lending me wisdom for the daughter I'd never had. "I'm all for independence, Dani, but husbands and wives — lovers, engaged couples, what have you — should talk things over. You don't want Matt to feel left out. He thinks he's marrying a movie actress. Will it change his feelings if he discovers his wife is a would-be dancer?"

Dani laughed. The wondrous sound filled the room, making it suddenly a happy place. "Oh, Emma," she said, tucking in a strand of hair that had come loose from the knot at her neck, "*Blood Along The River* is almost in the can. I want to stop the charade, at least when I'm off-camera. Matt and I aren't going to get married."

Recalling the heated argument Vida and I had overheard at the ski lodge, I wasn't completely surprised. "I've wondered," I said vaguely. "Somehow, you never seemed . . . devoted." It was an old-fashioned word, worthy of Vida, but I suddenly felt like a fogey. "I figured there might be someone else."

Dani had picked up a videotape that pictured an athletic young woman in a dance rehearsal costume doing something strenuous in a room with big skylights. Dani studied the cassette, then turned her gaze back to me. "There is someone else. There always was." She put the videotape down on top of the TV and laughed again. This time the musical sound was a trifle discordant. "Matt's in love, but not with me. I'd tell you who, but you'd print it in your paper. That wouldn't be right, I guess."

I was literally on the edge of my seat. "You could always go off the record."

Dani's gaze wandered around the room, to the mediocre watercolor of Mount Baldy, the half-naked gods and goddesses, the Harlequin masks, the carved trout, and the one good piece I hadn't noticed before: a small silver dancing girl, sweetly graceful, realistically posed.

Dani saw that I had followed her eyes. "I got that for my mother when I was in Rome last year on location. Isn't it pretty? She loves it."

It occurred to me that perhaps I had missed the little figurine because it hadn't been there earlier. If Dani wasn't going to talk about Matt Tabor's defection, perhaps she'd unload about her mother.

"Dani, what's with you and Patti? She's behaved as if you were the worst daughter who ever lived, yet here you are, in her house, talking about sending her gifts. What's going on? It's not fair to you for everybody in Alpine to think she hates your guts."

To my surprise, Dani opened a drawer in the end table next to her chair and pulled out a pack of cigarettes. "Do you mind?" she inquired. "I don't do this often."

"I don't do it at all. Any more." I made a face. "I wish I did sometimes. Go ahead."

Dani lighted up, her awkwardness with the cigarette indicating that she was telling the truth about her amateur smoker's status. "For a long time, Mom blamed me for what happened to Scarlett. She was convinced I'd been a rotten mother. It preyed on her mind, maybe because she'd lost her grandchild —" Dani paused and bit her lip, the words not coming so easily now " — and, in a way, her daughter at the same time. I was no comfort to her, I couldn't be, I needed too much comfort myself. So she cast me as the villainess, and it was only after I came home to Alpine and we talked and talked that she realized I wasn't at fault. Now things are much better." Dani smiled, a bit tremulously. "We're almost back to where we were six years ago, before I married Cody."

"She wasn't in favor of your marriage?"

"Oh, God, no!" Dani exhaled a thick cloud of smoke. "She tried to talk me out of it, said he was as bad as my father. Maybe worse. But I was young and headstrong and wouldn't listen. Why," she asked plaintively, "do we know so much more at eighteen than we do at twenty-four?"

I had to smile. "It goes with being a teenager. My son's out of that stage now, and one of these days, I'm going to become really smart. I hope."

Dani smiled, too. "I'll bet I'd like your son. I wish he were a little older. Maybe I could

fall in love with him. I haven't done that yet."
She made it sound like an item she was anxious
to check off on her list of life.

"You didn't love Cody?"

Her smile was wry, seen through the fog
of her cigarette. "No, it was a typical ado-
lescent crush. All heat and hormones. For both
of us."

I gripped my Coke and slipped farther back
onto the sofa. "You realize that the sheriff
thinks you're the last person to see Cody
alive?" I didn't know if Milo really believed
that, but it made sense to me. Dani's jaw
dropped and she began to shake her head in
denial, but I gave her no opportunity to contradict: "You were seen, out by the turnoff
to the Burl Creek Road. That's where you
lost your eyeliner. What on earth were you
and Cody doing out there that night?"

Dani scanned the ceiling: left, right, right,
left. I had the impression she was looking for
answers, the way she'd study a frame of film
for dramatic composition. "I had to see him,
just once. Not because I cared about him —
but to tie up some loose ends."

"Did you?"

"No. Not really. He was too drunk." She
fiddled with the cigarette, moving it from one
hand to the other.

I waited for her to say more, and when she

didn't, I posed another question. "Why did you drive out to the edge of town?" I knew I was pushing my luck with my prying, but Dani seemed more uneasy than annoyed.

"I didn't want to go up to his apartment." she replied, her voice steady. "It might have given him the wrong idea, especially since he'd been drinking. I picked him up in Matt's Zimmer and I drove without thinking." She waved away the cloud of smoke, the better to meet my gaze. "We used to live out that way, past the reservoir and the fish hatchery. I guess it was an automatic reflex on my part."

"Was he alive when you left him?"

"Yes." Her unblinking stare challenged me to disbelieve her.

"Then why didn't you drive him back to town?"

Dani touched the soft coil of hair at her neck. "He wanted to get out. He was being obnoxious. I figured the fresh air would do him good. And I was by the Burl Creek Road, so I could zip straight up to the ski lodge."

I studied Dani's face carefully. She seemed to be telling the truth, but her acting skills could probably convince me if she said there was a blizzard going on outside. It was hard for me to conceive of leaving an extremely drunk man out on a lonely road at midnight. But the man was Cody Graff, and if what I believed about him was true, he would not have invited common courtesy.

I was casting about for other, more pointed questions concerning Cody's death when I heard a car pull up outside. Dani looked down at her watch which was lying on the coffee table. "It's after three. Mom said she'd be home early. She was beat."

In more ways than one, I thought, watching Dani stub out her cigarette. I wondered what the daughter felt about the mother's passive resistance to Jack Blackwell's fists. But there was no chance to ask. Patti Marsh came into the house with a sack of groceries. From Safeway. I had a sudden urge to call Ed Bronsky.

"Hi, Dani," she said, then saw me sitting on the sofa. "What's this, more news you can get wrong in your paper? Or are you going through my checkbook?"

I started to make a rejoinder, but Dani merely smiled. "Don't have a tizzy, Mom. Emma and I were just philosophizing. Life, love, career choices. What did you get for dinner?"

Patti appeared appeased. "Beef ribs. Macaroni salad. Jojo potatoes. Safeway's got a great deli. I don't have to cook, all I have to do is pay a lot of money. But I've got that now, haven't I, chicken?" Despite the bruises, Patti looked quite smug.

"Right, Mom." Dani exchanged a conspiratorial glance with her mother. "Let's go to Paris. I'll show you how people really eat."

Suddenly, I felt like the original third wheel. All this mother-daughter camaraderie was making me oddly uncomfortable. Was it real? Maybe. Yet thus far so little about the Marshes and the Graffs and the rest of them seemed genuine. I stood up, making ready to leave.

"Hey," exclaimed Patti, doing a typical about-face, "don't run off. Have a drink. What have you got there?"

"Coke," I said. "But I have to drop a roll of film off at the photographer's —"

"Buddy Bayard's open until six," cut in Patti. "Have a real drink. Gin? Scotch? Bourbon? Vodka? Rum?"

I felt contrary enough to ask for tequila, but settled for bourbon. The truth was, I didn't like drinking strong alcohol during the day in summertime. But I decided to humor Patti Marsh. Her mood change made me think I might learn something. She had set the groceries on the counter in the kitchen and was now at the makeshift bar, mixing tonic with vodka and pouring me a bourbon over ice.

"Here, kiddo," she said, handing me my drink. "Has mild-mannered Milo given up yet?"

I was taken aback. "What?"

265

"The sheriff." Patti sat down in the cut-velvet chair and lighted a cigarette. "Hey, Dani — you cleaned this place! It looks like a frigging motel. You deserve a husband when you get married."

Dani smiled. "I deserve a man I can love. You should be so lucky, Mom."

"So should we all," I murmured, deciding that the bourbon didn't taste so unpalatable with the windows open and the living room feeling not quite like a mausoleum.

After a deep swig, Patti Marsh set her drink down on the coffee table. "Men. I could write a book on that subject." She gazed at me through a haze of smoke. "Can you use *asshole* in a title?"

I uttered a wry laugh. "Probably not."

Patti nodded. "I didn't think so. But you could say it in the book. On the pages inside, I mean." She took another gulp of vodka and settled back into the cut-velvet chair, the smoke from her cigarette swirling around her like a snake. "Twenty-four years. I waited twenty-four years." She glanced at Dani who looked faintly alarmed. "Oh, screw it, honey! What do we care? I already told Jack."

Dani gave a little jump, then reached for the package of cigarettes in the drawer. "You did?" She sounded incredulous.

"You bet. I didn't mind having a laugh at

his expense, but I don't want a broken jaw." Gingerly, she touched her cheek. "He was still pissed this morning, so I told him. God, I thought he'd have a heart attack!" She drank some more and laughed uproariously.

Dani cradled her almost-empty seltzer bottle in her slim hands. "Oh, Mom . . ." She sounded disapproving.

"Oh, hell!" Patti drank, smoked, waved her hand. "The bastard owed me! And you! Never mind!" She shot a finger in her daughter's direction. "Sure, sure, he's helped you with your career and all that crap. But that's now, not then, when we really needed it. Stop looking so prissy, kiddo." Patti turned to me; I knew I wore an utterly mystified expression. Who was she talking about? Blackwell? Or someone else? "Reid Hampton didn't pay me fifty grand because he cut down a bunch of frigging trees," Patti declared. "He owed me that money from way back. Reid Hampton's real name is Ray Marsh. The son of a bitch is Dani's father."

Chapter Fourteen

Vida was incredulous. She slammed the carriage of her typewriter so hard that I thought I'd have to do some more repair work.

"Reid Hampton is Ray Marsh? Oooooh . . . that's . . . *silly!*"

"It's true." I eased into Ed's chair. He and Carla had both left for the day, since it was now nearing five o'clock. Roger was out in the front office, driving Ginny Burmeister crazy. Or so I guessed. "You said yourself Ray went to California. He did, he'd always been fascinated by movies and he got a job as a gofer at Paramount. He changed his name — Reid, as in r-e-e-d, apparently being derived from Marsh and the Hampton coming from the side of the family that was related to the two Wades, American Revolution and Civil War generals."

"Oh, nonsense! Ray's family didn't have any distinguished ancestors hanging on their family tree. They were the sort who'd have been related to camp followers." Vida uttered a deep, impatient sigh. "Honestly, Emma, I can't believe I wouldn't have recognized him. I think Patti is pulling your leg."

"Not for fifty grand, she isn't," I countered. "Reid — Ray — gave her that check to make up for all the years he missed paying child support. Listen, Vida, you haven't seen Ray Marsh in almost twenty-five years. He's gotten older, grown a beard, dyed his hair. He worked his way up in the business, through the ranks. Then he launched his own production company about eight years ago. When he discovered that Dani had come to Hollywood, he must have felt a pang of conscience. He helped launch her career. He's been a patron and a father to Dani, at least in the last few years."

"Did she know who he was all along?" Vida was still looking skeptical.

"No. It was Patti who figured it out. She *did* recognize Reid. I remember how she looked at his photograph on my desk the day she came in to complain about the article on Dani. I suppose it was the eyes, because he wasn't wearing sunglasses in that picture. Then she went after him, threatening to reveal all if he didn't pony up."

Vida's forehead creased in a frown as she considered my explanation. "I'm slipping," she murmured. She gave me a look that bordered on the pathetic. "I'm turning into an old fool, just like everybody else. Do you want to put me out to pasture?"

"Vida!" I laughed, though more in exasperation than amusement. "Have you *seen* Reid Hampton up close since he came to Alpine?"

Vida rested her chin on her fist and thought for a moment. "No. But I did glance at those pictures."

"Big deal." I waved a hand in dismissal of Vida's nonexistent senility. "The problem is, I don't know what to do about using the information as a story. Patti blabbed everything to Jack Blackwell so he'd stop slapping her around and realize that she wasn't taking a payoff for his blasted trees. Jack won't keep quiet. And I'll bet Patti won't stop with Jack."

"So Ray — Reid — paid in vain. At least as far as Patti's silence is concerned. That's very ironic." Perplexity crossed Vida's face, but she appeared to be growing resigned to Reid Hampton's true identity. "How did Dani react to all this?"

"I guess she was shocked when Patti told her a few days ago. But she seems to be comfortable with it now. After all, she's known Reid for quite a while, and he's always been in her corner. Just like a father. In fact, she said she could never understand why he didn't make the obligatory pass at her."

As usual, Vida went straight to the heart of the matter: "That's nice, family reunion, dues paid, all that. But what has it got to do with Cody's murder?"

I gave a little shake of my head. "I don't know. Reid's never been at the top of my list as a suspect. The only motive I could think of was something to do with the trees, but it would have made more sense if he'd killed Jack, instead of one of Blackwell's underlings. Now I'm wondering if he might have killed Cody because he mistreated Dani — or the baby. You know, sort of expiating his own sins for walking out on Patti and Dani."

Vida didn't look impressed by my theory. "I don't hold with all this psychological claptrap. It's too convoluted. Whatever happened to financial gain, jealousy, revenge, and all those horrible secrets that only one person knows, at least in books?"

"Half of Alpine probably knows Reid's secret by now," I said dryly. "Maybe I can do a feature, 'From Alpine to L.A. — Father and Daughter Reunited on Sunset Boulevard' "

"Oh, good grief, you sound like Carla!" Vida rolled her eyes. She put the plastic cover on her typewriter, tugging it over the machine like a dressmaker trying to fit a size eight sheath on a size fourteen figure. "Let's talk motive."

I didn't answer right away. My personal apprehensions about the case still appalled me.

"I don't think we can talk motive until we deal with what happened to little Scarlett."

"You mean whether or not Cody killed her." Vida spoke briskly. "He did, of course. That's why Art Fremstad had to die. Brother or not, Curtis Graff would have been next, if he hadn't left town. As for Doc Dewey . . ." She slowly shook her head. "Maybe some people are still sacred. Or maybe Cody lost his nerve."

I dragged Ed's chair closer to Vida's desk. "Are you saying that Art, Curtis and Doc all knew that Cody murdered his baby? Oh, Vida!"

"Knew, or suspected. Dani, too — perhaps." Vida removed her glasses, but instead of the usual vigorous rubbing of her eyes, she gently massaged the lids. "Emma, some things are so awful. You don't want to believe them, your instinct is to turn away and pretend they couldn't possibly have happened. I wonder if that isn't what went on with Dani and some of the others as well. We humans are such a terrible mix of good and evil. Yet we must pretend that evil doesn't exist — or we'd go quite crazy."

For some moments, I gazed at Vida, moved by her little soliloquy. "If," I said at last, in a quiet voice, "we accept the fact that Cody caused that baby's death, we don't need any other motive. There's Dani, Patti, Curtis, even Reid. Or Jack Blackwell, acting on Patti's behalf."

"What about Matt Tabor? He's engaged to Dani."

I explained that the engagement was off, if indeed it had ever really been on. Vida took the news in stride. "A publicity romance. Oh, well." She gave a start. "So who was Matt quarrellng with up at the ski lodge?"

I admitted I didn't know. We were mulling over the possibilities when Roger charged into the news office, carrying a fake snake.

"Ginny went home," Roger announced. "She ran. I guess she doesn't like snakes." He put the wiggly creature next to me on Ed's desk. I gave Roger a half-smile. The snake moved. I let out a shriek and leaped from the chair.

"Damn it, Roger, that's real! Get that sucker out of here!" I was flat against the wall, while Vida gaped at the snake.

Roger's round face was wreathed in a cherubic smile. "It's just a little ol' garter snake, Mrs. Lord. They don't bite. Here, pick it up." He made as if to shove the snake in my direction.

"Out! Now!"

Roger took my measure, then darted a look at his grandmother, who was trying very hard not to laugh. "Do as Ms. Lord says, Roger. It's *her* office." Vida didn't sound too pleased with the concession.

With a heave of great reluctance, Roger grabbed the snake and exited. I hoped he would take the damned thing down the street, across Railroad Avenue, and leave it by the river. Which, I presumed, was where he'd found it in the first place. But knowing Roger, I suspected he would put the garter snake in one of the concrete planters that lined Front Street. Or, I thought with alarm, *in my car.*

I leaped across the office. "Vida, I've got to run. I'll call you tonight." Gathering up my belongings, I raced outside, but Roger was nowhere to be seen. The Jaguar appeared safe, devoid of snakes. I drove to Cal Vickers's Texaco station to get gas. Cal, who used to do business across from the General Motors dealership down the street, had moved last year to Alpine Way, directly in front of the shopping mall. He looked busy, with activity inside the garage; three cars, an RV, and a van lined up at the pumps; and a pickup parked in front of the snack shop that Cal had added at his new location. The pickup didn't strike any chords, but the young man who was standing by it did: Curtis Graff was waiting for Cal Vickers to finish with a customer.

Pulling the Jag up near the car wash, I got

out and strolled over to Curtis. He was wearing stone-washed jeans and a T-shirt with the sleeves cut out. When I called a greeting, he looked puzzled, then shaded his eyes against the western sun, and gave me a half-smile.

"Mrs. Lord," he said, "I didn't recognize you at first. I forgot to come in and get those newspapers. Are you closed?"

"Yes, but I can send them to you. Or your parents." I nodded at the pickup. "Is that your brother's?" It seemed a logical guess.

"Right." He patted a rusty red fender. "I'm selling it. But I thought Cal ought to give it a once-over. It's pretty beat-up, but I might as well get something out of it and use the money to pay off Cody's bills."

I nodded. "I suppose he had his share of debts like the rest of us."

"The usual." Curtis didn't seem too interested in his brother's financial obligations.

"I'm glad he and Marje didn't get themselves in too deep," I remarked, angling for an opening. "She strikes me as a sensible soul." The statement implied her fiancé was not.

"Marje is a good kid," said Curtis, pulling a pack of gum out of his back pocket and unwrapping a stick. As an afterthought, he offered me a piece.

"No, thanks," I said, recalling the last time

I'd tried a wad of bubble gum and had ended up at Dr. Starr's with a shiny gold crown, a large dent in my savings account, and the happiest dentist in Skykomish County. "Marje seems to be coping," I noted, still at a loss in my effort to get Curtis to open up.

"She's tough." Curtis chewed with vigor.

"I saw Dani and her mother today." Cal was coming our way, his wide, florid face beaming at us under his billed cap. "I suppose you can't blame her for dumping Cody off by the side of the road the night he died."

Curtis, who had been turning toward Cal, rocked slightly on his heels. "She told you that?"

I acted nonchalant. "Sure. Cal and Charlene saw them. Right, Cal?"

"What's that?" Cal took off his cap, used his forearm to wipe the perspiration from his brow, and grimaced into the sun.

"You and Char — you saw Dani Marsh and Cody Graff in that Zimmer last Saturday night." I ignored Curtis's scowl, which was uncannily reminiscent of that of his dead brother.

"We saw somebody," replied Cal, smoothing back the fringe of black hair that curled around his ears.

Curtis shot me a belligerent look. "What did Dani say?"

I gave a little shrug, shifting around to avoid the sun in its downward path over the mall: "She said he was too drunk to talk to. So she let him out of the car. I suppose she thought the fresh night air might revive him. It didn't." My own gaze was as harsh as his.

Under the sawed-off T-shirt, Curtis's shoulders relaxed. "He was smashed, all right. On drugs, too. It doesn't surprise me."

I was about to protest, but Cal spared me the effort. "Aw, Curt, Cody had his problems, but he wasn't mixed up with drugs. He'd come in here, once, twice a week, and josh around with me and the guys. I never saw him look squirrely. And I check eyes, just in case somebody is about to gas up and go off goofy. I've called Dodge half a dozen times to let him know I thought we had a druggie on the road."

Curtis made a disaparaging gesture with his hand. "You're no expert, Cal. Believe me, I knew my brother. I'm surprised nobody found out he was taking stuff before this."

"But he wasn't," I protested. "His death was caused by an antidepressant, not some illegal substance."

"Whatever," said Curtis, turning to Cal. "Hey, can you look over this pickup? I think the fuel pump . . ."

Feeling snubbed, I started to walk away.

I also felt frustrated. What had happened to my journalist's right to ask and the public's need to know? Or was I treading on ground so private that my lingering status as an outsider created a conspiracy of silence? Feeling the perspiration drip down my neck, I considered going through the car wash. Without the car. But Milo Dodge was pulling up in his Cherokee Chief. I ran over to meet him.

"Milo," I hissed, leaning into his open window, "get off your duff and go over and ask Curtis if he thinks Cody killed his little daughter."

From behind his sunglasses, Milo gaped at me. "Emma, are you nuts? I can't ask Curtis something like that!"

"If you don't, I will." I gave his regulation shirt collar a tug. "The trouble is, he won't tell me. But he might tell you. Come on, Milo, you're the sheriff. Do you want to get beat by Averill Fairbanks and his UFOs?"

Milo's long face worked in consternation. At last he uttered a sigh, presumably of surrender. "I've got to pick Honoria up by six-thirty . . . Oh, hell, I'll take Curtis out for a quick beer. This is no place to interrogate anybody." Milo got out of his Cherokee Chief, long legs unwinding onto the gas-stained tarmac.

Satisfied, I got back into the Jag and wheeled

it in behind the RV, which was about to leave. Curtis, Cal, and the sheriff now formed a tight little trio, hovering around the open hood of the pickup. My victory over Milo had proved almost too easy.

Five minutes later, I was on my way to the Grocery Basket, proving my loyalty to a home-grown merchant. I lingered in the frozen food section, feeling blissfully cool, and wondering if the forecast for ninety the next day was accurate. I hoped not.

I was tossing frozen chicken pies in my cart when I saw Donna Fremstad Wickstrom approaching. Her manner was frazzled, her attention riveted on the orange juice section. I reversed directions and came up alongside of Donna. To my surprise, she looked as if she'd been crying. A rumpled Kleenex was stuffed in the top of her polka dotted sundress.

"Heat got you down?" I asked guilelessly.

Donna didn't look fooled by my feigned innocence. "It's all this Cody Graff business that's got me down," she snapped. "First you and Vida, now the sheriff. I'm so upset I don't know what to do."

Feeling repentant, I put a hand on her arm. "I'm sorry, Donna, I know this is rough on you. What did Milo want?" My triumph with the sheriff now seemed easier to understand; maybe he wasn't as slow of wit as I sometimes thought him.

Donna lowered her head, chin almost resting on her breastbone. "It should make it easier . . . but it doesn't, not in a way," she murmured. Slowly, she raised her face to meet my gaze. "Sheriff Dodge thinks Art may have been murdered, maybe by Cody Graff. I'd rather believe that than think Art killed himself. But it makes me so *angry* . . ." She literally gnashed her teeth. "I wish Cody was still alive. I swear I'd kill him!"

I blinked. Had she? Donna and Steve Wickstrom had been at the Icicle Creek Tavern Saturday night. Had Donna, who must have known her late husband better than anyone, suspected that the suicide note was written by somebody else? I shivered, and not from the blast of cold air that poured out of the freezer as an elderly woman reached for a bag of frozen peas.

"Why do you think Cody killed Art?" I asked, keeping my voice low.

Donna rolled her cart back and forth, the wheels grating on the floor. "I don't know!" she whispered, the tears back in her eyes. "Art never did anything to Cody. That's what makes it so awful! It's like one of those gang stories you read in the Seattle papers, where somebody shoots somebody just to see what it's like. It doesn't make sense!"

It did, though, to me. Fleetingly, I wondered if I should say as much to Donna. Perhaps it would help. The irrational taking of a life is harder to bear than death with a reason. At least that's how my mind works.

"Donna," I said in a level voice, "I think Cody murdered his own baby. I also think Art knew that but didn't quite know what to do about it. Or if he did, he never had a chance. Cody killed him first."

As the words came out, Donna's face stiffened and her eyes grew huge. The knuckles clutching the grocery cart turned white. But the tears didn't fall. "Shit," breathed Donna. The cart rocked back and forth, but more gently now, as if she were rocking a baby. Hers, maybe. Or even little Scarlett, forever small, always ready to be soothed.

I waited. If Art had ever hinted his knowledge, or even suspicion, to his wife, perhaps she would remember it now. But Donna kept shaking her head and rocking the cart. "Shit," she said again, her voice leaden.

"He never said anything?" I asked quietly.

"No." She tucked the Kleenex farther down between her small breasts. "But he was worried. Or troubled." Donna looked straight at me. "That's why I could accept that note, even though it made me feel like such a failure, a wife who wasn't there for her husband. He

281

couldn't talk to me, he couldn't tell me how his job bothered him, he couldn't share his troubles, so he . . ." She lifted a hand, then let it flutter to her side, like a crippled bird.

"But that wasn't it" I said firmly.

Donna's chin shot up. "No. It wasn't. He was probably just mulling over what he should do. Art was like that, he never did anything on impulse. If only Sheriff Dodge had been in town, if only Art had talked to me, if only . . ." She sniffed hard, swallowing her tears.

"If only Cody Graff hadn't been a killer," I murmured.

Donna squared her slim shoulders. "But he was. And by God, I'd like to shake the hand of whoever killed him." With a tremulous, brave smile, she gave the cart an aggressive push and headed off down the aisle — to frozen vegetables, past whole grain waffles, and beyond ice cream, on special at $2.89 a half gallon.

I stood for a few moments, resting my fingers on the boneless ham I'd picked up in the meat department. Donna Fremstad Wickstrom was a courageous woman. Or a very clever one. Either way, it struck me how life and death could mingle with broccoli spears and party pizzas. We humans did not live by bread alone, but sometimes we died in the most unexpected ways. At the hands of a stranger. In the arms of a lover. Under the evil eye of a parent.

For the first time in days, I was too cold. I moved on, into the fresh, fragrant realm of produce.

I was still too cold.

Saturday brought the ninety-degree temperatures I'd dreaded. It also brought a phone call from my brother.

"Quit bitching," said Ben in his crackling voice. "It's almost a hundred and twenty in Tuba City. I'm thinking of saying mass tomorrow in the nude."

I laughed, then insisted he hang up. I wanted to pour out my troubles, but not on his long distance bill. He refused, saying that he'd been in Vegas the previous week and had won $500 at craps. "I found a shooter," he said. "I even hit boxcars."

For ten minutes, I regaled him with the Cody Graff murder; for two more I told him about Tom Cavanaugh. Ben addressed the latter first:

"Don't reject Tom's generosity. As a priest, I'm telling you that's selfishness and pride. As your brother, I'm telling you you're too damned stubborn. Tom can afford it, he wants to do it, let him. And listen, Emma, one of these days you're going to have to let him meet Adam. I've met Tom. He's a hell of a guy. Are you ashamed of him?"

"I'm ashamed that he's married," I said.

"So's he, probably. But that's a fact, and you have to admire him for sticking by Fruit Loops, or whatever her name is. I admire him for wanting to help you and Adam. Give the guy a break. After all, he's half Tom's. Adam looks more like his father than he does like you, Sluggly." The old nickname came from our extreme youth, a cross between Sluggo and Ugly. I'd always called him Stench. Fortunately, we had not lived up to our childhood monikers.

I mumbled something that was akin to agreement, then waited for his words of wisdom regarding the murder investigation. This time, his counsel came more slowly.

"It sounds to me as if nobody wants to admit this Cody guy got himself murdered. Why is that? Not because he didn't deserve it, right?"

"Right," I echoed into the receiver. "So what are you saying?"

I heard Ben speak away from the phone, presumably to a parishioner who had just arrived at the rectory he had described as about the size of a recycling bin. "I'm saying that everybody really does know Cody Graff was murdered." He paused, waiting for his slow little sister to let his words sink into her brain.

"But nobody wants to let on who did it."

I caught my breath. "Ben, do you mean somebody — maybe several somebodies — know who killed Cody?"

"That's what it sounds like to me." He paused, again speaking to another party. "Hey, Emma, I've got to run. I forgot I was hearing confessions this morning. It gets too damned hot to sit in that booth come late afternoon. Call me when you find out whodunit."

Chapter Fifteen

Vida was taking Roger to the Science Center in Seattle for the day. I considered it a wasted trip, since Roger didn't need any more ideas about how to wreak havoc. But her absence meant I couldn't confer with her about my encounters with Curtis Graff and Donna Wickstrom. As for Milo, I didn't know what his sleeping arrangements were, if any, with Honoria Whitman. I preferred not to call him and discover that maybe he hadn't yet gotten back from Startup.

The mail arrived early, before noon. Along with my Visa, Texaco, and Skykomish PUD bills, I received a manila envelope from Tom. Inside was an Alaska Airlines schedule, a cashier's check for $2500, and a short note.

"Dear Emma," the note read in Tom's sprawling, not always decipherable hand, "this should cover Adam's flight to Fairbanks, plus enough to bring him home before school starts or for the holidays. I'm sending you the schedule because I suspect (from what you've told me) that Adam may not always be specific about matters like time, place, etc. Your Loggerama edition looks good. What did you do — threaten Ed Bronsky with a chain saw? Love, Tom."

I was smiling as I tucked the note in my desk. The check seemed too generous, but I decided to take my brother's advice and not quibble. As for Tom's comment on *The Advocate*: he was on our mailing list. I wondered if he went through every issue. Probably not, but it made me feel good to know that at least he looked at the paper once in a while. And approved. I told myself that I didn't need any green lights from Tom for personal reasons, but that I respected his professional opinion. Maybe that wasn't quite true, but I knew it should be.

I wrote to Tom at once, thanking him for his generosity. The first paragraph sounded stiff; I tried to loosen up in paragraph two, telling him about Roger. I mentioned the murder investigation, the progress of the location shoot, the interminable hot, dry spell. I thanked him again, on Adam's behalf, on my own. I signed "Love, Emma," slipped the stationery into a matching envelope, and stuck on a stamp. Then I sat back to try and figure out what to tell my son. *Our* son.

Adam knew I'd had some contact with Tom over the years, but he'd shown a remarkable lack of curiosity about the relationship. When Adam was small, I rarely mentioned Tom.

About the time Adam stared school in Portland, he began to ask more questions. I was honest, if reserved. Kindergartners cannot understand the adult human heart. Ph.D.s can't either, but at least they like to talk about it. I merely told Adam that his father was a very good man who couldn't marry me and who didn't live close to us. Adam, growing up in an era of single parents, hadn't found his situation unique. Eventually, I told Adam what his father's name was, what he did for a living, that he had a wife and family in California. But it wasn't until he turned seventeen that he expressed a desire to meet Tom. I discouraged Adam; I hadn't heard anything of Tom in years. *Wait,* I cautioned.

And Adam had. It wasn't until he came home from Hawaii on Christmas break that I told him Tom Cavanaugh had been in Alpine. To my amazement, Adam sank into uncharacteristic gloom for three days. On Christmas Eve he came to himself and asked some pointed questions. Why had Tom come? Had he asked about Adam? Who were his other kids? Was he coming back?

I explained how Tom had visited on business, to advise me about the running of the newspaper, possibly even to make an investment. He had two other children: a boy Adam's age and a girl a couple of years younger. Yes, he'd not only asked about Adam, but he'd taken his picture with him. And some day, he might be back.

Oddly, Adam expressed no immediate desire to meet Tom, but he cheered up and the rest of the holiday went by happily. Now I had the cashier's check in hand, made out to me. I would cash it and put it in my savings, to parcel out to Adam as needed. But I would have to tell my son about it, because if he wanted to fly home before the semester started, he'd have to make his reservations soon.

I was sitting in the backyard under the evergreens, mulling over the best approach, when I heard Milo call my name. I shouted that I was outside. Milo loped around the corner of the house, carrying a small box.

"Here," he said, handing me the box and slipping onto the matching deck chair. "Honoria thought you might like it."

I carefully opened the box and searched through crumpled tissue paper. My hand touched something round and smooth. It was about the size of a tennis ball, and when I removed it from the box, I saw there was a hole about half an inch in diameter. The object itself was dark green with just a hint of white in the glaze. I held it out in front of me.

"Well!"

"Isn't that something?" said Milo, leaning forward and smiling in admiration.

"It sure is," I agreed, wishing I knew what that something was.

Milo must have noticed my puzzlement. "It's a vase," he asserted. "For a single flower, like a rose, or a daisy. You stick the stem in that hole. With water, of course."

I studied the would-be vase, rolling it on my palm. It was very heavy. "I like the color. But how do you keep it from tipping over?"

"What?" Milo frowned. "Oh, that's up to you to figure out. Honoria likes to think of her work as . . . how does she put it? *Involving* people. Art shouldn't just sit there, it should *do* something. Or make *you* do something. Isn't that fine?"

"It's very thoughtful." Which, I had to admit, it was. But short of floating the blasted thing in a mixing bowl full of water, I hadn't the foggiest notion what to do with Honoria's gift. "I'll drop her a note. Or call her." I gave Milo my brightest smile, not wanting him to think me ungrateful.

"She made me a pet cock." Milo looked very pleased.

"A *what?*" The heat must be getting to me. Surely I couldn't have heard Milo correctly.

"You know," he said, very seriously. "A

pet cock is a kind of valve. For releasing pressure."

I kept a straight face. "I think I'd rather have this," I said, hoisting the glazed ball-cum-vase. "I wouldn't know what to do with a pet cock."

I'd expected Milo to tumble to the double entendre, but it seemed his mind had wandered off to other matters. "Emma, I'm worried. Time's running out. The movie crew is going to leave Tuesday or Wednesday. Curtis Graff will probably take off tomorrow. I've got no reason to hold any of them."

"You haven't found any physical evidence?" Overhead, a pair of chipmunks chattered in the Douglas fir.

Milo shook his head. "Matt Tabor pitched a fit, but we went all over that fancy car of his a second time. All we could find besides those hairs was a thread that may or may not have come from Cody's jeans."

I made an appropriately sympathetic remark before offering Milo a beer. I took Honoria's gift into the house and returned with two cold bottles of Samuel Smith ale I'd found at the back of the refrigerator. For half an hour, Milo and I sipped and talked, getting nowhere. He was, however, intrigued by Ben's theory.

"Your brother must know people pretty well," he said, "being a priest and all." I allowed that was fairly accurate. Priest or not, Ben had his blind spots. "Now why," mused Milo, "would somebody know who the killer was and not say so?"

"The most obvious reason is that whoever knows wants to protect the person who killed Cody. That could be Dani and Patti, or Reid and Dani, or various combinations of people who care about each other." I moved my chair back a few inches as the sun rose high over the treetops. "It could also be fear. Cody's murderer might not stop there. Take Jack Blackwell, for example — I don't believe he poisoned Cody, but if he did, I think he's the type who would kill again to save himself. There's a ruthless quality about that man."

Milo gave a grunt of assent. "Hampton, too. Hell, I remember Ray Marsh — we went to high school together. He was a wrestler. I played basketball."

"But you didn't recognize him?" I asked.

"No. He was kind of scrawny then, wrestled at a hundred and twenty-six pounds. His hair was about the color of mine, only more washed-out." Milo brushed at his sandy forelock, a few strands of gray glinting in the sun. "By the time he walked out on Patti, he'd put on some weight, but he was still more boy than man."

I made a murmur of acknowledgment. The

flutter of bird's wings, the shadows cast by the evergreens, the heavy heat of midday were all conspiring to make me sleepy. My mind didn't want to dwell on murder. Yet Milo was right — we were running out of time. I was trying to stir myself into some kind of mental action when Milo's beeper went off.

"Damn," he mumbled, getting up and going into the house to use the phone. I leaned back in the deck chair, craning my neck to look out toward the street. I caught the rear end of Milo's Cherokee Chief. So far, he had resisted efforts to have a cellular phone installed in his off-duty vehicle.

He retuned with two more bottles of beer. They were warm. I knew he must have rummaged around under the sink to find them. "That was Bill Blatt," he said, sinking back into his deck chair. "There's some sort of ruckus going on up at the ski lodge. I told him and Sam Heppner to see what it was, and if it looked serious, to call me back. I suppose Henry Bardeen has a guest who tried to skip without paying the bill."

I eyed Milo curiously. Hadn't it dawned on him that trouble at the ski lodge might involve the movie crew? But of course there were other guests, perhaps half again as many non-Hollywood types. Milo must know his own business. I kept quiet.

"This theory about Art," he was saying, cradling the bottle of ale against his chest as he stretched out in the chair, "really threw me. I stopped to see Doc Dewey about it this morning, but he wasn't around. Or," he added with a wry glance in my direction, "if he was, Mrs. Dewey wasn't going to let me talk to him. She's pretty thick with Dot Parker, and I don't think Mrs. D. has forgiven me for arresting Durwood."

"Did Doc ever say anything to you about the Graff baby's death?" I was still trying to fight off my feeling of inertia.

"Never." Milo took a long drink of the warm ale. My own bottle rested on the grass, unopened. He sat up abruptly, an awkward jangle of long arms and legs. "You know, that's strange, Emma. If that baby had been murdered by Cody, wouldn't Doc have guessed? I mean, if Art was suspicious, Doc sure would have been."

"That's true." I gave him an accusing look. "You never told me what Curtis said last night."

"Curtis turned into a damned clam. He refused to talk about it, said it was too painful to bring up." Milo's face was rueful. "Maybe so, but it's driving me nuts with everybody pulling this hush-hush act. The only thing Curtis would say was that his brother was scum, that Marje Blatt was blind if she intended to marry him, and that Dani was misunderstood by a lot of people."

The beeper went off again. Milo swore and returned to the house. He emerged in less than a minute. "Goddamn, that tears it!" He started to drain his ale, thought better of it, and handed the bottle to me. "Billy and Sam had to arrest Matt Tabor. They're bringing him down to the office."

I struggled to my feet, my lethargy gone. "Why?"

Milo was already taking long hurried strides across the grass. I ran to keep up. "Assault with a deadly weapon," he called back over his shoulder. "Matt took a fireplace shovel to Reid Hampton. Reid's on his way to emergency. Maybe that'll get Doc Dewey away from his baseball game on TV."

I was torn between following Milo down to the sheriff's office and going to Alpine Community Hospital. Halfway from the front door to the carport, I made up my mind to head for the emergency room. Milo would tell me what went on with the booking of Matt Tabor, but I needed a first-hand report of what had happened to Reid Hampton.

The waiting room for Emergency was small, spartan, and air-conditioned. By the time I arrived, Reid Hampton had already been wheeled into an examining room. The nurse behind the reception desk was short, red-haired, and had a face that reminded me of a Pekingese. Her plastic name tag identified her as Ruth Sharp, R.N.

I told her who I was, which didn't seem to impress her in the least. "I'm checking on Mr. Hampton's condition," I said, trying to sound official.

Ruth Sharp arched her finely penciled eyebrows at me. "His condition? He just arrived. Why don't you call back later this afternoon." The suggestion was clearly intended as a dismissal.

"Where's Doc Dewey?" I asked, digging my heels into the gray-and-white-flecked carpet.

"Dr. Cecil Dewey or Dr. Gerald Dewey?" The nurse's pug nose twitched a bit, probably in disapproval.

"Either one," I replied, my patience on the wane. Behind her, a young woman carried a howling infant through the double doors.

Ruth Sharp looked down at some papers on her desk. She appeared to be debating whether or not to tell me anything. "Dr. Gerald Dewey isn't on call this weekend. Dr. Cecil Dewey isn't here yet. He's on his way, I believe. Perhaps you'd like to speak to Dr.

Simon Katz. He's up here from Monroe." She glanced at her watch, which looked as if it should have adorned the wrist of a railroad conductor. "Dr. Katz will be free in an hour or two."

I decided to wait for Doc Dewey. Stepping aside for the woman with the screaming child, I began to roam around the little waiting room. Ruth Sharp and the beleaguered mother had to shout to be heard over the youngster's cries. I had just sat down when the young woman approached and set the child next to me. It was a boy, about three, with very bright red cheeks, curly brown hair and a runny nose. I tried to smile; the boy let out another howl. I buried myself in a year-old copy of *National Geographic*. The child suddenly stopped crying, hopped off the chair, and began to run full tilt in circles around the waiting room. *Another miracle cure,* I thought, remembering the times I'd hauled Adam off to the doctor's, usually in the dead of night with the threat of snow, and had been certain he was near death. On virtually every occasion, it had taken him less than three minutes to recover his usual form and raise hell until we got into the examining room. On one particularly harrowing night, he had run away while I was filling out an admittance form. I had chased him all over Portland's Good Samaritan Hospital and through a side door, where he had jumped into a reflecting pool. It turned out that he had gas. It was a wonder I didn't have a stroke.

Twenty minutes passed before I saw Doc Dewey behind the window of the doors that led into the emergency area. I got up, careful not to trip over the whirling dervish who apparently was still awaiting the ministrations of Dr. Katz. Crossing the small room, I rapped softly on the glass. Doc turned, giving me a quizzical look.

"What is it, girlie?" he asked, opening the door a couple of inches. "You sick?"

I explained that I was performing in my professional capacity. "Reid Hampton's famous. It's a news story. What happened?"

Doc expelled a gruff little breath. "Reid Hampton, Ray Marsh, what a crock! Give me five minutes, we'll catch a cup of coffee." He nudged the door shut.

It was actually ten minutes before Doc Dewey shuffled into the vending machine area that served as the hospital cafeteria. I noticed that his hand shook as he carried his paper cup over to the table where I was sitting. Crock or not, his experience with Reid/Ray had seemingly unnerved him.

"Slight concussion," said Doc, easing himself into an orange vinyl chair. "He'll have

298

to stay overnight, but he should be all right. It's a good thing that Tabor fellow's got a swing like a bear with a crosscut saw."

"He really attacked Reid?" I realized I shouldn't be incredulous; movie people were known to be excitable. Still, I hated relying on clichés.

Doc drank his coffee as if he were parched. "Seems like it, all right. Reid — oh, hell, I'm going to call him Ray, I brought the kid into the world over forty years ago — said there was a row. Heather Bardeen was doing something upstairs outside their rooms and heard all the commotion, so she called her dad, who called the sheriff. I didn't ask Ray a lot of questions, because he has to keep quiet." Doc shook his head, the sparse white hairs looking limp. "Damned fools, all of 'em. What's this world coming to, Emma?" He looked at me as if I should know.

"Frankly, it's a miracle Matt didn't do some serious damage," I noted. "Reid — or Ray, if you will — is in terrific shape, but so's Matt and he's several years younger. They must have been going at it a while before the sheriff's deputies got there."

"Oh, yeah?" Doc eyed me inquisitively. "What are you trying to say, girlie?"

I considered. It wasn't advisable to toss irrational answers back at Doc. His shrewd blue eyes demanded judicious thinking. "I mean that if Matt really wanted to brain Reid, he could have done it. Or if they were going at it tooth and toenail, they'd both be here in the hospital."

Doc nodded once. "Good point. Makes you wonder, doesn't it?" He polished off his coffee and stood up, lifting himself out of the chair by hanging onto the table. "I'd better go see if Katz needs any more help. If not, I'll go home and watch some golf. The Red Sox won again — what do you think about that?"

I thought that was fine. On the way out we talked of Fenway Park, of the Green Monster, of Boggs and Clark and Clemens. "No relation to Carl or Samuel," remarked Doc as we passed through the now-empty waiting room. "Roger, I mean. At least that I know of. Carl and Samuel spelled it different from each other, but they were related all the same. Did you know that?"

I said I did. "Speaking of Roger, do you really think Vida's grandson needs medication, or just a good swift kick?"

For a fleeting instant, Doc looked appalled, then he broke into a grin. "If it were me, I'd prescribe the medication for his parents. Tranquilizers, heavy-duty. But I can't argue with Gerry. It wouldn't be right. My son knows what he's doing. And nowadays, you can't tell a parent to give their kid a good licking. That's child abuse."

I glanced over at the reception desk. Ruth Sharp, R.N., appeared absorbed in charts, but I doubted it. She struck me as a world-class eavesdropper. I lowered my voice:

"Was Cody Graff a child abuser?"

Doc's body gave off a tiny tremor, but his blue eyes were steadfast. "Yes."

I couldn't suppress a little gasp. The confirmation of my private beliefs came as a shock. Even when you fear the worst, you still hope for the best. "Did you know it at the time?" My voice was barely audible.

Doc nodded slowly. "I was pretty sure. The trouble was, I didn't know who did it. Then."

The soft thrum of a telephone sounded in the background. I put a hand on Doc's arm. "You mean you thought it might have been Dani?"

Doc was looking very grim. "Maybe. It wasn't obvious who it was. If you're going to ruin somebody's life, you want to be damned sure you got the right one."

Ruth Sharp was standing, leaning across the reception desk. "Dr. Dewey, a Mrs. Whipp is on her way in. She fell out of a lawn swing. Possible wrist fracture."

Doc rolled his eyes. "The Whipps are at it again." He adjusted his stethoscope and turned toward the emergency receiving area. "There goes the golf," he muttered. "A good thing it bores the bejeesus out of me." Doc disappeared behind the swinging doors.

"I had to let him go," Milo asserted in a peevish tone. "We have to wait to see if Reid Hampton presses charges."

I was sitting across from Milo in his little office, angling my chair to get the full benefit of the fan that was whirling at high speed on the floor. According to Milo, the quarrel had started over Reid's refusal to take Matt with him to Seattle to meet the film lab people.

"Sounds silly," said Milo, fingering a round blue object on his desk, "but I've known men to fight over dumber things."

"Was Matt penitent?" I asked.

Milo stuck his finger through the middle of the blue object. It was smaller than a dough-nut, but basically the same shape. "Actually, he was. Not at first — he was pretty bellig-erent. But then he simmered down and seemed worried about Hampton. I had to talk him out of going over to the hospital on his way back to the ski lodge."

"Alone?"

Milo stared, wearing the blue object like a big ring. "Yeah, why?"

I tilted my head to one side. "If Matt is

in love with somebody other than Dani, who is it? It's got to be a woman who is here in town, because Vida and I heard them quarreling. Who?"

Milo's hazel eyes wandered around the room. "Hell, I don't know, Emma. There are several other women on that movie crew. Are you sure you heard two voices? Maybe he was talking on the phone."

I reflected. "I thought we heard someone else, but I couldn't make out who it was. Matt was doing all the shouting."

"I'll bet he was on the phone," said Milo.

"Find out," I said. "I can give you the day and the time. Have Heather check it and see if Matt was making a call then."

"Why?" Milo was regarding me skeptically.

I had no rational answer. But unlike my exchange with Doc Dewey, I didn't feel the need for logic with Milo. "Just do it. Don't you believe in hunches?"

The disparaging expression on Milo's face told me he didn't. But I knew he'd do it anyway. I got up to leave, but paused in the doorway.

"Say, Milo, what's that blue thing you're fiddling with?"

Glancing down at his hand, Milo's long mouth twitched in a dry smile. "This? It's my pet cock. Want to play with it?"

I giggled. "No, thanks."

Sometimes Milo wasn't as dense as I thought he was.

I hoped Vida wouldn't be too late getting back from Seattle. It was too hot to do yard work, or clean house, or get a head start on the next issue of *The Advocate*. I flopped on the sofa and read for an hour, then took a chance and called Adam. He wasn't in, but I suddenly realized I hadn't collected all the items on his wish list. If Curtis Graff was leaving for Ketchikan the next day, I had to get cracking. In less than an hour, the mall would be closed. At least the stores were air-conditioned. The idea should have come to me sooner.

By six P.M., I had finished my shopping, coming as close as I could to Adam's specific desires. I stopped at the Venison Inn for dinner and was surprised to see Matt Tabor sitting alone at a window table. He wore his brooding look, and a feeble attempt by two young women seeking an autograph was rejected with a surly remark. My initial instinct to say hello died aborning. Matt was obviously in no mood for company.

But I was wrong. Five minutes later, Marje Blatt came into the restaurant and walked straight to Matt's table. He looked up and gave her a tight smile. It appeared Matt was expecting Marje.

As I ate my London broil, I watched the couple surreptitiously. Could Marje be the love of Matt's life? It didn't seem possible. How would they know each other? He'd been in Alpine for less than two weeks. She had been engaged to Cody Graff until his death. I chewed very slowly on my buttered carrots. But if somehow they were lovers, what would be more convenient than that Cody should die? I chewed some more, turning the carrots to pap. Matt apparently had a terrible temper and wasn't adverse to beating people up with a fireplace shovel. Marje, however, seemed of a more peaceable nature. But poison was said to be a woman's weapon. . . .

I tried to read the signals they gave off between them. Earnest conversation, a serious discussion, no physical contact, not so much as a smoldering glance. Their meal outlasted mine. I dawdled over my lemonade, wished I could smoke about six cigarettes, and finally left while they were still finishing their entrée.

The phone was ringing when I got in the house. I caught it just before it switched over to the answering machine. It was Milo.

"You were right, Emma. Or were you wrong?" He sounded vague. "Whatever. No call was made from Matt Tabor's room that morning. Whoever he was talking to was with him."

I told him about Matt and Marje. "I have to be honest, though," I cautioned. "I didn't see any sparks fly."

"Hmmmm." Milo was musing, and I could see him fingering his long chin. Or his pet cock. "Marje would have been at work that time of day, right?"

"Probably." My hunch was teasing me. "Are you keeping an eye on Matt?"

"Not really, why?"

"I just wondered." There was something I had to say, to tell Milo, to keep the hazily evolving idea alive in my mind. "How's Reid?"

"I haven't heard. What's up, Emma? You sound antsy."

"I am," I admitted. "Say, where's Curtis Graff staying? I've got to see him before he goes back to Alaska."

"He was at Patti's, but he may be at Cody's apartment, clearing stuff out. That's my guess. The number's in the book."

I found Cody Graff's listing before Milo did and I rang off. Curtis answered on the first ring. To my surprise, he offered to come up and collect Adam's parcels.

He arrived half an hour later, just as I felt the first breath of fresh air filter through the evergreens. Curtis was wearing a dress shirt, no tie, but tailored slacks. I couldn't help but stare.

"You look sharp," I said, showing him into the living room. "I don't have the gumption to get dressed up in this kind of weather."

He gave me a diffident smile. "I've got a dinner reservation in less than an hour at Café de Flore." His eyes roamed the living room, taking in my Monet and Turner prints, the stone fireplace, the braided rug my great-grandmother had made almost a century earlier. I expected him to comment on the decor, but instead he shoved his hands in his pockets and looked at me sideways. "I'm taking Dani to dinner. She could use an evening out."

"Well!" I cleared my throat. "That's nice, Curtis. She's been through hell." I collected myself and turned a level gaze on him. "Now — and a long time ago."

To my further surprise, Curtis sat down on the sofa. "I'm getting the idea that a lot of people know the truth about what happened — a long time ago. Maybe that's good."

I seated myself in the armchair opposite him. "You don't sound positive."

"I'm not." He was now looking away, in the direction of the tall oak cabinet that housed my alphabet soup collection of audio-visual pleasures: TV, VCR, CD player. Curtis's gray eyes had the same restless quality as his brother's, but there was no sign of Cody's sulkiness. "It's tough," Curtis said, after a long pause, "to know when you've done the right thing, isn't it? I mean, even if you've pondered long and hard, and you know it's the only way, you still don't feel easy in your mind."

Curtis's remarkable, if cryptic, little speech caught me off guard. "Life is very complicated," I said, falling back on a platitude. "Are you talking about dealing with other people or making independent choices?"

For some reason, my query brought a faint smile to Curtis's face. "Not independent. No, not at all. Let's just say it's about people." He rested one leg over the other knee, careful of the crease in his slacks. "I must sound weird. Coming back to Alpine after all these years has been an unreal experience."

"I should think so. It would feel odd under any circumstances, but with Cody getting killed, it must almost make you sorry you came."

"I had to come." His face had turned very earnest; the words almost sounded desperate. "But I'll be real glad to leave tomorrow night."

"Curtis," I said, hoping to strike a balance between friendly curiosity and professional interrogation, "why *did* you come?" I hoped my tone would imply that I had a right to know and that he had a duty to tell me.

His response came slowly. Curtis's teeth worried his lower lip and his fingers thrummed on his knee. "I wanted to see Dani."

"You care for her that much?"

Above the shake rooftop, I could hear the cawing of crows. A car took the corner too fast on Fir Street, causing the wheels to screech. On the other side of town, a Burlington Northern freight whistled as it slowed on its ascent into the mountains.

"Dani's special," Curtis said at last. "I don't mean because she's a movie star. She was always that way. Even when she was a kid, there was something different about her. She didn't *act* different, she just *was* different. It's hard to explain."

I had an inkling of what Curtis meant: Reid Hampton had described her as *luminous;* but the word was too extravagant. Dani Marsh struck me as more down-to-earth. "She seems like a very decent person. Vulnerable, too, the kind you'd want to protect."

Curtis nodded energetically. "That's it. She's tough in some ways, but not in others. Her mother is the other way around. I mean, Patti talks tough, but she really isn't. Dani's

309

the opposite. She's decent, all right. You got it." He seemed pleased with my analysis.

"I'm guessing that you weren't pleased when Dani married your brother."

"I sure wasn't." Curtis scowled at the memory. "Anybody could have told her it was a bad idea. I don't think it took her more than two weeks to figure it out for herself."

I was searching for another roundabout way to ask the obvious. It's not easy for a journalist to avoid direct questions. But unlike Vida, I couldn't be so blunt in casual conversation.

"Yet they stayed together for over a year," I remarked, "and went ahead and had a baby."

Curtis put both feet on the floor and stood up. "They stayed together for over a year. That's right." He moved in a semicircle, one hand ruffling the hair at the back of his neck.

Curtis didn't seem inclined to elaborate. "The baby's death must have sealed the fate of that marriage," I said. "How did Cody take it?"

Curtis gave me an odd look, part puzzled, part scornful. "He acted all broken up. He blamed Dani for going out."

"But Cody was with the baby," I pointed out.

Scorn vanquished puzzlement. "That's right." Curtis bit off the words.

"What happened that night, Curtis?" I'd finally managed to ask the direct question.

Curtis looked as if he were going to sit down again, but instead he wandered to the end of the sofa. Deep in thought, he gazed at the end table — at the telephone, answering machine, pen, notepad, and my prized Tiffany lily lamp. "Dani called the fire department. She was hysterical, almost impossible to understand. I was on active status, so I answered the phone. All I could figure out was that something terrible had happened." He was speaking dispassionately, divorcing himself from his memories. "A couple of other guys and I went out to their trailer home, ready for anything. Art Fremstad was already there. Dani was a little calmer, but still a mess. Cody was blubbering into his beer, trying to drink himself stupid. Little Scarlett was dead, probably had been for almost an hour."

He stopped, presumably gathering courage. Curtis moved the length of the coffee table, pausing by the floor lamp with its shade of geometric stained glass. "I got sick. I threw up in their bathroom." He hung his head. "Then Doc Dewey came. He asked Art and me a lot of questions. It dawned on me what he was getting at. But he never said anything. He just sort of looked at us, and at Dani and Cody, and said to send for Al Driggers and the hearse."

"But you knew then that the baby's death wasn't natural?"

Cody's face had darkened, his features looking sharp in the shadow cast by the lamp. "Not for sure. There were some marks on her face, but Cody said he'd tried to revive her. You don't want to think about the other possibility."

"No," I breathed. "Of course not. Especially when it's your own brother and his child."

Curtis wrapped his fingers around the lamp's slim column and stared straight at me. "But," he said softly, "it wasn't his child."

I sucked in my breath. My jaw must have dropped, and I knew I was gaping stupidly at Curtis. "What . . ." I began, but Curtis's face had closed up, as if he had given everything he had, and the larder was empty. Judging from the blank look in his gray eyes, his soul was empty, too.

"I'd better go meet Dani," he said in his normal voice. "It takes a while to drive down to Café de Flore if there's heavy traffic coming over the pass on a Saturday night. You got Adam's stuff?"

I did, having hastily packed everything into a large cardboard box just before Curtis arrived. I thanked him, wished him well, and hoped he enjoyed his dinner. It was almost dark when I watched him go down the walk to the street where Cody's pickup was parked. I wondered if Curtis intended to drive it to Café de Flore or if Dani was going to borrow Matt's Zimmer.

Most of all, I wondered about little Scarlett's father. Perhaps Curtis had been suffering from grief as well as shock when he'd thrown up in his brother's bathroom. It struck me as very likely that Curtis Graff hadn't lost a niece that summer night, but a daughter.

It was after ten o'clock when Vida called. "Did you have a good time?" I asked, envisioning the Pacific Science Center in ruins.

"Yes, yes, never mind that," she said in a voice that sounded as if her engine was racing. "Listen, Emma, I just tucked Roger in and went through his belongings to get his dirty clothes. I found the medicine young Doc Dewey gave him. Amy had sent it along, but Roger forgot to tell me." Vida took a deep breath while I waited for her to launch a new attack on the modern approach to child-rearing. "Emma, it's Haloperidol. *Doesn't that beat all?*"

Chapter Sixteen

I drove over to Vida's in my bathrobe. She couldn't leave Roger, of course, lest he parboil a burglar or engage in some other childish prank. Insisting that I see for myself, and convinced that despite modern electronic switching equipment in the telephone company's central office, our words could be overheard, Vida had asked me to come to her house.

I arrived just as she was putting a green-edged cloth over the cage of her canary, Cupcake. "Roger's asleep," she said in a whisper. "The poor little fellow is all worn out. He had no idea those security guards could run so fast at the Center."

I decided not to ask why Roger was being chased, and could only hope that he also had been chastened. At the sound of the tea kettle, Vida whisked into the kitchen. I followed her while she made tea.

"Here's the stuff," she said, pointing to an innocent-looking bottle on the counter. "It's also called Haldol."

I read the label, with its usual cautions. "Okay," I said, sitting down at her Formica-covered kitchen table, "so we know the drug existed in this form in this town. So what?"

Vida, unlike most people I know, actually serves tea in teacups. She carried a Radford's yellow rose pattern for me and an English garden scene by Royal Albert for herself. "Emma — look at that label." She blew on her tea and waited for my reaction.

I started to read aloud, but Vida gave a vigorous shake of her head. "I'm not talking about what's there — I'm talking about what's not." Her eyebrows arched above the tortoiseshell frames. "No pharmacy label. Young Doc Dewey took it right off the shelf in his office."

"Oh!" I sighed at my obtuseness. But I still didn't see Vida's point. I admitted as much.

"It means," said Vida, "that this stuff — which was what Cody ingested — was available at the clinic. Someone could have gone in to see either of the Deweys and made off with a bottle of it and poisoned Cody."

The theory fell flat with me. "No, Vida. They lock up drugs. You know that."

Vida's chin jutted. "I know they don't. They're really rather careless. Back by the lab, they have a room which is part dispensary, part supply closet. It's never locked. I walked right in once and helped myself to one of those travel-sized boxes of Kleenex for the car. I think we should check with Marje and see who had appointments in the week or two before Cody died."

"I suppose." I fingered the little bottle as if it could give me inspiration, then set it back down on the table, accidentally knocking it against Vida's cut-glass sugar bowl. The small sound triggered a random thought in my brain, but I couldn't grasp it quickly enough. "There are other sources," I suggested. "Parker's Pharmacy. The hospital."

"Certainly," agreed Vida. "But I daresay either of those places is more secure. I still opt for the clinic."

I rested my chin on my hand, mulling over the idea. Certainly there was one person involved with Cody who had access to the clinic's supply of Haloperidol: Marje Blatt. But maybe it wasn't wise to say so to Vida.

In the end, after we had hashed over the doings of the day in Alpine, I hinted to Vida that Marje couldn't be dismissed as a suspect.

"We can't leave anyone out," I said. "That's what Milo and I were discussing this afternoon — how somebody may be protecting somebody else."

Vida, who was still exclaiming over Matt Tabor's attack on Reid Hampton, frowned at me. "Are you making too much of Marje having dinner with Matt? Really, I admit it's a bit odd, but I'm sure Marje will explain it to her old auntie. After all, Matt may be a movie star, but basically he's probably just a young man who enjoys the company of a pretty girl."

"When he isn't out creaming his director with a shovel?" I threw Vida a caustic look. "Come on, Vida, who do you think Matt was arguing with the other morning up at the lodge?" I watched her roll her eyes, but didn't wait for her answer. "It wasn't Marje, I'll admit. I don't know why your niece was being wined and dined by Matt Tabor, but I doubt it had anything to do with her feminine charms. Am I right?"

"Probably." Vida looked exasperated.

"So who was the other half of the lovers' quarrel?"

Setting her teacup in its matching saucer, Vida drew herself up in her customary majestic style. "Really, it's so galling. It shouldn't be, of course, but it is, because I'm a woman. I suppose I hate to see good men go to waste." She pursed her lips, glanced into her now empty cup as if she were going to read the dregs, and gave a little shudder. "Obviously, the great love of Matt Tabor's life is Reid Hampton."

It made sense that when Reid Hampton found himself up against a double exposure, he chose the lesser revelation of the two secrets. Patti Marsh knew her husband. Perhaps Reid's homosexuality had caused the breakup of their marriage, rather than his unwillingness to take on the responsibility of a wife and child. Reid Hampton, or Ray Marsh, had paid $50,000 to Patti Marsh not to keep his real identity a secret, but to guard his sexual preference.

Vida and I both doubted that Reid was ashamed of being gay. Instead, we figured that he didn't want his hot new protégé, Matt Tabor, to be labeled anything but a raging macho man. Box office was the bottom line, and a hero who called his male director Honey wouldn't bring in the paying customers. And if the trade reports were accurate, Reid Hampton's production company desperately needed a hot ticket.

Just before midnight, I pleaded exhaustion, more from the heat than any stress or strain. Naturally, Vida was tired, but she seemed too involved in the murder case to wind down. She was particularly fascinated by the notion that Curtis Graff might have been little Scarlett's father, a lapse on Dani's part that Vida found not only excusable, but commendable.

As Vida escorted me to the front door, she gave the sleeve of my bathrobe a little shake. "We're getting close, Emma. I can feel it."

I offered a weary smile. "What you're feeling is polished cotton, Vida. And I feel as if my head is full of cotton wool. Good night."

"I mean it," she shouted, heedless of her sleeping neighbors. "We're hot on the heels of that killer!"

I got into the Jaguar and locked the doors. I only hoped that the killer wasn't hot on our heels as well.

Father Fitz was on vacation, replaced by a young priest from Wenatchee who was into social justice. With my own quest for justice nibbling at my attention, I caught only the high points of his sermon. Everyone is equal. Christianity is not a passive state. Taking action is better than not taking action. Society is upside down. Purify your soul, but if you can't handle that, clean up the water. At least it was better than listening to Father Fitz rant about fast young women with shingled hair or the atrocities of the Bataan Death March.

After mass, I strolled out into the parking lot. Beyond Mount Baldy, a few wispy clouds teased the land with the promise of better things to come, such as rain. Ninety again today, with no break in sight. No precipitation in the five-day forecast, fire danger in the extreme. I slumped into the Jaguar and headed home.

I was pulling into the driveway when the young priest's sermon hit me like a punch in the stomach. With a squeal of tires, I put the car into reverse and headed straight for Vida.

Vida's first reaction was that I was crazy. Ten minutes later, over tall glasses of iced tea, she began to accept my inspired theory.

"I don't see how you can prove it, though," she remarked, keeping one eye on me and the other on Roger, who was out in the front yard catching bugs in a jar.

"I'm going to have to rely on Milo. I thought of asking everybody who was at the Icicle Creek Tavern, but I've covered too many court cases to not know how much conflicting testimony eyewitnesses can come up with. I'm afraid it would be a waste of time." I gave Vida a semi-reproachful look. "I wish you'd been there."

Vida lifted her chin. "I did my duty at Mugs Ahoy. You can't expect me to be everywhere."

"I know." My smile was meant to placate. "It's just that you're a better observer than Milo is, for all of his law enforcement experience."

"That's because he's only a man," said Vida, pouring more iced tea from a fat green pitcher. "They don't notice things the way other people do, Emma. Their vision is limited, as if they're wearing blinders. They rarely see the whole picture."

"True," I agreed in a vague voice, wishing I could lay claim to seeing more than I had. The bar stools on which Carla, Ginny, and I had been seated hadn't given us a particularly good vantage point except for the immediate vicinity. There were too many bobbing heads and moving bodies blocking our view. As for Carla, she was a hopeless witness. I might expect better of Ginny but in cursory conversations during the past few days, she hadn't been able to tell me any more than I already knew. The tavern had been such a jumble of people, noise, and movement that isolated incidents were hard to recall. After more than a week, I could barely keep a coherent account in my own mind.

Vida had gotten up to call to Roger through the screen door "No bees, dear. Just grasshoppers." She paused as Roger responded in a voice I couldn't hear. Vida gave a shake of her head. "I can't tell which are boys and which are girls, either, Roger." She turned to her chair, still shaking her head. "He wants to dress the grasshoppers, according to sex. Isn't he the one?"

Resisting the urge to ask *one what?* I started to steer the conversation back to the topic at hand. But despite the distraction, Vida was already there. "You're forgetting someone," she said, pushing her glasses farther up on her nose. "I have a feeling that one of those people at the tavern would make an exemplary witness."

I winced as I saw Roger go from A to Z in a single bound, trampling a bed of asters and zinnias. "Who?"

"The sort of person who isn't as physically active as most people." The glasses slipped a notch. Vida regarded me over their rims. "Honoria Whitman."

Vida couldn't come to Startup with me because she wasn't sure when her daughter and son-in-law would be back. I almost suggested we take Roger along, stopped long enough to question my sanity, and said I might give Milo a call. But Vida informed me that Milo had gone to Seattle to take his son to the Mariners' game. Briefly, I cursed Milo for appearing to regard Cody Graff's murder less seriously than I did.

There was heavy traffic going both ways on Stevens Pass. The sun beat down on the broad highway; the south fork of the Skykomish River was so low you could walk across it; and I had to search to find patches of snow in the mountains that lined both sides of the road. My directions to Honoria's house had been derived from Milo's description. Feeling guilty because I hadn't phoned ahead, I stopped in Gold Bar to call Honoria.

To my relief, she was in; to my surprise, she sounded genuinely glad that I was coming. I took the turn she had given me and wound my way a quarter of a mile on a dirt road through overhanging vine maples.

Honoria's house probably had once been a summer cottage. But somewhere between the need for indoor plumbing and rising real estate prices, the cedar shake dwelling had been renovated. Tucked among the trees near a sluggish creek inching through ferns and cattails, the little house possessed a certain charm.

Honoria was sitting in her wheelchair on the front porch, which spanned the width of the cottage. "I made separators," she said as I trudged up the ramp to join her. "Kahlua, brandy, and milk. Not really a hot weather drink, but somehow it sounded wholesome."

"It does at that," I agreed, sitting in a rough-hewn chair that was surprisingly comfortable. For the first quarter of an hour, we sipped our separators and made polite if congenial conversation. I thanked Honoria for her gift, emphasizing that I intended to find one perfect rose to set in the hole.

Honoria laughed, a delightful, husky sound. "Oh, Emma! Did Milo tell you it was a *vase?*"

she laughed some more, shaking her head on her graceful neck. "It's nothing! It's just a . . . *thing*. But Milo is so practical, I had to tell him it was . . . useful." Her laughter subsided into a rich giggle.

I laughed, too, but not quite as heartily. "And I thought it was a small bowling ball for a one-fingered amateur," I murmured. "Oh, dear."

Honoria giggled again and tucked her linen shirt into her neatly pressed slacks. "It's the shapes and the textures I like," she explained, growing more serious. "I don't see why pottery always has to be useful. It's like any other art. It can be whatever you want it to be, which in this case, is really nothing but a blob. Except to the Milos of this world, bless them. They're so *practical,* they can fix dripping faucets and replace fuel pumps and shingle your roof. We'd be lost without them."

I had visions of Milo with a ladder, scrambling about on Honoria's roof in the middle of a winter windstorm. I tried to refocus, with Milo on my roof, but all I saw was him asking me to move the ladder and help him get down. Just the same, I admired Honoria's candor. Indeed, I admired Honoria. Only in the most perverse corner of my often perverse soul did I wish I didn't.

It was time to get down to business. My

curiosity was rampant, not only on a professional level, but because I sensed that I was on the right track in discovering the killer's identity. If only Honoria were as keen an observer as Vida thought she was . . .

I began by asking Honoria if Milo had questioned her — in his official capacity — about the Icicle Creek Tavern. He had, she assured me, but there had been very little she could tell him. As a newcomer, she didn't know most of the people involved. It was only after the fact that she had discovered their identities.

"Dani Marsh and Matt Tabor, of course," she said, refilling my glass from a green and yellow carafe I presumed she had created. "I recognized them from their movies. But the others . . ." She gave a simple shrug. "They were new to me."

"You were sitting near the bar, and fairly close to Cody and Marje," I pointed out. "Do you remember anything about Cody being served that last beer?"

Honoria paid me the compliment of pausing long enough to consider my question seriously. "Milo asked me that, too. At the time, I told him I didn't. But the more I tried to remember . . ." Her oval face puckered in concentration. "So much was going on, with those angry exchanges between all sorts of people, including Matt Tabor and

Cody Graff . . . Dani's mother, that was easy to figure out, there *is* a resemblance . . . And Reid Hampton — I'm sure I've seen his picture in some film magazine or the newspaper — and the timber company fellow . . . It was all so distracting, and yet predictable." Honoria gave me a helpless look. "Do you know what I mean? It was almost like a movie, the cliché barroom brawl scene."

Recalling that my reaction had been similar, I tipped my head in assent. "Do you mean *phony?*" I asked.

Again, Honoria stopped to consider my query. "Phony . . . not that, but not exactly genuine, either. It was as if everyone was playing a part, not staged in that sense, not rehearsed, but doing what was expected of them." She made a sudden impatient wave of her hand. "I can't quite get a fix on it. I do know, however, that I was quite fascinated, and in watching all the action, I didn't pay strict attention to where the beer was going."

"That," I said, "may have been intentional."

Honoria's gray eyes locked with mine. "I see." She ran her tongue over her upper lip. "Why?"

"I'm not sure," I admitted. "Maybe as cover for the murder."

The gray eyes grew very wide. "But . . . that would mean that somebody else — other than the killer — was involved."

My gaze kept a steady pace with Honoria's. "That's right. At least I'm guessing it is." I leaned forward on my rough-planked chair. It was very quiet at Honoria's place, the highway sounds muffled by the trees, the slow-winding creek making barely a gurgle, the leaves unruffled by the still, warm air. Only the occasional chatter of a chipmunk or caw of a crow broke the silence. "Beyond all the fuss and furor, what else did you see, Honoria?"

She slumped slightly in the wheelchair, her eyes following a shaft of sunlight between the vine maples and the cottonwood trees. "That's what I've been trying to remember. I don't think I saw anything. Except," she went on, more slowly and with great care, "there was that awkward moment — for me, that is — when Patti got playful with Milo. You understand," said Honoria, returning her gaze to my attentive face, "that I wasn't reacting in a possessive way. It was more as if I were watching Milo take a test — how would he handle the situation? He passed beautifully."

Momentarily sidetracked by Honoria's apparent concern for my feelings about Milo, assuming I had any, I smiled wryly. "He palmed her off on Janet and Al Driggers, knowing full well that if anybody was up to the task, it would be Janet."

"Yes, and it raised him a notch in my esteem." Honoria paused to sip from her drink and watch a pair of blue jays hop around a slim cedar tree just off the porch. "But I didn't want him to catch me staring at him like a teacher watching a pupil, so I made myself look the other way. You may recall that we were sitting at the far end of the bar, near the rest rooms and fairly close to Cody and his fiancée."

I nodded. I remembered that part well enough. "Most of the time, my view of you was blocked by all the action. But I remember catching your eye when things seemed to simmer down."

"Exactly," agreed Honoria. "But before that, while Milo was getting rid of Patti, I kept my eyes on the bar itself. That timber fellow — Blackwell? — was serving the service station man a beer, I think, and the doctor poured one for somebody else. Dani took it off the bar and handed it to Marje Blatt who carried it over to Cody. I suppose he drank it." Her gaze was meaningful, yet it conveyed a question.

"I suppose he did," I replied, wishing that Honoria could have arrived at the Icicle Creek

Tavern earlier. She had confirmed some of my suspicions, but not quite all of them. For a full minute, we let the silence wrap around us, feeling the heat of the day and the tension of the moment. "That's it?" I finally asked.

Honoria made a rueful face. "I'm afraid so. I didn't see Dani or Marje slip anything into that beer mug. And I didn't notice if anyone went up to Cody after that. Milo came back and the next thing I knew, Cody and Marje had left the tavern." With a helpless gesture of her graceful hands, Honoria gave me an apologetic look. "I'm not much help, am I?"

I tried to make my expression encouraging. "Every tiny bit helps. This is Milo's job, after all." Maybe it was wrong of me to meddle; certainly it wasn't fair to criticize the sheriff's handling of a difficult case.

Honoria raised her glass. "To Milo, then."

I nodded as we clicked glasses. Something clicked in my brain as well.

"I think you just showed me a missing link," I asserted, noting the puzzled expression on Honoria's face. "Now we'll let Milo take over. Let's hope he passes this test as well as he did the one at the Icicle Creek Tavern."

Chapter Seventeen

My hands were tied until evening, when Milo returned from Seattle. By then, Vida should be free of Roger, though I realized she would not regard his departure with the same enthusiasm I would. Meanwhile, I made another attempt to call my son in Ketchikan. He was working, I was told, and wouldn't be back until ten, my time. Maybe, I thought, I should set aside some of Tom's $2500 to help defray the cost of long distance.

I spent what was left of the afternoon piecing together the evidence, most of which was circumstantial, as well as guesswork. Much of what I'd learned had nothing to do with Cody Graff's murder. At least not on the surface. The relationship between Patti Marsh and Jack Blackwell was, alas, what it was: an abusive man and a woman who could defend herself only against those who meant her no serious harm. I didn't know if Reid Hampton had abused Patti, but their daughter apparently had carried on the family tradition by marrying Cody Graff. And Cody, fueled by jealously or maybe just a vicious streak, had smothered little Scarlett, and then killed Art

Fremstad. For five years, Cody Graff must have figured he'd gotten away with murder.

Dani must have realized early on in her marriage that Cody was a nasty piece of work. My guess was that she'd sought consolation from his brother, who had been more than willing to give her his all. Curtis had said he and Cody had fallen out over a girl. Had he meant Dani? Or Scarlett? Or both? Dani had run away to Los Angeles; Curtis had fled to Alaska No doubt both had been horrified as well as grief-stricken. And probably afraid.

In California, Dani had found not only a mentor but a father. I couldn't help but speculate that the lure of Hollywood had been in their blood, sending each of them from the evergreens of Alpine to the palm trees of L.A. As for Reid Hampton, the revelation of his real identity didn't perturb him as much as any hint of his relationship with Matt Tabor. But I didn't think that their feelings for each other had anything to do with Cody's death. Reid had tried to cover up his sexual preference for professional, not personal, reasons. He had promoted a nonexistent romance between Dani and Matt while dating women — such as me — casually but publicly. Who better to ask out for an evening than the local newspaper publisher? Nor did I think that Matt's jealous rage was aimed in my direction

— if Reid Hampton was straying, the object of his affections could be anybody, and probably another man. Again, I felt that episode had very little to do with Cody's murder.

I could also dismiss the ruckus between Jack Blackwell and Reid Hampton. Strictly business, to be settled by their lawyers, not with their fists. Matt might make a show of defending Reid's rights, and Jack had certainly pitched a fit over Patti's fifty grand, but nobody was going to kill one of Blackwell lumber's employees because of financial gain or loss.

The key, I kept telling myself, was what Marje Blatt and Dani Marsh and so many others had told me all along: that Cody Graff had not been murdered, that his death was accidental, that he had overdosed. I didn't believe that for a minute.

The problem was that the tighter I pulled the pieces together, the less I liked my conclusions. There is a truism in the news business that as long as a journalist is on the scent of a story, real emotions are held at bay. Once all the facts are gathered, personal reaction sets in. On this oppressive, humid evening in August, I had reached that point. I was almost sure I knew who the killer was, and I didn't like the answer one bit. I didn't even much like myself for coming up with such a terrible solution. The combination of too much heat and too little wisdom was making me feel depressed and faintly nauseous. Maybe I was hungry. Food, which can usually sustain me through almost any crisis, is not quite as appealing when the temperature nudges ninety.

As I got up from my writing desk to forage in the kitchen, I realized I was dizzy. I stumbled over the phone cord and went down hard. The wind was knocked out of me, but it was my left foot that hurt badly. Writhing about, I regained my breath and tried to pull myself up.

The foot did not want to bear my weight. I knelt on my right knee, feeling tears of pain sting my eyes. It had been a few minutes after seven when I'd last looked at my watch. Would Milo be home? Would Vida have bade Roger good-bye? Should I call the hospital?

Feeling foolish as well as awkward, I stretched for the phone. It rang in my hand. My voice was feeble as I said hello.

"Mom? Hey, you sound weird. Did I screw up the time change again? I got off early and somebody told me you'd called a couple of times."

For once, my son's voice was not the most welcome sound in the world. "Oh, Adam," I began dismally, "I just fell flat on my face."

"What did you do, break your beak?" He

sounded more amused than alarmed. "Hey, if you knocked out your front teeth, you can probably use the dental insurance to get caps."

In spite of my pain, I laughed. "It's my foot. Or ankle. Not nearly so mirth-making as the prizefighter or jack-o-lantern look."

"No, that's pretty boring," Adam agreed, beginning to show a bit of concern. "Can you walk?"

"I can't even get up." I was, however, edging my way onto the sofa. "It's okay, I'll get somebody to check it out for me tonight. How are you?" God forbid, I didn't want my son to worry about his mother. God give me reason — would Adam really spare me a pang?

To my amazement — and probably God's as well — he did. "You better have it X-rayed, Mom. Remember the time I fell out of that old pear tree next door to our house in Portland and I crawled around for two days before you decided it wasn't just a sprain?"

"Right," I said in a guilty voice. "It was your third crash-and-burn in less than a month. I was getting blasé. Adam, I got a letter from your father." Wincing as I pulled myself onto the sofa, I waited for my son's reaction.

"No kidding." His voice had dropped an octave. "What about?"

I explained, in as businesslike a tone as I could, caught as I was in a web of pain and a wash of uncertainty. "So," I concluded, "this is your father's way of making a contribution to your education. I haven't yet checked on what the airfare is between Ketchikan and Fairbanks, but —"

"I have," Adam put in, again amazing me. "Jeez, Mom, that $2500 will pay for a ton of trips. Maybe I can come home before school starts. Or go to Japan."

"Japan!" For just an instant, my foot didn't hurt any more. My son's irresponsibility had obliterated my suffering. "Adam! Don't be an idiot! That isn't what Tom intended." I tried to simmer down and lower my voice. "Why would you want to go to Japan anyway? Now, I mean."

"Don't you remember Miko Nagakawa, that major babe I met just before I moved from Honolulu? She lives in Kyoto. I called her last week and she said it would be cool for me to come over any time."

"It's not cool," I said sternly. The foot was throbbing again, so hard I was sure I could hear it. "Let her come over here. As I recall, her father owns about six corporations and a couple of third world countries."

Eventually, it seemed that I had talked Adam out of his notion to fly to Japan. As a veteran of the motherhood wars, I've learned never to be certain of anything. But he was definite — as definite as any young person his age — about flying home for the Labor Day weekend. I didn't argue that one. I'd be too glad to see him.

"You go take care of your knee," he said, obviously no longer obsessed with my dilemma. "But give me his address, okay?"

"What?" I stopped, aware that Adam never called Tom by name, almost never referred to him as *father*. "Oh — you mean . . ." I faltered, feeling the moment's awkwardness.

"That's right." Adam suddenly sounded older. "I want to write a thank-you letter. To . . . *him*."

When I hung up, the tears in my eyes weren't just from pain.

Vida drove me to Doc Dewey's, half-carrying me to her car. She is literally a tower of strength, and I thanked her profusely.

"Don't be silly," she snapped. "If I didn't know better, I'd think you did this on purpose."

I gave her a sidelong look as we drove down Fourth Street in the twilight. "Maybe I did." Vida merely snorted.

Doc had directed us to go to the clinic, rather than the emergency room of the hospital. Young Doc was on duty and the father didn't want the son to think he was usurping patients. Or so Doc informed Vida when she made the call from my house.

"I can run an X-ray machine as well as any whippersnapper," Doc said, pushing a wheelchair toward us. "It's all these damned specialists who can't do anything but tend to one part of your anatomy. Take a bone man: he'd be out of luck trying to tell you what to do with a sore throat. Or a urologist — now there's a fellow who may know an asshole when he sees one on the examining table, but can't deal with one in real life. Specialists — no sense of a patient's overall well-being, girlies. Take my word for it."

Vida had wheeled me into the room which contained the portable X-ray unit while Doc lectured us and adjusted the equipment. He was wearing a faded cotton sports shirt and baggy suntan pants. His face was drawn and his color seemed off, especially since we'd had so much sun in recent weeks.

With Vida's help, I got up on the examining table. Doc was still griping about certain segments of the medical profession, interspersed with directions on how I should hold my battered body.

"A first-year resident can make between twenty-five and thirty thousand these days," he was saying as he clicked on the X-ray machine. "Hell, I didn't make that much in the

337

first five years I was in practice. Try to turn your ankle to the right, girlie. Oh, I know, everybody talks about inflation, but I still say — no, no, a little more to the right . . . That's better — the problem is, these young people are spoiled today, they've been given everything . . ."

Doc rambled on. I realized Vida had slipped out of the room. Gritting my teeth, I tried to keep the ankle from flopping over into a less painful position.

"Just one more," Doc was saying. "Straight. Point that toe, girlie."

I winced some more, but Doc was quick. He took the films into the little darkroom while I tried to relax. I was beginning to recover from the shock of the fall, which I felt should be a good sign. But even as I collected my wits and stared at the ceiling, my nerves became unraveled for different, more tragic reasons. By the time Doc emerged from the darkroom, I was feeling giddy.

"No break," he said, plastering the three X-rays up against the wall under a strong light. His thin fingers trailed the outline of my foot bones. "It's a bad sprain, though, girlie. Keep off it for about three days. You want crutches?"

My mind, which had been wandering in circles over Cody Graff's corpse, snapped back to earth with a thud. "Oh, Lord! I never could manage crutches!"

Doc eyed me sharply. "Can you stay home from work for three days?"

"No," I admitted with a heavy sigh as he helped me sit up. "I'd better get the damned crutches." At least there were no stairs at *The Advocate* or inside my house.

Doc pushed me back into the waiting room just as Vida came out of the supply closet. I was too preoccupied with figuring out how to avoid getting blisters under my arms to notice that she was holding something in her hand.

"Here, Doc," she said, unfolding her fingers. A small glass bottle caught the overhead light. "I found some more Haloperidol syrup. Do we congratulate you or call the sheriff?"

What little color Doc had retained was sapped by Vida's words. His drawn face turned haggard and his hands shook as he groped for the back of the nearest vinyl chair. He seemed to shrivel up inside his shirt and pants. I realized that his clothes weren't baggy so much as they were ill-fitting. Doc had lost a considerable amount of weight. My heart sank even deeper. "Call 'em," he replied. "And don't forget Al Driggers. I don't want to cheat him out of an undertaking job."

★ ★ ★

We sat in Doc's office for close to an hour, with the night enfolding the clinic like a shroud and the wind finally blowing up through the river valley between the mountains. Doc was behind his desk. Vida had the patient's seat. And I languished in the wheelchair.

I'd interviewed murderers before. Some were sullen; some were self-righteous; some were scared to death. There had been a few I'd felt sorry for, but there had never been one I'd admired. Until now. Doc might not have acted in self-defense, but he'd killed Cody to save others. In effect, he'd defended the community. Cecil Dewey had devoted a lifetime to saving lives. Now he'd taken one, but only to spare others. The earnest young priest, with his call for justice, had jolted my mind. It was Doc himself who had said only God could straighten out the Marsh family's problems. But Doc had decided not to wait for divine intervention.

"I couldn't let Cody marry Marje," Doc said flatly, after he'd recovered from the shock of being discovered and ushered us into his private office. "She's been like a daughter to me and she wouldn't listen to reason. But I knew that what happened to Dani and little Scarlett could happen to Marje and her baby some day. Cody was a vicious spoiled brat with no conscience."

"He had charm," Vida put in. "*I* couldn't see it, but those girls could. Girls can be so silly."

Doc nodded, a gesture that seemed to tax him. "Dani and Marje may seem unalike, but they're not. Basically, they're small-town girlies who figure they can reform the Cody Graffs of this world." He gave a sad shake of his head. "No woman can do that with any man, let alone a bad apple like Cody."

Silence filled the room for a few moments, while the three of us contemplated the futility of trying to improve on nature. It was Vida who spoke next, her elbow resting on Doc's desk and looking for all the world like a patient giving advice to her doctor.

"It was the denials that gave you away," she said. "Nobody — at least among the people who could be considered suspect — would admit it was murder. When Emma and I finally discovered that little Scarlett hadn't died of SIDS, we assumed that either Dani or Cody had killed her. Then we figured that Art Fremstad must have realized the truth, so he was pushed over the falls. That didn't seem like the work of a woman, especially a little thing like Dani. So it had to be Cody, and of course it was Cody who was poisoned."

Doc inclined his head. His eyelids seemed very heavy, but when he looked up at us, his gaze was as shrewd as ever. "I knew, too. I went around looking over my shoulder for almost a year. And Curtis — I think he guessed, but he didn't want to turn in his own brother, and he was in love with Dani."

"Was the baby his?" I asked.

Doc frowned. "I've never been sure, but I think so. Which may be why Cody killed the poor little thing. But I wouldn't have put it past him to do it to his own. God help us, it happens. My problem was that I wasn't positive who had smothered that tyke. And maybe I was wrong. It's not the kind of thing you run around asking people to help you make up your mind. If it had been Dani, she'd left town and there was nothing I could do about her. As for Cody, as long as he wasn't remarried or living with some woman who had kids, I figured it was best to let sleeping dogs lie. I could have done an autopsy, but I didn't have the heart for it. And somehow, knowing that one of the parents — maybe both, as it turned out, if Curtis was Scarlett's father — were innocent, I couldn't put them through that. It was a mistake, of course."

I gave Doc a sympathetic look. "But it didn't happen again, and that was the main thing."

342

Doc turned very grave. "It might have saved Art Fremstad, if I'd acted fast enough."

Vida's jaw thrust out. "You and Curtis and even Dani might have ended up dead, too, Doc. You can't look at it like that."

Doc shrugged. I scooted the chair forward a few inches. "All along I kept feeling as if I were watching scenes from a movie," I said, unable to keep from wondering how long it would be before I could get some painkiller inside my aching body. "How much of all that was make-believe?"

Doc scratched his bald spot. "Not as much as you'd think. Patti always blamed Dani, and Dani was never sure what had happened. But when Curtis came back to town and told Dani and Patti what he thought was true, they joined forces. Then Reid and that actor fellow got into the act, too. After all, Scarlett was Reid's granddaughter as much as Patti's. They came to me one evening and asked what I thought. Then they asked what ought to be done about it." He stared at his hands which were lying flat on the desk. "I'd already tried to talk Marje out of marrying Cody. Now it seemed that I was being asked to administer justice. I considered going to Milo, but what could we prove? It never occurred to me that Art Fremstad had been murdered, at least not by anyone around here. Maybe

I didn't want to believe it. Art wasn't the suicidal type, that's for sure. But," Doc went on and his words were meant for me, rather than Vida; "a small town is the center of the universe to the people who live there. Even though we know better, we like to believe that its imperfections aren't as bad as other places."

I tried to give Doc a thin smile of understanding. "So you and the others formed a sort of pact?"

"There was never much said out loud." Doc leaned back in his chair and let out a weary sigh. "The rest of them had somehow designated me as their avenging angel. They tried to create a smokescreen by carrying on as if they were all still mad at each other — at least Dani and Patti did — but the only one who was really disturbed by Dani's return to Alpine was Cody. He may have hated her, but mostly I think he was afraid of her. I'd bet my bottom dollar he would have liked to have landed that axe right in her gizzard."

"I was never in favor of Marje marrying Cody, either," shrilled Vida. "I said something to her parents once, which wasn't enough, because my brother and his wife are both dumb as a brick wall. And Marje thought I was being an old fogey."

"But," I noted quietly, "Marje knew, didn't she?"

Doc again nodded. "I told her. After he was dead. She carried on something fierce when she heard he'd been hit by a car. She called me at the hotel in Seattle that Sunday, all upset. I didn't let on then, I hoped maybe the whole thing would actually be passed off as an accident. But after Cody's autopsy, I called her back a couple of days later and told her what Cody had done to little Scarlett. She cried some more. But she thanked me."

"For what?" The question fell out of my mouth.

Doc gave a little grunt. "For saving her, I guess." He glanced at Vida, then looked back at me. "If I'd told her earlier what I thought Cody had done to that baby, she might not have believed me. Even if she had, there would have been another foolish girl and another innocent baby. Nobody — not Dani, not Patti, not Curtis, not me, by God — wanted that. I think Marje guessed . . . what I'd done to Cody."

Vida nodded vigorously. "Of course she did. Marje tried to divert Billy Blatt and Milo by saying Cody was taking Haloperidol. But he wasn't. You and Marje were really the only ones who could have put the stuff into Cody's beer. In fact, you put it in all three of his beers, didn't you, Doc?"

He gave a little grunt of assent. "I had to be sure. Nobody can calculate an individual's tolerance."

"I guessed that," I put in. "Cody was already showing signs of drunkenness when I got to the tavern with Carla and Ginny. You were the only one on duty behind the bar and you'd been there the whole time, doing your two-hour stint. I wondered about the bottles of Haloperidol, then I remembered that clicking sound in your pocket. Although it didn't register at the time, it was glass striking glass. I finally realized that when Honoria and I toasted Milo."

Vida shot me a sidelong glance, but this was no time to get distracted. "I thought the person with the poison" — I was careful to avoid the word *killer*, which seemed so ill-suited to Doc — "might be taking a risk by bringing the stuff into the tavern, but if you were found with it, no one would think twice. You're a doctor. Still, I had to wonder if you were concerned about being found out."

Letting out a disdainful breath, he scowled at me. "I sure was! My family, my reputation, the whole works, would — will — be hurt. I didn't want that to happen. I may have killed somebody, but I'm not nuts."

"Of course not," Vida agreed. "You carried it off beautifully. This is all conjecture, Doc. I doubt that a serious case could be made against you."

"Oh, I don't know," mused Doc. "It could be done if we had a decent prosecutor in this county." He seemed quite untroubled, however, his clinical air intact.

"Witnesses are so unreliable," Vida remarked. "Dani passed the mug along, but someone might have seen her tamper with it."

"Actually," I noted, "Jack Blackwell could have done it, since he was behind the bar. He had no motive, unless he was acting on behalf of Patti. But I ruled him out when Honoria Whitman told me he hadn't touched Cody's beer. Neither did Reid or Matt or Patti herself. Honoria never mentioned Donna Fremstad Wickstrom. I doubt she knew who Donna was, but I never seriously considered her anyway because I honestly don't think she knew Cody killed Art until the last few days. If she did, and had wanted revenge, she would have acted much sooner." I paused, my voice tired and my ankle making my ears ring with pain. "Curtis Graff was there, but he was nowhere near his brother. That left you and Marje, Doc. And I had to believe Honoria would have seen Marje if she'd been the one with the Haloperidol." Oddly enough, the once-unfamiliar word slipped easily off my tongue. I was beginning to know its name all too well. "But Vida's right. Conflicting testimony, no concrete evidence — it's all circumstantial."

Vida was making stabbing gestures on Doc's desk with her forefinger. "Tell me this, Doc — was it planned that Dani would drive Cody out and dump him by the Burl Creek Road?"

Doc's tired face wrinkled up, then sagged again. "No. There was no plan, as such. But I think Dani knew what I'd done and she hoped to make it look like an accident, so she borrowed Matt's car — more smokescreen, maybe — and went over to Cody's. I'm surprised he could get as far as the street, but he must have, unless she had help."

"Maybe she did," I suggested. "Maybe there were two cars." Had Dani lost her eyeliner while she was trying to get Cody out of the car? Or had Patti, perhaps with Reid Hampton in tow, actually dropped it? The point was now moot. "Reid or Matt or even Curtis might have been driving the other one."

"Could be." Doc looked as if not only the subject at hand, but the world itself had gotten very tiresome. "When are you going to call Milo?" The question was put to Vida.

For once, she actually squirmed. "Ooooh . . . I don't know — he may not be back

348

from Seattle yet." Her hand went to her glasses, then her hair, and finally came to rest on the edge of the desk. "Doc, what did they tell you in Seattle?"

He lifted his hands, which still trembled slightly. "Three months, six at most. It's lymphatic. I diagnosed myself, you know."

"I should think so," Vida retorted, bridling a bit at the mere suggestion that Doc would allow some big city specialist to figure out his condition.

Doc was on his feet, moving toward the door. "Parker's is closed," he said. "I'll get something out of the supply closet for you, girlie."

"Okay," I said, much relieved. I had the good sense not to tell him to skip the Haloperidol.

Chapter Eighteen

Milo showed me how to shift my body and thus keep my weight on my hands rather than my armpits. I thanked my lucky stars I only weighed a hundred and twenty-five pounds. I cursed the Fates that had made every ounce so clumsy.

"Damn," said Milo, after he'd finished his demonstration and was lapping up a beer, "what do I do now?"

"That," I replied, lying on the sofa like a nineteenth-century tubercular heroine, with a bowl of popcorn as an unlikely prop, "is up to you."

"Hell." Milo was staring at Honoria's ceramic blob which I had put on the coffee table for want of a better venue. "This puts me in a terrible spot," he muttered. "If I arrest Doc, the whole town will hate me and I could lose the election to Hitler. If I don't make an arrest, I'm a goner, too."

I moved my ankle, complete with tightly wrapped Ace bandage, slightly to the left. "You have to see that justice is done, Milo." I put absolutely no emotion into my words. The truth was, I didn't have much left.

"Yeah, sure, right . . ." Milo's annoyance could have been with me or with the concept. Maybe both. Finally it dawned on him that he wasn't the only professional who was on the hook. Since it was almost midnight and we'd been hashing Cody Graff's death over since ten-thirty, it was about time. But as Vida says: *men aren't like other people.* I could hardly have expected him to consider anybody's position but his own so quickly.

"Say, Emma," he said, rolling the beer can between his hands. "What are you going to do about this? You've got one hell of a story."

I gave him my most innocent gaze. "Only if you make an arrest, Sheriff. Otherwise, I've got hearsay and a libel suit." It was a non-story, and I mustn't beat myself over the head for suppressing the news.

"Oh." Milo slumped with disappointment. I didn't add that if I were back in Portland, working on *The Oregonian,* I would have used the information I had to rock City Hall. If some doctor had poisoned somebody else, no matter how benign the killer or how malignant the victim, I would have seen it as my professional duty to bring the culprit to justice. But that was Portland, and this was Alpine. I knew Doc Dewey. I knew Cody Graff. I knew what had gone before, and what might have been. I would rather burn *The Advocate* to the ground than sully Doc's reputation.

"Cancer, huh?" murmured Milo. I nodded. Milo swore. "What'll we do without Doc?" There was a plaintive note in the sheriff's voice.

"There's young Doc, and I suppose he'll get somebody new. It would have happened eventually. Doc must be seventy, at least."

"Seventy-four," said Milo, into his beer can. The words echoed; the can must be empty.

"Go get another beer," I urged. "And bring me some milk instead of Pepsi this time. I'm getting high enough on Percodan."

Milo complied, loping back with a glass of milk and a Miller. The ale was gone. Reclining in the rocker, Milo closed his eyes. "Everybody says it was an accident. An overdose maybe." He spoke musingly. "It's Art I'm thinking of . . ."

"Donna knows the truth," I put in. "Isn't that enough?"

Milo's eyes flickered open. "It is if she tells it."

"She'll only have to tell it once."

"True."

We lapsed into silence. In the distance, I could hear the midnight train, followed by a roll of thunder. I smiled to myself. Perhaps the heat wave was breaking, at least for a day or so. All up and down the Cascades, I could imagine rain beginning to fall, up on the mountain crests, down into the foothills, onto the hillsides, and eventually, with luck, all over Alpine.

"I could stall." Milo lifted his head from the back of the rocker.

"For six months? A year?"

"People forget."

"In Alpine?"

Milo gave me a twisted grin. "No. But they get sidetracked. And sometimes even when they don't forget, they forgive."

I smiled back at Milo. "Go for it."

Milo's grin widened, then he sobered abruptly. "Go for what, Emma?"

Our gazes locked. I heard myself let out a little gasp. Then I started to giggle. "Oh, Milo, you dope, you know what I mean! Besides, right now, I'm a helpless cripple. What about Honoria?"

Milo turned sheepish. "She's a helpless cripple, too."

"Oh, dear. You know the strangest women!" My giggles were verging on hysteria, the result of emotion, pain, and Percodan. "I should go to bed."

A bit clumsily, Milo got to his feet. He loomed over me. "How are you going to get there?"

"Damned if I know," I admitted.

Milo sighed. "I'll help. Then I'll sleep on the couch. Don't argue. Nobody's waiting up for me at home. Damn it, Emma, why can't we be as sexually irresponsible as our children?"

"We weren't raised that way," I replied. And wondered what that said about the likes of Milo and me as parents. By the time I put my head on the pillow in my bed and Milo had settled down in the living room, I decided that maybe our children were smarter than we were. Or was it that our own parents had been wiser? Again, maybe it was the Percodan. . . .

" 'Robert Cohn was once middleweight boxing champion of Princeton.' " Cal Vickers paused to clear his throat, take a sip of beer from his mug, and receive a glance of approval from Vida. " 'Do not think that I am very much impressed by that as a boxing title, but it meant a lot to Cohn.' "

Cal's monotone droned on, as he read the opening chapter of Ernest Hemingway's *The Sun Also Rises*. I sat back on my orange crate, while the crowd of customers at the Icicle Creek Tavern listened to the fourth reader of the evening.

Vida's brainstorm had been a success. Over fifty patrons had brought an eclectic array of books to the Saturday night gathering. New paperbacks from the drugstore rack, old novels culled from boxes in dusty attics, books checked out on seldom used or often abused library cards, even a collection of Latvian recipes, rested on the tavern's rough tabletops and blemished bar.

During the past six days, we had had a rainstorm that lasted less than an hour, a minor earthquake with the epicenter just south of the Canadian border in Whatcom County, and the resumption of our hot, dry summer. Reid Hampton had been released from the hospital, had apparently made up with Matt Tabor, and *Blood Along the River* was proclaimed a wrap about the same time *The Advocate* hit the street on Wednesday. Our building was still the color of Vida's canary, but we were promised it would be repainted in thirty days. I disposed of my crutches on Thursday, though I still walked with a limp that Doc Dewey informed me would last until Labor Day. But it was mid-August, and if I peeked at the calendar, autumn would officially commence in just a little over a month. But I didn't peek. I never do — for fear that somehow I will jinx the change of seasons.

Milo was sitting between Honoria and me, wedged in at the same table the two of them had shared the night Cody Graff had been poisoned. Two weeks had passed since Cody had staggered out the door on Marje Blatt's arm. It seemed like a lifetime. On Monday, Milo had announced that the investigation of Cody's death was closed. He and Doc Dewey, who was the county coroner, after all, had come to the conclusion that Cody had accidentally overdosed. I wrote the story for Wednesday's front page, but kept it to under two inches of copy, buried in the lower left corner. No one called or wrote to question the article. Maybe that was because the much longer piece that surrounded the Graff announcement had dealt with Tacoma City Light's desire to build a dam on the Skykomish River. Since such a project might threaten the already meager number of fish in the river, Alpiners took umbrage and personally blamed me for such a harebrained scheme. The locals knew their priorities, and Cody Graff was no longer numbered among them.

Fuzzy Baugh was now reading a Tennessee Williams play, changing his voice up and down, depending upon the speaker's sex. The relic of a New Orleans accent that remained in Fuzzy's voice lent authenticity, which was a blessing — because he couldn't act worth a hoot. Vida, seated on a tall stool behind the bar, kept a poker face; I tried not to snicker when I caught her eye.

Feeling a jab in my shoulder, I craned my neck, careful not to upset my orange crate. Patti Marsh and Jack Blackwell stood behind me. She carried a Jackie Collins paperback; he held a hardcover Elmore Leonard.

Patti leaned over to whisper in my ear. "Dani called from L.A. this afternoon. She's decided to make at least one more movie."

"For Reid?"

Patti's laugh was on the wry side. "Yeah. Costarring Matt. Reid — Ray — thinks they're *hot*."

"They certainly looked hot in all those winter clothes," I replied, forgetting to whisper. Fuzzy Baugh frowned at me in his most mayoral manner, then resumed reading Maggie the Cat's impassioned lines to her husband Brick.

Patti started to edge away, but Blackwell stayed put. He addressed his words not to me, however, but to Milo. "It looks like you're unopposed, Dodge. You feeling comfortable?"

Fuzzy had concluded his scene, so Milo was able to speak in his normal voice. "I do now. Averill Fairbanks had me worried for a minute there."

Blackwell snorted in disdain. "Averill! He's nuts." When Milo didn't argue, Jack slapped the sheriff's shoulder. "Don't get too cozy under that badge, pal." His grin wasn't exactly sinister, but it would have gone well with a curling mustache and a flowing black cape. Jack Blackwell might not be as evil as he seemed, but I still didn't like him much. I was betting he always rooted for Leonard's sleaziest characters. "I'm going to the courthouse Monday and file for sheriff myself."

Milo choked on a mouthful of small pretzels. "*You* . . ." It was hard to tell if the word was a question or an accusation.

"Why not?" said Blackwell, as Vida introduced the local dentist, Dr. Bob Starr, who had brought along Lawrence Sanders's latest deadly sin. "It's not that hard to run a timber company when the woods are shut down for two to three months at a time with this lousy hot weather. Who knows? The way things are going, it could be curtains for the whole frigging industry. It might be smart to have a sideline." He gave Patti a light slap on the behind. "Let's go, babe. Milo wants to play games with his pair under the table. His guns, I mean." Blackwell leered at Honoria, then at me, and sauntered off in the wake of Patti's swaying hips.

"Damn," breathed Milo.

Honoria surveyed him over the rim of her plastic wine glass. "He won't beat you." Her tone brooked no argument.

"It's still a pain," said Milo. But he gave

Honoria a grateful smile.

"It's a democracy," I noted, trying to keep my voice down so that Dr. Starr's audience could hear him say something other than "Wider."

"Maybe Blackwell's kidding," said Milo as the dentist stepped down to polite applause.

"Maybe," I allowed. Honoria said nothing.

Vida was standing up, thanking all those who had participated in the reading and everyone who had brought a book. Of our trio, only Honoria had read aloud, leading off the program with Anne Lindbergh's *Gift from the Sea*. Milo had brought a book on fly-fishing, which he admitted he'd never opened. I toted a much-worn, two generations-old copy of *Winnie-the-Pooh*.

". . . to continue reading, not because you have to, but because you want to," Vida was saying. "If you think back to the early days of Alpine, what did those first settlers do in the long winter evenings?"

"Screw!" It was, of course, Janet Driggers.

Vida gave her a flinty smile. "Besides that. We are, after all, a small town, so they must have done something else. They read. And they did it by Coleman lantern for the first twenty years or more. Alpine was always a remarkably literate town. I'd hate to see that reputation lost." She paused, turning to her left. "To end this fine evening of books and beer, I'd like to present one of our most beloved and distinguished citizens. Ladies and gentlemen, I give you Dr. Cecil Dewey."

Doc was wearing a suit and tie with a white dress shirt. He looked shrunken, yet undaunted. His hands no longer shook as he held them up to quiet the raucous ovation. I glanced at Milo, whose long face was wistful. Did Honoria know? Probably not. She was wearing her most serene expression as Doc read from Samuel Clemens's speech delivered on the occasion of his seventieth birthday. Doc spoke in a clear, strong voice:

" '. . . This is my swan-song . . . Threescore years and ten! It is the Scriptural statute of limitations . . . You have served your term, well or less well, and you are mustered out . . . you are emancipated, compulsions are not for you . . . You pay the time-worn duty bills if you choose, or decline if you prefer — and without prejudice — for they are not legally collectable.

" '. . . Keep me in your remembrance, and . . . wishing you well in all affection, and that when you . . . shall arrive at Pier No. 70 you may step aboard your waiting ship with a reconciled spirit, and lay your course toward the sinking sun with a contented heart.' "

Until then, I'd never seen Vida with tears in her eyes.

Doc's funeral was held on the Saturday after Thanksgiving at Trinity Episcopal Church. The rector, the gaunt-faced Regis Bartleby, whose ascetic appearance belied his horselike appetite, gave a fine eulogy. Fuzzy Baugh's words were fulsome, and Young Doc's reminiscences were suitably personal. But the truth was, I thought Doc had given himself a better send-off at the Icicle Creek Tavern on that August evening three months earlier.

There was snow on the ground, almost six inches of it, and the forecast called for more throughout the weekend. Indeed, it had started snowing in early November, typical for Alpine. We might not see bare earth until April.

Though in fact, we were seeing it now, as we stood around Doc's grave and waited for the casket to be lowered. I had one hand on Vida's tweed coat sleeve, and Adam draped an arm around my shoulders. He had gotten in from Fairbanks Wednesday afternoon, his second trip home in three months.

The rector intoned the final prayers as a few flakes of new snow drifted down over the cemetery. The church had been packed, and at least a hundred brave souls had ventured up the hill for the burial service. Milo, newly reelected in a walk over Jack Blackwell, had been one of the pallbearers, along with Dr. Starr, Fuzzy Baugh, and Durwood Parker, who, thankfully, had not been required to drive. At the head of the grave, Doc's widow was leaning on her son, clutching a rumpled handkerchief in her gloved hand and looking very brave. When Regis Bartleby presented the American flag to Mrs. Dewey, Young Doc kissed his mother's cheek.

"Medical Corps, Army Air Force, World War II," whispered Vida. "Stationed in England, 1943 to 1945."

"I know," I whispered back. "I read your obit."

Under her black felt bowler, Vida frowned at me. "It's not finished."

Out of the corner of my eye, I saw Donna Fremstad Wickstrom approach the grave. She hesitated, teetering on her high heeled calfskin boots, then dropped a single white rose onto the casket. I turned back to Vida.

"Yes, it is," I said.

Vida gazed at Mrs. Dewey and Young Doc. Marje Blatt had joined them. She hugged Mrs. Dewey and glanced in her aunt's direction. Marje smiled.

"You're right," said Vida. "It's finished."

★ ★ ★

Adam wanted to get a tan. "Two days at Malibu," he said for the fifth time. "That's all. Hey, Mom, I've got mucho money. I can come home for Christmas, then Easter, maybe even a midwinter break. But, man, I've got to catch some rays."

"You're not a native; you're a changeling," I accused. We had just dropped Vida off after the reception at the Dewey house. Adam was driving, having developed a love as great as mine for the green Jaguar. "If you fly to L.A. tomorrow, even for two days, you'll miss Monday and Tuesday classes. Wait until Christmas break. You'll have over three weeks of freedom."

To my surprise, Adam seemed to be considering my suggestion. Surreptitiously, I watched his profile. As he matured and the angles sharpened, the likeness to his father grew even more apparent. Except for his eyes and twenty years of bills, there was nothing to show my claim on this son of mine.

"Okay," he finally agreed, leaning back into the leather bucket seat as he maneuvered the slippery corner onto Fir Street. The snow was coming down harder now. With a sinking feeling, it occurred to me that by tomorrow afternoon, the pass might be closed.

"It's not snowing in Seattle," I said suddenly. "Do you want to drive in tonight, catch a Sonics game if they're in town, and stay over?"

Adam eased into my driveway. "Sonics — or Warriors?"

I started to make a face of noncomprehension before his meaning dawned on me. "The sun doesn't shine in the Bay Area this time of year, not even where the Golden State Warriors play. At least not much. Were you talking L.A. or S.F.?"

"L.A.," he answered, his brown-eyed gaze level with mine. "But now I'm thinking S.F. I could fly down there and be back in Fairbanks Monday morning."

I kept my voice steady. "Is that what you want to do?"

Adam looked away, to the windshield, which was already almost covered with thick flakes of snow. "I'm not sure. I'd call first."

"Good thinking." I should be giving him advice, I told myself. Or encouragement. Or something. Instead, I waited.

"Would he pitch a four-star fit?" Adam continued to stare at the white windshield.

"Probably not. As long as it wasn't awkward for Mrs. Cavanaugh."

Now he turned again to face me. "Do you want to come?"

364

"No." I gave a single shake of my head. "Not this time."

"It's the first time," Adam pointed out.

Let's hope it's not the only time, I thought, and was astonished at my reaction. "That's okay."

Adam opened the car door. "I'll call now, then check the flights," he said into a flurry blowing out of the north.

"I'll get the number," I responded, careful to watch my footing on the surface of newly fallen snow. There were times when my ankle still hurt.

Inside the house, I busied myself while Adam took up the phone. On my knees, I shoved crumpled newspaper under the grate, piled up kindling, and dumped a couple of logs on top. Striking a match, I tensed as I heard Adam's voice, tentative but clear.

"Hi, this is Adam Lord. Your son."

I caught my breath. How like Adam to be so direct! What must Tom be thinking? I tried to picture him at the other end, gripping the receiver and chewing on his lower lip.

Adam was laughing. "Right, I'm in Alpine . . . Yeah, well, I've got all this money. . . . Huh? Right, she's fine, she's here playing with matches. . . . No, not till Monday, so I thought maybe I'd fly down to — okay, sure, right. . . . No, I haven't checked with the airlines yet." Still grinning, Adam glanced over at me and gave a thumbs-up sign. "I'll call you when I land. What? Call ahead from Sea-Tac? Okay. Thanks . . . sir."

I struck a match and set off the fire. But it was Adam who had lighted up the world.